There was no good reason to get involved with Tori

Walker knew there was no reason to let her get to him, to believe there could be something between them and a million reasons why he shouldn't think about her, shouldn't dream about her.

She was caustic and guarded and fake.

She was beautiful and smart and more caring than even she realized.

Hell.

He edged closer. She didn't back up, didn't move closer. She simply watched him, that coy half-smile of hers playing on her lips. "Did you want something, Detective?" she asked, all cocky and confident and challenging.

"Yeah," he said gruffly, sliding his hand behind her neck to hold her head. Tugged her hair so her face tipped toward him. Her eyes flashed and widened, her hands went to his chest, laid there, not pushing or pulling, just heating his skin. "I want something."

Dear Reader,

Thank you so much for picking up a copy of *In this Town*, the final book in The Truth about the Sullivans trilogy. It's never easy to say goodbye, and I have to admit that after spending the past year writing about Mystic Point, I'll miss these characters. While it wasn't always smooth sailing, I had a great time with the Sullivan sisters as they learned the truth about the past and found hope and love for brighter futures.

But *In this Town* isn't just the third book of a trilogy, it's also my tenth book for Harlequin Superromance!

Wow. Ten books. I can hardly believe it.

It truly is a dream come true, one born years ago when I was a young, stay-at-home mother. Honestly, the idea of writing romances for Harlequin Books hit me out of the blue but when it did, it took hold with an intensity unlike anything I'd ever known.

I wanted to be a writer. That was it. A simple declaration but one that changed the course of my life. Now I'm living that dream but I couldn't have done it without the support of my family and readers.

So I want to thank you for your part in making my dream come true. Thank you for reading my stories, for sharing in the beliefs that love should be celebrated and that there's nothing better than a happy ending.

Please visit my website, www.bethandrews.net or drop me a line at beth@bethandrews.net or P.O. Box 714, Bradford, PA 16701. I'd love to hear from you.

Happy reading!

Beth Andrews

In This Town

BETH ANDREWS

HARLEQUIN®

entertain, enrich, inspire™

Recycling programs
for this product may
not exist in your area.

ISBN-13: 978-0-373-71806-1

IN THIS TOWN

Copyright © 2012 by Beth Burgoon

www.Harlequin.com

Printed in U.S.A.

ABOUT THE AUTHOR

Romance Writers of America RITA® Award winner Beth Andrews's big dream came true when she sold her first book to Harlequin Superromance. Beth and her two teenage daughters outnumber...oops...*live* with her husband in Northwestern Pennsylvania. When not writing, Beth can be found texting her son at college, video-chatting with her son at college or, her son's favorite, sending him money. Learn more about Beth and her books by visiting her website, www.bethandrews.net.

Books by Beth Andrews

HARLEQUIN SUPERROMANCE

Other titles by this author available in ebook format.

To Andy.
Thanks for being my biggest fan.

Acknowledgments
Special thanks to Assistant Chief Mike Ward of the
Bradford, PA, Police Department.

CHAPTER ONE

MASSACHUSETTS STATE POLICE detective Walker Bertrand shifted in the hard seat and drummed his fingers on his thigh. He'd been in the small, coastal tourist trap of Mystic Point for all of forty minutes, the past thirty of those spent in this chair while the district attorney and mayor did their best to tactfully explain to the police chief and his assistant chief why they were in a shitload of trouble.

Though Walker was certain explanations weren't necessary. Ross Taylor and Layne Sullivan had to know that sleeping together would cause them problems. If not, they deserved to have their badges taken away from them.

Walker leaned forward, let his hands dangle loosely between his knees while silently urging Jack Pomeroy, the long-winded D.A., to wind things the hell up so Walker could get to work. Finally, and with a great deal of reluctance and regret on his puffy face, Pomeroy handed Chief Taylor a paper.

Taylor's expression remained impassive as he read the allegations against him and Sullivan. To Walker's right, Mayor Seagren looked as if he'd rather perform dental surgery on himself—minus Novocain—than be the bearer of bad news to his two highest ranking police officers.

Walker let his gaze slide over Assistant Chief Layne Sullivan.

Women were a mystery, one of life's greatest. But being the only son in a family with four daughters gave Walker a certain edge. He'd been surrounded by females since birth, after all. He understood them. Knew how they worked and could easily read their moods, gauge their thoughts.

Not that he needed a PhD in the psychology of women to know Sullivan's mood was hostile, her thoughts contemplating murder.

His murder.

Waves of animosity rolled off her, battered Walker with resentment and anger. She didn't want him here. Not in her town. Not sitting across from the chief in her police department. Not sticking his nose into her professional life and career.

Life was tough that way.

Being a cop meant he often went where he wasn't wanted.

He didn't take it personally.

Walker stretched his legs out in front of him and met Sullivan's heated gaze with a bland one of his own—which only seemed to piss her off more.

"If you fire Chief Taylor," she said to the mayor, her long, lean body practically vibrating with outrage, her fisted hands on her hips, "then I quit."

A passionate response, though a bit predictable for his tastes. Had it been brought on by respect for her boss, the man who—from all accounts—had won the position she'd wanted for herself? Devotion to the man she was sleeping with? Or loyalty to her partner in crime?

Taylor set down the paper. "They're not firing me."

Not yet.

Maybe not at all. But everyone in the room knew it was a distinct possibility.

"Any matters regarding termination of employment are up to Mystic Point's city council and mayor," Pomeroy pointed out. "Not me or Detective Bertrand."

Sullivan jerked her head in Walker's direction. "Then why is he here?"

"I'm here to help," he said easily.

He was there to get to the truth.

Working for the state attorney general's office, Walker was often tasked with investigating alleged wrongdoings in local government. City council members and mayors and police chiefs who abused their power or took bribes. Police departments accused of everything from cover-ups and mishandled cases to illegally obtaining evidence.

Most cops considered him the enemy. A traitor to the brotherhood, one who tore through the Blue Line and turned his back on his comrades in arms so he'd get promoted, maybe receive a few accolades as he climbed higher and higher in his career.

They could think whatever they wanted. Walker knew he was part of the system, a valuable part that helped maintain a balance. That rid the ranks of dirty cops and politicians. He dug for the truth, a messy, time-consuming, often thankless job.

He was damned good at it.

Sullivan bared her teeth and he wouldn't be surprised if she leaped at him and took a big chunk out of his hide. "We don't need your help."

"The D.A. thinks you do," William Seagren said, the bald spot on his crown shiny with sweat.

"This is ridiculous," Sullivan snapped. "Ross didn't do anything wrong."

"Then he has nothing to worry about," Walker said before Seagren could respond.

Sullivan snorted. "Nothing except the fact that an investigation like this could ruin his reputation, not to mention have an adverse effect on how he's viewed by the officers under his command and the community. They'll question his capabilities, his ethics and morals."

She was passionate, Walker would give her that. And, if he was being honest, he could see what had tempted Taylor into pursuing a sexual relationship with her. Her dark hair was pulled back into a ponytail that reached the middle of her back, her features sharp. The uniform she wore accentuated the curves of her hips, her breasts.

Yeah, she was a looker. But Taylor should've had more restraint. More control.

Walker would have.

"Maybe Chief Taylor should've considered the consequences before he became personally involved with one of those officers under his command," Walker said, then casually touched the top of his head, just in case the laserlike glare she shot his way had ignited his hair on fire.

Mayor Seagren cleared his throat. "Now, Layne, surely you can understand why we have to look into this matter."

"Understand that you're accusing us of—" she grabbed the paper Chief Taylor had set down and skimmed it "—neglect of duty and ethical violations and…corruption?" Her eyes wide, she crumpled the edge of the paper in her fist. "God, Billy, that's a felony."

"So is conspiracy to obstruct justice," Walker pointed out, tired of the bullshit. Of how Pomeroy and Seagren coddled these two. This was why he'd been brought in, because no one in the county could be trusted to do the job. To remain impartial. To not get personally involved with these people, with this town.

"I'm here," Walker told Sullivan in what he thought was a highly reasonable tone. "There's going to be an investigation—nothing will change that so you might as well accept it. And you might want to start worrying less about your supervisor and more about how this investigation is going to affect you and your career."

She growled at him. The woman actually growled.

"Captain," the chief said mildly. Admonishingly.

Her expression didn't soften and there was no sign his quiet censure affected her in the least but after sending Walker one more of her "Burn in hell!" looks, Sullivan walked to the wall next to the desk, leaned back and stared straight ahead.

Interesting. Not just her acquiescence, but the entire interaction between her and Taylor. Nothing in their body language gave away the fact that they were lovers. There were no touches, no fleeting, longing glances. Taylor had even addressed her by rank, instead of her name. The smart choice given the circumstances and Walker's presence.

Then again, maybe the chief and captain always maintained a certain propriety while at work, foolishly believing they could keep their professional and personal lives separate.

They couldn't. No one could. Sex changed things. Emotions clouded good judgment. Private fights, hurt feelings, even the rush of the good times and the pull of desire eventually leaked out of the bedroom and into the office. Tensions built, resentment simmered within the ranks of the department, causing low morale, bitterness and accusations.

Walker would determine whether those accusations were based on fact, fiction or something in between.

"How does this work?" Taylor asked in his Boston accent. There was no visible anger, no worry in his eyes. His tone was calm, his shoulders relaxed. As if he had nothing to hide, had done nothing wrong despite the evidence to the contrary.

If Walker had been the type of cop to go with his gut, he might believe Taylor was sincere. As honest and honorable as his record with the Boston P.D. indicated.

Instincts were all well and good, and Walker didn't discount his, but neither did he put all his faith in them, either. He trusted his head, not some nebulous feeling. He gathered the facts, saw his cases from every angle, analyzed everyone and everything and then, and only then, did he come to a conclusion.

Pomeroy shifted forward, his tie caught on the shelf of his round stomach. "Detective Bertrand is in charge of seeing if the accusations against you both have merit."

"Until he completes that investigation," Mayor Seagren said, "you will be placed on administrative leave—"

Sullivan muttered something that sounded suspiciously like "Nazi witch hunt" but Walker couldn't be sure.

"With pay," the mayor continued. "Meade will take over in the interim."

"Meade's a good choice." Taylor faced Walker. "You can expect our full cooperation. Isn't that right, Captain?"

"Of course," she said as if that never should have even been in doubt despite her obviously wanting to rip out his still-beating heart and chuck it out the window.

Mayor Seagren stood. "Before we get to the rest—"

"There's more?" Sullivan asked incredulously.

"I just want to state for the record that I fully expect Detective Bertrand's investigation to discover the allegations against you both to be completely unfounded."

"They will be," Taylor said as if anything less was not only unacceptable but unfathomable.

Sullivan shoved away from the wall, offended and irritated. Then again, that seemed to be her standard expression. "Since we're going on record, I'd like to say that this is a complete waste of time. Chief Taylor and I have done nothing wrong."

Taylor pinched the bridge of his nose. "Captain Sullivan—"

"No. I will not stand here with my thumbs up my ass while our reputations are dragged through the mud and our ethics questioned." She began to pace, her long legs eating up the short distance of the office, her ponytail swinging behind her. "We did everything by the book. Everything. And now, months after we reported our personal relationship—as per MPPD's regulations—there are suddenly questions about how we conduct ourselves and do our jobs? It's bullshit."

"Just because there are no departmental rules forbidding relationships within the Mystic Point police department," Walker said, "doesn't mean that getting...personal...with your superior officer was a good idea."

She stepped toward him. "You are seriously starting to piss me off."

Walker held her gaze. "Careful. Wouldn't want to add an assault charge to that list of allegations."

Her grin was cocky with a healthy dose of mean tossed in. "Want to bet? And the next time you address me, make sure you do so properly. Do you understand me, Detective?"

She was pulling rank on him. He couldn't help but admire her for it.

"Oh, I understand perfectly." He paused long enough to let her know he couldn't be intimidated. "Captain."

Taylor stood. "We'll leave our badges and service weapons with Lieutenant Meade."

Pomeroy grunted as he got to his feet. "Before you do, there's one more thing...."

He nodded at Walker, who reached for the envelope

pressed between the arm of the chair and his side, and handed it to Taylor. The chief's hesitation was so slight, most people probably wouldn't have noticed it.

Walker wasn't most people.

Taylor read the report, his expression darkening, the first sign of emotion he'd shown since being told his professional life was under scrutiny.

Sullivan crossed over to him. "What is it?"

He handed the paperwork to her. Walker had to give her credit, she didn't give anything away. No shock crossed her face.

No guilt.

"How did you get a hold of this?" Taylor asked, his voice gruff. Demanding. "This report should've been sent directly to me."

"Considering the accusations against you and Captain Sullivan," Pomeroy said, "I thought it best to have it sent to my office first. And, due to the findings of those reports, the district attorney's office, along with the state attorney general, think it'd be best if the investigation into Dale York's death was handled by someone outside the Mystic Point police department."

"That's right," Walker said, in response to the way Taylor's mouth flattened, the horror in Sullivan's eyes. He grinned. "I'm taking over."

FUNNY TO THINK that once upon a time, Tori Mott had actually believed in fairy tales. Oh, not the ones about glass slippers or mermaids who longed to be human. And don't even try to tell her that when a beautiful girl shows up at the house of seven miniature men all they want from her is to cook and clean while she sings to a bunch of woodland animals.

Please. Men, no matter their height, all wanted the same thing and there was nothing G-rated about it.

She also never bought into the idea that some handsome prince would ride up and carry her off, far from a mundane life of endless toil. No, Tori used to believe something much more dangerous, much more insidious than poisoned apples and ravenous, transvestite wolves who liked girls in red hoods.

She'd actually bought into the idea that she could escape her small hometown, could go somewhere far away from the rumors, the envy and resentment and, worst of all, the pity she'd lived with her entire life. That she could make her dreams, all her big plans, come true. And that finally, she'd achieve the greatest lie of them all.

A happy ending.

Talk about delusional, Tori thought as she wove her way between tables in the Ludlow Street Café's dining room. Nothing like life coming along and giving some poor fool dreamer a sharp smack upside the head to knock some much needed sense into her. Getting pregnant at eighteen did that for her. Made her realize that sure, sometimes dreams did come true.

Just not for her.

So she'd stopped wishing and hoping for spectacular and had settled for average. Which had turned out to be a good life.

If good didn't quite live up to the expectations she'd built for her future when she'd been a teenager, she had no one to blame but herself.

"Here you go," she said to Mr. Jeffries as she set his usual breakfast—two eggs over easy, white toast and three slices of bacon—in front of him. "Can I get you anything else?"

"More coffee when you get a chance, dear," he said, smiling at her as innocently as a baby.

The smile, combined with the fact that he looked like a harmless grandfather with his round cheeks, ill-advised comb-over and a seemingly endless supply of blindingly bright bow ties, hid that he was a groper.

Tori wouldn't have minded if he'd been a better tipper. Or if he had roaming hands with some of the other above-legal-age waitresses at the café. But nope. She, and only she, was lucky enough to get what he deemed a *love tap*—but was actually more of a hopeful squeeze.

So when she caught sight of his age-spotted hand heading her way, she neatly sidestepped. "No problem. I'll be back in a second with that coffee," she said, making sure to sound pleasant and courteous.

Then, because for all his faults, Mr. Jeffries was a regular customer and only a minor nuisance, she amped up the usual amount of wiggle to her hips as she walked away. Just to give him something to look at.

Young, old or in between, men all liked to look. But only she decided who got to touch.

She grabbed the coffeepot and refilled Mr. Jeffries's cup, leaving another handful of creamers at his table since he always pocketed several before he went home. Half the café's tables and booths were filled, voices and the occasional laugh mixing with the sounds of silverware scraping plates, of dishes being cleared. The air smelled of strong coffee, toasted bread, bacon and deep fried potatoes, the odors clinging to her hair, the tiny particles of grease permeating her clothes, her skin. By the end of her nine-hour shift, she'd smell like a walking, talking French fry.

The joys of working in the food industry. Smelly clothes, greasy hair and tired, aching feet. But it was the only thing she'd ever known, as she'd been waiting tables here for the past fifteen years. *Fifteen years*. Literally half her life.

She wasn't sure whether to be proud she'd stuck with something for so long…

Or depressed as hell.

She exhaled heavily as if she could blow away the tension that question caused. No sense being either. This was her job, her life.

But…God…what if? What if something more, something different was possible?

The thought, the mere idea of leaving Mystic Point, of finally going after the life she'd always wanted, was exhilarating. Empowering.

Scary as hell.

Her phone buzzed in her pocket, snapping her out of the crazy fantasy of ever leaving Mystic Point. The back door to the café opened and Nora Sullivan stepped into the narrow hallway as Tori checked her phone. Great. Layne was calling. Again. She glanced at Nora.

Stuck between her sisters. The curse of being the middle child.

She clicked Ignore on her phone and faced Nora. "Well, hello there, stranger," Tori said, her own black skirt feeling too short, too tight compared to her sister's orange dress, the hem of which skimmed just above Nora's knees. "Haven't seen you in a while."

If Nora noted the censure in Tori's tone, the light accusation, it didn't show in her easy smile or blue eyes.

When had her baby sister become so adept at camouflaging her feelings? Or maybe Tori had just lost her ability to read her? Neither thought sat well.

"Good morning," Nora said cheerfully, as if they'd last seen each other yesterday instead of two weeks ago. As if nothing was wrong.

Tori knew better.

She tossed the old grounds from the coffeepot into the garbage. "It's a little early to be so chipper. Even for you."

That was Nora's thing. Being bright and sunny and optimistic. Hey, whatever got her gears grinding, but honestly, just the thought of being that freaking merry all the time gave Tori a headache.

"Did Layne get a hold of you?" Nora asked, smoothing a hand over her blond hair.

God forbid even a single strand try to escape the tight twist she insisted was professional-looking but was really an affront to stylish hairstyles everywhere.

"She wants us to meet her at the station."

"I know, she told me. Three times."

Waving at someone in the dining room, Nora scrunched up her nose. "She called me twice and sent four text messages. She's nothing if not persistent."

"Yeah, persistent. Demanding. Bossy. Annoying—my personal favorite. And for the love of God, don't do that thing with your nose," Tori continued, adding fresh grounds to the pot. "You look like a rabid bunny ready to tear the heads off innocent children."

"Please, I'm adorable and you know it."

"True. But the problem is that you know it. Layne and I shouldn't have told you you were pretty so often when you were little. We created a monster."

Nora waved that away. "You created a self-assured, confident, independent woman, but that's neither here nor there," she said, sounding like the attorney she was. "What is here and there is that we need to get going or we'll be late. You can ride with me and Griffin."

"I won't be anything," Tori said, rinsing the coffeepot before filling it with chilled, distilled water, "because I'm not going."

Nora stared at her as if she'd suddenly declared she was going to shave off her eyebrows. "Of course you're going."

"Why? Because Layne wants me to? In case you haven't noticed, I'm working and I will continue to work until my shift ends at two. I'm not about to drop what I'm doing, leave Celeste in a bind and abandon my customers and co-workers just because my older sister decrees it."

Layne wasn't the boss of her. A fact her older sister didn't seem to be aware of.

Tori hated that Layne demanded she drop everything whenever the whim hit her. Tori may not be the assistant chief of police like Layne or an attorney like Nora, but she had a job, one she took seriously. One she couldn't afford to be away from—literally. Ever since her divorce, she'd barely been able to make ends meet.

No one told her the price of freedom would be so damn high.

"I don't think Layne would've asked you to leave work if she didn't feel it was important," Nora said, proving that, despite her angelic face, she could be as stubborn as her sisters. "So, come on." She clapped her hands lightly, her tone high-pitched as if she was calling a hesitant puppy. If she whistled, Tori might have to hurt her. "Let's go."

Tori turned on the machine. "Look, don't think you can avoid me for weeks—"

"Don't be ridiculous," Nora said, her arms crossed, her cheeks pink.

"—and then waltz in here and make demands. I'm not going. Deal with it."

"First of all," Nora said, hurrying after Tori as she walked toward the other side of the restaurant, "I haven't been avoiding you."

Tori stepped into the large alcove separating the dining room from the kitchen. "Ever since you started sleeping with Griffin York you've barely been around. Does he keep you chained to the bed?"

Sharon Cameron's booming laugh drowned out whatever Nora had been about to say. "He could chain me to the bed," Sharon said. "I'd even bring my own restraints."

"Not helping," Tori called to her coworker as Sharon took several place settings back into the dining room.

Patty Tarcher, a rotund, gray-haired, sixty-year-old grandmother of ten set food-laden plates from the order window onto a tray. "I say enjoy it while you can," Patty told Nora. "Once they hit fifty, men's libidos drop like a rock in the ocean. Never to be seen again." Balancing the tray with one hand, she snagged an extra set of silverware off the long table behind them and peered over the top of her glasses at the sisters. "That's why God invented those little blue pills. Things are magic, I tell you. Pure magic."

"Way more information than anyone ever needed to know," Tori said.

"Thanks, Patty, but Griffin's and my relationship isn't based solely on sex," Nora said, humor underlying her prim tone.

Patty frowned. "Now that's a shame. Those are the best kind."

Tori and Nora watched Patty leave. "Oh, my God," Tori breathed. "I'm going to need to scrub my brain to get rid of the image of Patty and Stan putting that little blue pill to use."

Nora's lips twitched. "Isn't Stan the guy who plays Santa at the annual Christmas party?"

"Ugh. Stop. Now I'm imagining him dressed as a jolly old elf." At Nora's laugh, Tori grinned. "I miss you, baby girl."

For some reason, that comment made Nora look guilty. Tori's eyes narrowed. No doubt about it, something was going on—she just had no idea what. But she was sure whatever it was, Griffin was to blame.

"I miss you, too," Nora said, rearranging the stack of wrapped silverware. "I've just been busy—"

"Tori," Celeste Vitello, the café's owner, called from the other side of the window. "Order up."

"Busy," Tori repeated, placing plates onto a tray. "Right. Too busy for your family."

Nora sighed. "You know it's not that way between me and Griffin, right?"

"Not what way?"

"Just sex."

That was Nora's first problem. She should keep whatever was between her and Griffin purely physical. Keep her heart out of it. "Does it matter?" she asked, lifting the tray and walking into the dining room.

Never one to give up anything easily, Nora caught up with Tori as she set omelets in front of a twenty-something couple.

"Of course it matters," Nora said when Tori returned the tray to the alcove. "You're my sister."

"And yet you continue to ignore my sage advice about Griffin."

"Because you're wrong about him." Her tone gentled. "He's a good man. I lo—"

"Oh, no. No, no, no." Tori covered her ears. "Do not start spouting off about your great love for him. Let me keep believing it's only physical between you two and will someday soon come to an end. It's the only way I'll be able to sleep at night."

Nora crossed her arms. "You know, instead of blaming me for this perceived distance between us lately, you might want to start considering how you're partly to blame."

Tori's eyes widened. "Because I don't like your boy-friend?"

"Because you don't respect my ability to make decisions for myself. Most women would be happy to hear their baby sister is in a serious, committed relationship with a man who loves her."

Tori couldn't help it. She laughed. "Honey, I'm not most women."

She may not have Nora's brains or Layne's ability to frighten the masses with one scowl—and legally carry a gun—but she did know men. It was one of her greatest strengths. And Griffin York was trouble.

Okay, so he was the best kind of trouble, the kind that came wrapped in a brooding, darkly handsome, super sexy package.

A pretty exterior for sure, but underneath? A cynical, bitter person who only hurt those who tried to get close to him. Who tried to love him.

Took one to know one, after all.

"Speak of the devil," she murmured as she stepped out to check her customers' drinks and noticed Griffin come in through the front door. The man looked like the poster child for the Bad Boy Club in his work boots, faded jeans and battered leather jacket.

She crossed to the drink station only to be followed by Nora. A moment later, Griffin joined them, making Tori feel cornered.

"Is she coming?" he asked Nora.

"Yes," Nora said at the same time Tori spoke.

"No."

He rubbed his thumb along the underside of his jaw. "Glad that's cleared up."

Nora took a hold of Tori's arm and gently tugged her into the hallway. "I'm sorry this is a bad time for you,"

Nora said, and Tori knew she meant it. Nora rarely said anything she didn't mean. Tori almost envied her ability to be so open and honest. So willing to put her true self out there for others to judge. "But we all know this must be about the case."

The case. Their mother's murder case. Tori bit the inside of her lower lip. Hard. She was tired of hearing about it, thinking about it. It was over. Done. The man who'd killed their mother eighteen years ago, who'd left Valerie Sullivan's body to rot and decay like so much garbage in the woods, was dead himself.

As his son stood before her, looking so much like his father, with his dark, tousled hair and slight dimple in his chin, it was all she could do not to throw herself at him, slap and scratch him. Try to inflict some of the pain her mother had suffered at his father's hands on him.

"There's nothing to discuss," Tori said, hating that she cast Dale York's sins onto his only child. Especially when so many people cast her mother's sins onto her. "No sense rehashing it all. It won't change anything. Won't bring Mom back or ensure that Dale is rotting in hell as punishment for what he did."

"I could carry her out of here for you," Griffin said to Nora, conveniently pretending Tori hadn't spoken.

He'd fit in with her family just fine after all. They tended to ignore her, too. Underestimated her.

"We could toss her in the trunk," he added. "Let Layne deal with her when we get to the station." He rolled his shoulders as if warming up for some heavy lifting, his focus on Tori, his gaze assessing. "What do you go? About one twenty-five?"

A sound of outrage escaped her even as she sucked in her stomach. "I'll have you know—" she jabbed a finger at Griffin's chest, wished it was a fork "—I weigh one-fifteen."

Give or take…oh…five pounds.

"If you say so." Then he smirked.

Her hands fisted. God, what she wouldn't give to knock that stupid grin off his face.

She tossed her hair back, her high heels bringing them almost eye to eye. "Listen, as much as I'm sure you two enjoy playing Bonnie and Clyde in your spare time, leave me out of it. Because if you lay one greasy finger on me, I'll have Layne arrest you for assault after I've taken my hedge clippers to your—"

"Now, now," Nora said. "No need to get all threatening and violent. It was only an idea." She patted Griffin's arm. "A sweet one."

Tori gaped at her usually levelheaded sister. "There is something seriously wrong with you. What did he do? Perform a lobotomy on you while you were sleeping?"

"We need to go," Griffin told Nora.

She sighed, as if dealing with Tori taxed the last of her usually limitless energy and patience. Well, it wasn't exactly a day at the beach on Tori's side of things, either.

Nora nodded. "I guess we'll just tell Layne she couldn't get away."

It took a moment for Tori to realize she was the "she" Nora was talking about. "Okay, first of all, I'm standing right here and you acting as if I'm not is really irritating. Secondly, I don't need you or anyone making excuses for me." Didn't want anyone doing so. She stood up for herself. Took care of herself.

After she'd realized the hard lesson that no one else was going to take care of her.

Too bad taking care of herself and her son wasn't as easy as she'd thought it would be.

Nora sent her a beseeching look, one made all the more powerful by her sister's sweetness. "Layne really wanted us both there. She wants you there."

Tori's resolve started dissolving like sugar in hot water. "I guess she's going to be disappointed, then," she said lightly before brushing past Griffin and heading back to work.

But guilt nudged her, hard and insistent as a toothache. Damn Nora. Damn Tori's love for her. That's what love did. It trapped you. Made you worry all the time about pleasing someone else, about putting your own wants and needs aside.

Love made you weak.

And Tori couldn't afford to be anything but strong.

CHAPTER TWO

"WHAT ARE YOU doing?" Celeste Vitello asked Tori.

Tori set a stack of dirty dishes into a heavy, plastic bin. "Giving Mr. Jeffries a lap dance," she said dryly, glancing at her boss. "You?"

"Now that is a horrifying thought." Celeste's dark, wildly curly short hair was held back from her face with a wide, black headband making her brown eyes appear larger, her cheekbones more pronounced. A white apron covered her stretchy black pants and orange T-shirt. "And while I admire your clever wit as much as, if not more than, the next person, shouldn't you get going? Layne wanted you at the station at nine and it's already eight fifty-five."

Using the back of her hand, Tori brushed her long bangs aside. "Not you, too."

"Me, too, what?"

"You've joined the Layne Brigade," Tori said, tossing silverware into the bin with a loud clang. "Bad enough she sent Nora over here to fetch me like I'm some sort of disobedient child, now you're waving at me from the front seat of the bandwagon? For God's sake, don't drink the Kool-Aid, people. Fight the power."

She wasn't surprised Celeste knew about Layne's important meeting. Layne probably called her, too. Or else Nora had swung by the kitchen to tell Celeste Tori was being stubborn.

Nora always had been a little tattletale.

Celeste pressed the tips of her forefingers against her temples as if seeking inner peace or warding off a headache. "Times like this make me wonder if you and Layne will ever outgrow your sibling rivalry."

"She started it."

Layne always started it with her judgmental attitude, bossiness and overinflated sense of superiority. As if she had some sort of holy light shining down on her just because she was the firstborn.

Celeste shifted out of the way of a customer, smiled and greeted him before edging closer to Tori and lowering her voice. "I'm officially giving you the time off. Now go be with your sisters."

Tori didn't want to leave, didn't want to fall into line just because Layne demanded it. "Thanks, but I'd rather finish my shift."

She gathered the crumpled napkins and empty containers of creamer and tossed them into the bin. But she felt Celeste watching her, studying her. It was annoying. Unnerving.

Not that she'd ever let anyone see even the slightest hint of nerves, of doubts. People saw only what she allowed. Her thoughts, her feelings were her own until she decided to share them.

"Patty," Celeste said to the other waitress as she walked past, "could you cover Tori's tables? She has a family emergency."

"Sure thing. Here," she said to Tori, "I'll take that back for you."

But when Patty took a hold of the bin, Tori's fingers tightened. A subtle tug-of-war ensued, causing the dishes to clank together. Patty's eyes flashed and she yanked hard. Tori's grip slipped. She stumbled back, bumping into the table with enough force to knock it against a chair.

With a triumphant grin, Patty tossed her head and walked away.

Tori straightened and stepped toward Patty's retreating back, ready to…well…she wasn't sure what exactly but she was afraid it included her lunging at the older woman and taking her down in a headlock.

Knowing Tori all too well, Celeste blocked her path. "Let's go to my office. We can discuss—"

"There's nothing to discuss." Fighting her building temper, Tori smoothed her skirt over her hips, tugged down the hem. "I'm not leaving."

Celeste raised her eyebrows. "My office. Now."

Damn. Celeste rarely used that no-nonsense tone with anybody, let alone Tori, which only made it that much more effective when she did resort to it.

Aware that they'd drawn several curious glances, Tori forced her lips up into her patented coy smile and sauntered across the dining room. Kept her movements graceful and unhurried even when she reached the empty hallway.

At the end of the hall, she entered the office. Weak sunlight filtered in through the two narrow windows, casting shadows on the dark carpet. Framed photographs of Tori and her sisters, along with one of their father, Tim, and Celeste decorated the wall to her left. Several smaller ones, all of Tori's son, Brandon, ranging from newborn to last year's school picture, were scattered on the bookshelf to the right. A huge, ugly cherry desk that had belonged to Celeste's grandfather took up more than its fair share of space, along with a three-drawer metal filing cabinet and two wooden chairs.

Walking in, Celeste flipped on the overhead lights then shut the door.

Tori crossed her arms. "I cannot believe you played the boss card on me."

Okay, so technically Celeste *was* her boss. But in addition to that, she was also her father's girlfriend and before that she'd been her mother's best friend. Celeste had been one of the few people who'd seen something valuable in Valerie Sullivan.

And in Tori.

Celeste loved her without expectation, without judgment. Some days Tori thought she was the only person who did.

"I do whatever it takes," Celeste said as she sat behind the desk. "You know that."

She did. Tori admired her for it and for what she'd made of her life. Celeste had her own successful business, one she'd built by herself from the ground up. The only thing Tori didn't understand was why Celeste gave her heart to men whose only real love, their obsession, was the sea.

Maybe it was in her blood. Her grandmother had married a fisherman, and her mother eloped with a navy petty officer, only to be left alone when he chose the sea over his young wife and baby daughter. At nineteen, Celeste lost her fiancé when the fishing boat he'd been on had gone down during a Nor'easter.

And now, for the past eight years, she'd been in a relationship with Tori's father, another fisherman who always, always, chose the call of the ocean over her. Just as he'd done with his wife and daughters.

Which proved that no man was worth giving your time, your attention and most especially your heart to.

"Sit down," Celeste said, gesturing to the chair in front of the desk, "and tell me what's going on with you."

Tori plopped onto the chair. "Nothing's going on. Since

when is wanting to cover my own shift, my full shift, a crime?"

"Honey, you were fighting a woman twice your age over dirty dishes."

"Patty's stronger than she looks. Those water aerobics are really working."

"I'm sure they are." Opening a drawer to her right, Celeste pulled out a bag of mini chocolate bars. Tori didn't think it was a coincidence Celeste's stash of candy and the loaded handgun she kept for protection were housed in the same space.

No one touched Celeste's chocolates without permission.

"What's wrong?" she asked, taking three candies from the bag before sliding it toward Tori.

Her voice was kind, worry clear in her brown eyes. It reminded Tori of when she'd sat in this very same chair as a scared, pregnant teenager. Only they knew Celeste was the first person she'd told. The person who'd held her as she'd cried, more terrified than she'd ever been in her life. So afraid of disappointing her family, of Greg turning his back on her, of being responsible—completely, totally, fully responsible—for the life growing inside her.

Humiliated and angry that she'd ended up just like her mother.

"What's the point of my going?" Tori asked, unable to stop the words from spilling out. "No matter what evidence they found or new theory Layne has, it won't change anything."

She wanted to move forward and forget the past. Not rehash it.

"Don't you want to know what happened?" Celeste asked quietly. "Don't you want to know the truth?"

Tori didn't believe in the truth. It was too easily manipulated, too easily hidden. She should know. Her own life was nothing but smoke and mirrors, shifting and reflecting what she wanted people to see. Giving them only what she wanted them to have.

"The truth is that Dale York killed Mom. And now he's dead. What else is there?"

She didn't expect a real answer but the look on Celeste's face told her the older woman was keeping something from her. See? Everyone lied. Everyone kept secrets. Even someone as good and honest as Celeste.

"What's going on?" Tori asked, her fingers aching from gripping the arms of the chair so tightly.

Unwrapping a candy, Celeste glanced around as if someone was going to suddenly materialize out of thin air to overhear their conversation. "I think Layne might be in trouble."

Tori exhaled a short laugh, the tension in her easing. "My big sister doesn't get into trouble. She gets everyone else out of it."

Layne had always been there to help Tori and Nora with their homework, made sure they had dinner, lunch money and went to bed at a decent hour. She'd been more of a mother to them than Valerie had ever been.

She never let her sisters forget it.

Tori appreciated the sacrifices Layne had made, how she'd taken care of them. She also resented the hell out of her for not seeing that she and Nora no longer needed her to be their substitute mom. They needed her to be their sister.

"Donna called me," Celeste said of her good friend and Chief Taylor's secretary. "She told me Mayor Seagren and the district attorney had an early morning meeting with both Ross and Layne."

"Ross and the mayor are always huddled up about

something." Billy Seagren loved nothing more than hanging out at the police station. She wouldn't be surprised if he hadn't asked Ross to make him some sort of unofficial deputy complete with shiny gold star.

"A special investigator sent from the attorney general's office was there, too. Donna isn't sure what's going on but there's been some sort of complaint against both Ross and Layne. Something is wrong," Celeste said. "I can feel it. And I think you should go to this meeting, not because Layne told you to, but because she needs you there."

Her mouth twisting, Tori tucked her hair behind her ear. Layne didn't need her. No one did. Not her sisters or her father. Not even her own son.

"Can I get back to work now?" she asked, sounding as petulant and defiant as Brandon. That he came by his attitude naturally only irritated her more. Would it kill him to mimic a few of her positive traits?

Celeste sighed, her disappointment clear. Nothing new there. Tori was always disappointing someone. "If that's what you really want…"

"It is," Tori said, already walking out of the office. She headed toward the dining room, but stopped at the doorway, her stomach turning. Whirling around, she crossed to the break room, circled the table, her stride short because of her tight skirt.

The guilt was back. As if she didn't have enough of the useless stuff already. She was a mother, wasn't she? She'd been dealing with guilt on a daily basis ever since Brandon was born. Was she good enough? Smart enough? Did she have enough patience? Give him enough time and attention and love?

It had only increased since she and Greg had told Brandon they were splitting up a year ago. She'd seen the accusation in her son's eyes. He'd known she'd instigated the divorce, blamed her for ripping their family apart. He'd yet to forgive her.

So, yeah, full quota of guilt here, thanks just the same. And Layne did not need her. She prided herself on not needing anyone. It was a sentiment—one of very few—she and Tori shared. One learned by watching their parents' dysfunctional marriage, by having a selfish, vain mother, a father who ran off to sea every chance he got.

It was too risky to count on someone to be there for you. Better, safer, to rely on yourself.

Besides, it shouldn't matter to Tori what was going on with Layne. They weren't close, not like Tori and Nora. Or at least, she and Nora had been close until her baby sister decided to hook up with the son of the man who'd killed their mother.

Discovering the truth about their mother should have brought them together, but instead they'd drifted apart. Living their own lives.

Whatever trouble Layne was in was just that. Hers. Tori had enough problems of her own to deal with.

She grabbed her purse from her locker and headed back into the hallway. Celeste stood in the kitchen doorway talking with Joe, the café's breakfast cook. Tori kept her gaze straight ahead as she passed them.

"Hey," Celeste called, stopping Tori at the door. "Let me know as soon as you find out what's going on."

Tori lifted a hand to indicate she heard then hurried outside. The sun peered through the clouds and a cool breeze lifted the ends of her hair as she clicked the unlock button on her car keys. She slid behind the wheel of her ancient Toyota, cranked the engine and pulled out, heading toward the police station.

Family ties. They bound and choked and twisted and

tangled a person up until they couldn't break free. But if you took on one Sullivan, you took on all of them.

God help you then.

THE BRUNETTE KNEW how to make an entrance.

She demanded attention. Walker studied the woman gliding into Chief Taylor's office, her heels tapping against the floor. A lot of it.

A small smile playing on her lips, she slid her gaze around the room before landing on him. Though her expression didn't change, he had the sense she was sizing him up, trying to figure out how big of a threat he was.

Her eyes met his and attraction, instantaneous and primal, slammed into him, had his next breath lodging itself in his chest with painful intensity. Jesus, but she was like a walking wet dream, all lush curves, long legs and full, slicked red lips. Her hair was chin length, the ends razor sharp, with a heavy fringe of bangs.

Awareness, feminine and powerful, entered her light brown eyes as she drew closer. If they'd been anywhere else but the police station—a bar, the grocery store… hell…a car wash—he would've tried to get her number, her name, her interest. An invitation into her bed.

But they weren't somewhere else. So he gave her his most intimidating scowl.

Her smile amped up a few degrees, her walk turned into an out-and-out slink, the movements sensual and, if he wasn't mistaken, practiced.

She knew what effect she had, knew what men thought of when they saw her.

It wasn't sex. Or at least, not just sex. It was something darker, more dangerous. She brought out a man's natural instincts to mate, to possess a woman in the most heated, basic and elemental way possible.

"Hail, hail," she murmured, her tone smoky and seductive, her features too similar to those of Captain Sullivan to be anyone other than the missing sister, Tori Mott, "the gang's all here."

He felt Taylor watching him, judging his reaction. Deliberately turning away from the brunette, he met the chief's gaze coolly. To prove he was in charge, of this case and his body.

"You're late," the assistant chief said in a brusque, disapproving tone.

Mrs. Mott lifted a shoulder in a negligent shrug that caused her sister's lips to thin. "Am I?" she asked. She sat next to Nora Sullivan and crossed her legs, her skirt sliding up, exposing her thighs. "So sorry."

Captain Sullivan balanced her weight on the balls of her feet. "No one is checking out your legs, so tone down the sex kitten act."

"I don't have an act. Although it really is a pity about no one noticing my legs. I've always considered them my best feature."

"God, Tori, do you have to antagonize her?" Nora asked, sending Walker a nervous glance.

"A girl has to find her fun somewhere." She glanced at Walker, her lips curved as if inviting him in on the joke, but her eyes were watchful. Guarded. Hiding secrets and her true intentions.

And he realized her legs weren't her best feature, not by a long shot. Those eyes were.

Leaning forward, she held out her hand. "I'm Tori Mott. And you are…?"

"Satan," Captain Sullivan said under her breath.

Chief Taylor sighed heavily. Nora Sullivan made a choking sound. And still, Mrs. Mott held her hand out to Walker, her eyebrows raised in question. In challenge.

"Detective Bertrand," he said, taking her hand.

He maintained eye contact as he held on for the proper amount of time. She pressed her lips together as if fighting a smile. Because of her sister's comment? Or because he hadn't been able to hide his reaction, not completely, at the sharp sting of desire that had accompanied the contact of her soft skin against his?

He wasn't sure he wanted to know.

"I thought Satan was your special pet name just for me," Griffin York, the dark-haired man next to the blonde, said to Captain Sullivan. "I'm hurt."

Sullivan didn't blush. Didn't squirm in abject embarrassment or worry over retribution. The set of her shoulders, the tightness of her mouth, told Walker she didn't respect his authority or the job he was there to do.

So be it. There was nothing he liked more than a challenge.

If Sullivan thought she could intimidate him with her bad attitude and sharp tongue, she was way off base. Hostility, both blatant and subtle, came with the job description. Most cops weren't thrilled at having an outsider come into their department, digging into their lives, jeopardizing their careers and reputations.

Then again, he wouldn't be here if Taylor and Sullivan had followed the rules.

"Bertrand is from the state attorney general's office," Taylor said, linking his hands together on top of the desk. "He asked us to call you all together for this meeting."

Asked. Demanded. Walker gave a mental shrug. As long as he got the result he wanted—a jump start on his investigation—he wouldn't quibble with the chief's word choice.

"Is that so?" Mrs. Mott asked, scrutinizing him as if there was more going on in her head than which skirt would best showcase that top-notch ass of hers. But then she blinked and her expression turned sultry again. "And why would a detective from such a grand and lofty state office be interested in the five of us?"

"Things like conflict of interest, mishandling of cases, corruption, misconduct and, of course, murder always interest the state."

The blonde Sullivan slid to the edge of her seat, her knees pressed together. "What are you talking about?" She turned to Captain Sullivan. "What is he talking about?"

The captain opened her mouth but Taylor held up his hand.

"There have been several complaints made against Assistant Chief Sullivan and me," Taylor said as calmly as if he was discussing the score of last night's Red Sox game. Either he had that much confidence the charges were unfounded or he put up one hell of a front. "Bertrand is here to launch a formal investigation into those allegations."

The blonde's eyes widened and Walker wondered if they were going to pop out of her pretty head and roll across the floor. She leaped to her feet. Walker stood as well, his hand hovering over his gun.

"Oh, for God's sake," Sullivan said wearily, "that's hardly necessary. Look at her—" She waved a hand in her sister's direction. "Does she really look violent?"

"Don't let the angel face fool you," York told Walker. "If she ever gets her hands on a crowbar, you'd better watch out."

"Not helping," Nora Sullivan said as she dug into her purse. She pulled out a cell phone.

"What are you doing?" Captain Sullivan asked.

Nora pressed a button, held the phone to her ear. "Calling Uncle Kenny. You need legal representation in order to fight these charges." She met Walker's eyes, lifted her chin. "These *bogus,* inflammatory charges."

That's right. She was an attorney, worked for her uncle who had, at one point, been the county's D.A. Tangled web and all that. Christ but this investigation was going to be a pain in his ass.

But at least he wouldn't be bored.

"It's an investigation," Captain Sullivan said, taking the phone from her sister and shutting it off. "And Ross and I are scheduled to meet with an attorney from the union this afternoon." She touched the blonde's arm. "Don't worry. It'll all work out."

"You're in trouble," Nora said, her voice thick.

Walker hoped she didn't let loose with the waterworks. Crying was one of the many ways women manipulated men. Growing up, his sisters often used tears to get what they wanted from their father and, later, him.

It was Walker's own damn fault such a low-down, rotten, dirty trick still managed to work on him.

Captain Sullivan shook her head. "The truth will come out. Isn't that what you always say?"

The blonde glanced over her shoulder at York, who tugged her back to her seat.

But not before Walker noticed how Nora blanched, the color leaking out of her face.

Seemed Tori Mott wasn't the only Sullivan woman with secrets.

"Is that why you dragged me away from work?" Mrs. Mott asked. "So you could tell us you're getting your hand slapped?"

"It's more than a hand slap," the blonde said heatedly. "This is serious, Tori."

"Ah, but Tori's never serious," Captain Sullivan said. "Isn't that right?"

Mrs. Mott studied her nails. "Why should I be? You're serious enough for both of us."

"We asked you here," Taylor said, obviously having dealt with these three enough times to know when to intervene before things got out of hand, "because the toxicology reports on Dale York came back."

Mrs. Mott frowned. "It's been what…two months? The autopsy was done the day after he died."

Taylor stood and rounded his desk, handing the report Walker had given him earlier to Nora. "Toxicology reports take anywhere from six to eight weeks to complete."

"His heart gave out," Mrs. Mott said. "It was fitting, though I'd sort of hoped he would suffer more before kicking it. Either way, it was no big loss to humanity." She glanced at York, her mouth a thin line. "No offense."

York flicked his green gaze at her. There was no love lost between them, that was for sure. Something to take into account.

Nora held the report out, her hand trembling. "This can't be right."

Taylor sat on the edge of his immaculate desk. "It's right. The coroner was wrong. A heart attack wasn't what killed Dale."

"So what did?" the younger York asked.

"Cyanide."

"Cyanide?" Mrs. Mott repeated, snatching the report from Nora. "That makes no sense."

Walker crossed his arms, wished he could take off his suit jacket, loosen his tie. "It makes perfect sense. Mr. York was poisoned. Besides being here to look into the issues regarding the chief and assistant chief, I'm also in charge of Mr. York's murder case."

Letting that sink in, Walker let his gaze shift from one person to the next. "And I can't help but wonder if the person who killed him is in this room."

CHAPTER THREE

FEAR TURNED TORI'S blood to ice, tightened her throat. Through the roaring in her head she could barely make out Layne's gruff—and no doubt, pithy—reaction to the detective's words. Nora's indignant cry. Bertrand's rumbling response. Then they were all talking, Layne letting Bertrand know he couldn't intimidate them, Nora threatening legal action, Griffin trying to calm Nora down. But it was all muted, as if Tori heard it through a filter. Only one thought filled her head, demanded her full attention.

Someone had murdered Dale.

The nightmare that had started at the beginning of summer when Ross's niece drunkenly stumbled upon their mother's remains wasn't over. It was getting worse. With the news of the true cause of Dale's death, talk about Tori's family would only grow. Once again, the Sullivans would be the subject of rumors and speculation. Of suspicions and doubts.

She could handle it, she assured herself, as could Layne—hadn't they endured it their entire lives? But Nora didn't deserve to have her name dragged through the mud. And Brandon...God...her son was only twelve. Still so much a child despite a recent growth spurt and a bad attitude that rivaled any teenager's. He shouldn't have to be subjected to the nasty gossip, the whispered innuendos. She had to protect him. Had to get him out of Mystic Point.

The back of her neck prickled with unease and she

raised her eyes to the man towering over her, his gaze discerning, his mouth unsmiling. Dale had been killed and this man—an outsider who knew nothing of them, of what they'd been through—wanted to pin the blame on one of them.

Anger, denial, flowed through her, caused the mask she wore as easily as a second skin to slip. Only for a moment, but she must've given her true thoughts away because in his eyes, she saw a flicker of triumph. As if he'd somehow won their silent battle of wills.

She smirked. Had the satisfaction of seeing his expression darken.

No one beat her at her own game.

"So someone killed Dale," she said, her tone loud enough to get everyone's attention. She tossed the paper onto Ross's desk, fluffed her bangs with her fingers. "It's not like his death is a big loss to society."

"Tori," Nora warned, watching Detective Bertrand nervously, her hand gripping Griffin's.

"What? I'm not going to sit here and pretend to grieve over a bastard like Dale York."

She resented the implication that she should act as if she was anything less than thrilled that he no longer walked the earth. That she should feel guilty.

Bertrand pulled a small notebook out of his suit pocket. "Mrs. Mott, are you saying you're happy Dale York is dead?"

"Don't answer that," Nora and Layne both ordered quickly.

They had her back. Always. Just as she had theirs.

Instead of feeling trapped by the bond between her and her sisters as she usually did, Tori felt...relieved. Their sisterly ties were tenuous at best, but they held strong when it mattered.

Tori sent Bertrand a look from underneath her lashes, one she'd perfected at the age of twelve when she'd realized her looks would take her a hell of a lot further than her brains ever could. "I'm sorry, Detective, but I'm afraid my legal counsel has advised me against answering that question."

His lips thinned. Obviously he hadn't liked her remark. Not her problem. Despite what most guys seemed to hope, she hadn't been put on this earth for the sole reason of making men happy. Oh, she knew what they wanted from her. For her to lie on her back and make their little hearts flutter.

They could just keep wanting.

Because while she had no qualms about using their desire for her, their attraction to her against them if it suited her purpose, she didn't sleep around. Never had.

But that hadn't stopped the rumors in high school from circulating. Hadn't stopped men from hitting on her, from trying to charm her into their beds even when she'd worn another man's ring.

He didn't seem the least bit affected by her charms. But she'd felt the heat arc between them when their eyes had first met. He wasn't as immune to her as he'd like her to believe.

As for her, well, sure she'd felt a slight…zing…upon first seeing him. She was only human after all and he was tall, broad-shouldered and blond, his handsome face sharply planed, his bottom lip thicker than the top.

Then again, she felt the same zing when she saw a picture of a shirtless David Beckham so she wasn't about to take any reaction to the detective's good looks seriously.

"I'd like to ask you all some questions regarding your whereabouts the night Dale York died," Bertrand said.

"None of us are answering any questions without legal

counsel present," Nora said, standing and staring down the enigmatic detective as if she could put a chink in his armor with just the force of her will.

God bless her little sister's confidence but Tori could've told her not to bother. Someone like Bertrand couldn't be intimidated. No, if a woman wanted to get underneath the detective's steely exterior, shake that air of superiority he wore as easily as his dark, expensive-looking suit, she had to be clever. Manipulative.

She had to be willing to use her body, her looks, to get what she wanted. Like their mother. Like Tori.

"That's fine," Bertrand told Nora as if he expected no less than them all dragging attorneys in here before saying another word. "I'd like to set up times to speak with you all—individually."

"Divide and conquer, eh?" Tori asked.

He slid an unreadable glance her way.

"My secretary can set up interview times," Ross said, straightening.

"Griffin has to get back to work," Nora blurted, her fingers twisting together.

Griffin, in the act of getting to his feet, stilled. "I do?"

She nodded slowly, her eyes on his. "Yes. You do. You have that car coming in at ten for that thing. Remember?"

Griffin may be sex on a stick, but he wasn't dumb. Then again, a blind person could see what Nora was pulling. "Right," Griffin said. "The car with the thing. Important customer."

"Yes," Nora said in a rush. "Very important." She blinked innocently at Bertrand—no one did innocent like Nora. "Do you think Griffin could set up his interview time first?"

Before Bertrand could call her on her bullshit, Ross stepped in. "After we've set up Mr. York's interview, I'll show you to the office you can use while you're here," he told Bertrand.

The detective looked ready to argue but Griffin was already walking away. They all watched him leave and Ross crossed to the door, stopped and sent Bertrand a raised brow look.

Bertrand nodded stiffly at Tori and her sisters. He had to be pissed, but he gave nothing away, kept his expression clear, his movements easy as he joined Ross.

She wrapped her arms around herself, chewed on her lower lip thoughtfully as she watched his back. A man who could hide his emotions so well was dangerous. Best to keep that in mind.

"What the hell was that about?" Layne asked Nora after the door closed behind the cops.

"I wanted to talk to you both alone."

"Next time," Tori said, "just hold up a sign saying Trying to Get Rid of You! It would've been more subtle."

"It worked, didn't it?" Nora turned to Layne. "Okay, no bull, no sugarcoating, just give us the truth, the unequivocal truth. How bad is it?"

Layne swallowed and wiped her palms down the front of her uniform. "It's bad. But nothing I can't handle," she added quickly.

Tori's stomach dropped. Layne was worried. Scared. Neither of which Tori was used to seeing on her sister's face. Couldn't say she liked seeing them now.

"How bad is 'bad'?" she asked, not sure she wanted to know.

"Ross and I are suspended," she said, as if forcing the words out.

"What?" Nora slapped her hands onto her hips, her cheeks flush with anger. "The mayor suspended you? What is he thinking?"

Layne took the band from around her hair and slid it onto her wrist, then combed her fingers through the long strands, her movements jerky and agitated. "He's thinking there are questions that need to be answered. Charges of wrongdoing that need to be investigated."

Tori shook her head. "But you didn't do anything wrong."

Layne always played by the rules. Plus she'd never do anything to jeopardize the career she loved so much.

"Neither one of us did anything wrong." Layne smoothed her hair back, wrapped the band around it again before letting her arms drop to her sides. "But it doesn't look good," she admitted flatly as if she didn't care her entire life was blowing up in front of her. Tori knew better. "It looks like Ross and I used our positions to cover up facts about Dale's death—even though we didn't know he was murdered until an hour ago."

"Why bring in someone?" Tori asked. "Why not let another officer from Mystic Point investigate Dale's murder? Someone from the county to look into the accusations against you and Ross?"

Layne shook her head but it was Nora who answered. "Too big a risk of an investigator from the county having a connection to someone here. Plus, it's no secret Jack Pomeroy and Uncle Kenny are good friends. Pomeroy even worked under Ken when he was D.A."

"It's better this way," Layne said, somehow sounding as if she really meant it. "There will be no questions about the validity of the investigation when our names are cleared."

Okay, Tori could understand that. But it didn't mean she had to be happy that Bertrand was going to be around for a while, dredging up the past when she'd finally thought they could all move forward.

"What can we do to help?" Tori asked.

Gratitude entered Layne's hazel eyes, softened her expression. "Just cooperate with Bertrand. Tell the truth."

"I don't trust him," Nora said, her arms crossed, her shoulders hunched. "You heard what he said. He thinks one of us killed Dale."

"It's his job to suspect everyone." Layne's soothing tone couldn't disguise the apprehension beneath her words. "But we have nothing to hide so we have nothing to worry about."

"Well, *we* may have nothing to hide," Tori said, "but what about Griffin?"

Nora whirled on her. "Don't. Start."

"Griffin was with Nora the night Dale died," Layne pointed out, all logical and coplike. "But Tori's right, he's going to be looked at," she told Nora. "We're all going to be looked at—even Ross because of his relationship with me. We all had motive for wanting Dale dead."

Nora went white. Swayed. Tori held her arm, ready to catch her in case she passed out. "Hey, you okay? Honey, you don't look so good. Sit down."

Nora shook her off, stumbled a few feet away. Her eyes were wide and bleak, her lips trembling. "No. Thanks, I'm fine, I'm just… It's all…crazy. I just…I have to go."

"What?" Tori watched, her mouth open, as Nora grabbed her purse and jacket.

Layne reached out to their younger sister. "Nora—"

"I'm sorry," she said, backing away from them both, her purse clutched to her chest. "I'm really sorry."

Nora slipped out of the room, closing the door softly behind her.

Tori turned to Layne. "We need to hold an intervention. Your place or mine?"

"An intervention for what?"

"To get Nora to tell us what's going on with her. She's obviously keeping something from us."

"I know, but she'll come to us when she's ready."

Tori wasn't so sure. What if they lost her? "You don't think whatever it is it has anything to do with Dale's death. Do you?"

"Of course not. And that's just what Bertrand wants. Us doubting each other, turning against each other."

"You cops are a sneaky breed, you know that?"

"Look, I don't know much about Bertrand but if he works for the A.G.'s office, it means he's good. Really good. We have to be careful." She searched Tori's eyes. "We have to be able to trust each other and count on each other no matter what happens. We have to stick together. It's the only way we'll get through this."

Like they'd done when their mom disappeared and so many other times. No matter the differences between them, her love for her sisters, her commitment to them, was a blessing. And a burden. And she couldn't break free.

"No matter what," Tori repeated, squeezing Layne's hand. "Together."

WALKER'S GAZE SWEPT the Ludlow Street Café's dining room as he headed toward a booth in the back. Busy place. Busier than he would've thought given that it was midafternoon on a Tuesday. Then again, his quick research told him it did a brisk business, one that increased during the summer months when tourists came in droves to the small town.

Sliding into the booth so that he faced the door, he noted the other two visible exits before he turned his coffee cup over. He inspected it and, finding no lipstick smudges, set it on the saucer and waited.

He tapped his fingers against the top of the table.

Searched the room again. Rolled his shoulders back and finally gave in and took off his suit coat and laid it on the seat next to him. Christ, but he hated waiting. Much preferred doing to sitting, though so far today he'd done a hell of a lot of the latter.

But that didn't mean he couldn't be patient when need be. It took time to gather evidence, to sift through facts and unearth the truth. That's what he'd done for the past four hours. Read reports—thoroughly, patiently—anything and everything that had to do with Valerie Sullivan's disappearance and Dale York's background. Dale's criminal record alone had taken up almost an hour of Walker's time, encompassing the years from when Dale legally became an adult until he, too, disappeared from Mystic Point eighteen years ago.

Now it was time to move this investigation into the opening stages.

"Well, hello there, Detective."

Cursing himself for letting her sneak up on him, Walker looked up and met Tori's eyes. Her lips were curved in a flirtatious smile, a coffeepot in her hand. His stomach did one slow roll even as his instincts kicked in—the ones telling him he was ass-deep in trouble.

"Mrs. Mott," he said, keeping his tone polite and formal.

"Don't tell me, you were passing by, minding your business, when you heard one of our famous doughnuts calling your name?"

He liked her voice. The sound of it, all husky and inviting and sexy. The thought, unbidden and unwanted, floated into his brain. He pushed it back out.

"Actually I was hoping to run into you."

She leaned forward to pour coffee into his cup. Her shirt gaped slightly, giving him an enticing view of creamy skin and the soft swell of her breast. She straightened and he jerked his gaze down to the table. But not before catching sight of the humor lighting her eyes.

She was laughing at him. No doubt she thought he was just another man to be crushed under one of her skyscraper heels.

"Were you, now?" she asked. "And why is that?"

He sipped the coffee to ease the dryness of his throat, realized it was better than expected and took another, longer drink. Just because she was sexy enough to make a man's hands sweat didn't mean he had to fall all over himself like some goddamn horny teenager.

It was clear she was used to calling the shots. So was he.

Whether personal or professional, he preferred relationships where he was in charge. Where he was the one to walk away.

He had a feeling no man walked away from her.

"I was hoping to ask you a few questions," he said.

She shifted her weight to her left leg, causing the material of her skirt to stretch across her hips. "And here I thought that was why we set up my interview. Friday afternoon at three forty-five if I'm not mistaken."

He could be patient, he reminded himself. But that didn't mean he had to like it. Didn't mean he couldn't do whatever it took to hurry up the process. "I'm free now," he said mildly.

"Well, isn't that convenient, you coming into this restaurant and sitting in my booth five minutes before my shift ends?"

Walker met her eyes, kept his hands still, didn't want anything to give him away. "Yes. Very convenient."

She made a sound, sort of a hum, then she smiled slowly. "Can I get you something to go with your coffee?"

The scents of grilled meat and French fries reminded

him he hadn't eaten since breakfast, made his mouth water. But he wouldn't order food from her, wouldn't eat in front of her. He couldn't. If they'd been at the police station, he'd never pull out a sandwich and bite into it during an interview.

And that's what this was. Just another interview, a way for him to get information out of her. Not some chummy lunch date. No matter how hungry he was.

"I'm good," he said, lifting his cup for another sip. "Thanks."

"Let me just put this down and we'll have ourselves a nice little chat, hmm?"

He watched her walk away. What living, breathing, heterosexual man wouldn't? Returning a few minutes later, she slid into the seat across from him and set down a bottle of water and a plate with a thick slice of apple pie.

"I hope you don't mind if I eat while you interrogate me," she said, unwrapping a napkin from around a set of silverware. "I skipped lunch."

"This isn't an interrogation."

Tori raised her eyebrows, used her fork to break off the point of the pie, releasing the scents of cooked apples and cinnamon. "Isn't it?"

"Just a few questions."

"I'm going to be in big trouble, you know," she told him in that throaty voice of hers right before she slid the bite of pie into her mouth, her glossy red lips wrapping around the fork.

He narrowed his eyes. In trouble? She was trouble. The kind most men had a hard time resisting.

Luckily he wasn't most men.

"Why would you be in trouble?" he asked.

"Talking to you without a lawyer present?" She shook

her head, forked up another bite. "My sisters aren't going to be too happy with me."

"That happen often? Your sisters being unhappy with you?"

She sipped her water, eyed him over the top of the bottle. "More often than not."

That, at least, had the ring of truth to it. But if it bothered her, he couldn't tell. Which only pissed him off. He read people for a living but with her, he was at a loss. And that made her dangerous. Intriguing.

He drank more coffee to hide his frown. No, not intriguing. She was a means to an end, that was all. The weak link in this case, the one person he figured he had a good shot of using to catch a break in his investigation.

He wouldn't get far with either Chief Taylor or Layne Sullivan—they were both cops, from all accounts good ones. Or at least they had been before they'd started sleeping together, raising suspicions they had let their personal feelings get in the way of their professional ethics. Nora Sullivan had graduated at the top of her class in law school, was smart and savvier than her angelic looks indicated. Her boyfriend, Griffin York, had been through the system himself as a teenager.

Walker chose Tori because she didn't know the legal system, not like her sisters. Because he'd guessed she was stubborn enough, arrogant enough, not to listen to her sisters' warnings about keeping her mouth shut.

She was all flash, no substance, and he wouldn't have to dig far to get to what was inside of her. She was obvious. Fake. He had no use for her, or her… What had her sister called it?

Her sex kitten act.

No, he had no use and little respect for women like her, who used their looks and their bodies to get what they wanted. But he couldn't help but wonder if he'd somehow underestimated her.

Shaking his head, he cleared that crazy thought right out of his mind.

"I have four sisters," he said, trying to draw her out, ease her into trusting him.

"Four? You have my sympathy."

"It wasn't so bad."

"I find that hard to believe. We don't have a brother but we did torment our younger cousin. When he was little, we used to dress him up in our old clothes, shoes, the works. I think there were even a few times when Nora and his sister put makeup on him and did his nails. Bright pink polish."

Walker worked to hide a wince. "No painted nails." At least not that he can remember—thank God. Though there was no way he was telling her about the time Leslie and Kelly, his older sisters, dressed him as Goldilocks for Halloween. Complete with curled hair. "Your cousin, that's Anthony Sullivan, correct?"

Her hesitation was slight, her gaze thoughtful. "It is. Luckily he turned out okay. So far, anyway." Her gaze drifted over Walker. "Seems like you turned out all right yourself."

"So far," he repeated solemnly.

Her lips twitched and he wondered what it would be like to see her smile. A real smile, not one of the practiced ones she shared so readily.

He cleared his throat. Rotated his coffee cup. "I'm grateful to have had my sisters, actually. They taught me a lot about how females think."

Tori laughed, the husky, sexy sound washing over him, scraping against his nerve endings.

"I don't doubt you learned quite a bit about the female psyche during your formative years, but don't go deluding yourself, Detective." Leaning forward, she lowered her voice. "No man knows what women think unless a woman wants him to know."

Then she winked at him, eased back and took another bite of pie.

And he felt as if he'd been hit by a two-by-four.

Damn, but she was good. "Maybe not," he agreed, "but I learned that sisters are always arguing. Someone was always mad at someone else, usually two or three against one but every once in a while they'd all just be pissed at each other."

Finished with her pie, Tori slid the plate away and took a sip of water. "Yes, sisters fight. They argue, yell and hold grudges. But the best part about sisters is no matter what's been said, the names been called or threats made, if they truly love each other, sisters always have each other's backs. And that's despite all the crap, the envy and sibling rivalry, despite knowing each other their entire lives and seeing each other at their best and worst. So if your grand plan here is to create some sort of rift between me and my sisters, don't bother. We've managed that rift all on our own."

Her eyes glittered, her mouth a thin line. Walker couldn't help but think this was the first honest reaction he'd seen from her. Unlike her flirting and coy smiles, this—her anger and frustration—was real.

And more appealing than he would've liked.

"But it doesn't matter," she continued. "Because when it comes to the Sullivan sisters, it's always been us against them." Her eyes met his and he noted the truth in them, the challenge. "And that's how it'll stay."

TORI FORCED HERSELF to sit back, to lower her hands to her lap so Bertrand couldn't see how her fingers curled. At least she wasn't the only one whose control had slipped. He looked ready to chew up his coffee cup, his eyebrows drawn, his shoulders rigid. Yet he still gave off a superior air, as if he was better than her, more capable of winning this game they were playing. As if he was so much smarter than her.

He judged her. And found her lacking. She wanted to climb onto the table, loosen his neatly knotted tie, run her fingers through his hair and muss him up, just to prove he wasn't as unaffected by her as he'd like her to believe.

To prove to them both he was like every other man she'd ever known—easily swayed by a pretty face. Men who only looked skin-deep so that's all she gave them.

All they deserved.

"Mrs. Mott, I can assure you it was not my intention to try to create problems between you and your sisters," the good detective said in that way that made him sound as if he was sitting on something rather uncomfortable.

Tori exhaled softly, worked up a small grin, felt her heart rate slow, her anger cool. "Wasn't it?" And if she believed that, she was an even bigger fool than he thought. "Well, then, let's just say my advice still stands. In case you change your mind and start thinking you can get me to turn against my sisters." She twisted the cap back onto her empty water bottle, waved at Sandy, one of the waitresses working the afternoon shift, then started sliding out of the booth. "If that's all—"

"It's not." He indicated the seat.

One foot out of the booth, she stilled. Her fingers tightened on the bottle. She didn't take well to being told what to do, not even silently. But she'd agreed to speak with him here, on her own instead of having every word she uttered vetted by some lawyer Layne and Nora had chosen, because she had nothing to hide. At least, nothing that had to do with his investigation.

She sat back, stretched her arm across the back of the booth, inhaled deeply and arched her back ever-so-subtly.

His gaze dipped—just for a second—to her breasts.

Looked like he was human after all.

She ignored the way her heart pounded, how her skin warmed from his quick glance. "I'm all yours, Detective Bertrand."

His eyes stayed flat and so cool she shivered.

"Somehow," he murmured, "I doubt that."

CHAPTER FOUR

WORKING TO KEEP her expression unchanged, Tori slid her arm down, pretending she was reaching over to straighten the metal napkin holder. She wished she could cross her arms over her chest, hunch her shoulders and duck her head, but that would be surrendering.

She could handle him; she could handle any man. It was what she did.

Bertrand pulled a notebook from his pocket. "Were you aware that Dale York had arrived in Mystic Point in July of this year?"

"Of course."

"When did you become aware of Mr. York's presence in town?" he asked when it became clear she wasn't about to offer more information.

"I'm not sure of the exact date."

He wrote something. "You must've been surprised he was back."

"Yes." Just thinking about it, about Dale walking around her town, made her throat constrict. "Yes, I certainly was surprised."

Surprised. Furious. More scared than she'd ever been in her life.

When Layne had come into the café that hot July day and told Tori that Dale was in town, Tori's first instinct had been to grab her son and run. To somehow escape what she'd known would only be more heartache and pain. To try to escape the past.

Her family had only just begun to come to terms with the fact that after all these years, Dale would probably never be found, would never be brought to justice for murdering their mother. The cops had tried to track him down but it was as if he had vanished from the face of the earth the night he left town.

Until he waltzed into the Mystic Point police station, hard-eyed and cocky, and claimed he wanted to cooperate with the investigation.

"Did you and Mr. York cross paths during the two weeks he was in Mystic Point?"

"Once," she said with a casual wave of her hand, as if their encounter had been of no importance. "But then, I'm guessing you already know that, don't you?"

Again he waited, giving her a look that said he had one nerve left and she was getting on it.

She blinked innocently at him. Well, as innocently as possible.

He flipped through his notebook. "You were listed as a witness to an assault the night of July 17 at a bar called the Yacht Pub." He lifted his head, his pen poised over paper. "Is that correct?"

"If it's in your handy dandy notebook, I'd say it must be."

He set the notebook aside, laid his hands flat on the table. "Mrs. Mott, police reports indicate you were a witness to an altercation that night between Dale York and his son, Griffin. Your sister Nora also witnessed the event and your other sister, Captain Sullivan, was the arresting officer."

Tori's stomach grew queasy. She was starting to see how bad this all looked to someone on the outside. How it could be construed that her family had conspired against the man who killed their mother. "That's right."

"You and your sister Nora went to the bar together?"

"No. I was with a group of friends. Nora was there when I arrived."

"She was alone?"

"She was with Griffin." Tori tipped her bottle, watched a drop of water slide to the top, then flipped it again. She'd been so upset seeing her sister sitting next to Griffin York at the Yacht Pub, the bar where their mother had tended bar. Where Val and Dale had started their affair.

"You went to school together, you and Griffin York."

"We did. Although we hardly ran around with the same crowd. I was half of Mystic Point High's hottest couple and he was the ultimate bad boy, hauling around that chip on his shoulder, a perpetual smirk on his face."

"You don't like him," Bertrand said.

Truth or lie? She had no problem with lies but sensed it wouldn't hurt to tell the truth in this instance. "Those are some seriously well-honed investigating skills, Detective."

"The police report also indicated that Griffin started the fight."

She may not like Griffin, wasn't sure she trusted him, but Nora did. Nora loved him. "Dale instigated it."

"How?"

"He got grabby with Nora." An exaggeration, one Tori didn't regret. As far as she was concerned, Griffin had every reason and every right to have laid into Dale that night. "Griffin punched him. They fought. Layne broke it up—"

"By using her Taser on Dale."

"He charged at her," Tori said, straightening. Bertrand was trying to turn things around, make it seem as if Layne had used unnecessary force because they all hated Dale.

"She was defending herself and trying to get the situation under control. Besides, it wasn't like she shot him."

"This morning at Chief Taylor's office, you said you were glad Dale York was dead."

She narrowed her eyes. Wasn't he clever, trying to trip her up with his lightning-fast questions? "Actually you asked if I was happy Dale was dead. I didn't answer. But I will now. Yes. I'm glad he's dead."

"Mrs. Mott, where were you the night Dale York died?"

"You think I killed Dale?" she asked, wondering if she'd made a mistake, a big one, in agreeing to speak with Bertrand here, now, on her own.

"I think you hated him," Bertrand said, watching her carefully. "That you were angry there wasn't enough evidence to charge him with your mother's murder."

"Right on both counts. But I didn't kill him."

"Your whereabouts that night?" he asked again.

"I was at the country club with the rest of my family. It was my cousin's engagement party."

He jotted that in his damn notebook. She wanted to snatch it up, take it into the kitchen and burn it on the stove.

"What time did you leave the party?"

"Midnight? Maybe a little later." She tossed the empty bottle aside. It rolled across the table, stopping at the salt and pepper shaker holder. "Look, it was late and—"

"Were you drinking that night?"

"I had a few glasses of wine." Had needed them considering her ex, Greg, had been there with his new girlfriend. Colleen Gibbs taught at the same school as Tori's cousin Erin so Tori had spent a tense evening watching them cozy up to each other. Even though Tori knew she'd made the right decision asking Greg for a divorce, seeing him with her, seeing how happy he was with another woman—when she'd failed so miserably at being his wife—hurt.

"Were your sisters there?"

"My sisters, my father and Celeste—"

"Celeste Vitello, your father's girlfriend and owner of this establishment?"

Nerves tumbled in Tori's stomach. She hadn't been far off the mark with her smartass comment about his investigation skills. He was good, better than she'd expected.

Lesson learned.

"Yes," she ground out, hating that he'd pushed her into being unable to muster up any pretense of indifference. "Ross was there, too, as was Griffin—for an hour or so—not to mention my uncle and his family and around two hundred of my cousin and her fiancé's closest friends."

"Where did you go when you left the party?"

"Home."

"Alone?"

Now she smiled, slow and easy. "I had several men offer me their…company…but yes, I was alone."

Bertrand looked at her as if he didn't believe her. "Your son didn't go home with you?"

Her son. He knew about Brandon. She snorted silently. Of course he did. He probably knew what color panties she had on, what she liked to eat for breakfast and how much money she made in tips last year.

"Brandon went home with his father." He preferred being at his father's house. Preferred being with Greg and Colleen over Tori.

She was surprised Bertrand didn't know that as well.

"So no one can verify your whereabouts during the hours of midnight until Dale York's body was found at approximately 6:00 a.m.?"

"Nope."

He leaned forward. "Mrs. Mott, did you kill Dale York?"

She mimicked his stance and tone. "No, Detective Bertrand, I did not. Although as far as I'm concerned, whoever did kill him did the world a favor."

"There's no proof Dale York killed your mother," he said, all emotionally closed off and professional. "What if he was innocent?"

"Just because there's no proof doesn't mean he wasn't guilty. I would've thought they'd have taught you that at the police academy." She slid to her feet, reached back for the water bottle.

"What are you doing?" he asked, looking completely confused and irritated.

"This is called leaving. It's what happens when I get tired of a conversation or am bored. I'm both. And since you've asked me all your very important questions, I see no reason for us to have our official meeting Friday afternoon. But before we both go our separate ways, there is one thing I want to say."

"I can hardly wait," he muttered.

"This thing with Layne, it's a load of crap. She doesn't break the rules…she makes sure the rules are maintained. And Ross? He's as by-the-book as they come."

"He's sleeping with a subordinate officer. Wait," he said, holding up a hand, "don't tell me. They're in love and love trumps everything else, even rules, regulations and law and order?"

"I have no idea if they're in love or in lust or just scratching an itch until something or someone else comes along. All I know is that they're two unattached adults and neither one would let their personal relationship interfere with their jobs. And they sure as hell wouldn't create some sort of grand conspiracy."

"I guess that'll be determined. I'll determine it."

"You're an arrogant one, aren't you?" she asked softly. "Confident. As if your badge gives you the right to look down on the rest of us mere mortals. I thought a good cop waited until he had all the facts before deciding whether someone was guilty, but you...you've already judged us. And found us guilty."

He held her gaze, not the least bit cowed by her sharp words, her acerbic tone. "I'm trying to get to the truth."

"I hope you find it because it's going to prove that neither my sister nor Ross have done anything illegal or unethical. It's also going to show that no one in my family killed Dale York."

She walked away. And prayed that she was right. Because if Bertrand discovered something, anything, that could be used against her sister or any member of her family, they were screwed.

LATE FRIDAY AFTERNOON, Anthony Sullivan pulled a coffee cup from the dispenser. Ever since his freshman year at Boston University, he stopped at this same store whenever he got back into town. Some habits were hard to break.

The bell on the door rang and he glanced over—and wished he'd attended a twelve-step program for lovers of bad convenience store coffee.

It was her. Jessica Taylor. He knew he should look away, but his eyes locked on her. She held the door, said something to the short redhead who waitressed with her at the café. Then she laughed, the sound seeming to float across the store to wrap around him. Torture him.

Goddamn her.

Ducking his head, he watched the chemically enhanced vanilla-flavored coffee squirt into the takeout cup. His shoulders ached with tension. His chest was tight, as if he'd explode if he took a full breath.

They'd met here, right here at this very spot, well over three months ago. When he'd run in for a coffee, he hadn't known his entire life was about to change. But then he'd turned and saw her and it was as if he'd been struck by lightning. As if everything out of order in his life had neatly fallen into place.

He'd been such an idiot.

Anthony sensed her approaching, caught sight of her from the corner of his eye. She was close enough he could smell her light perfume. Could reach out and trace his finger down the softness of her cheek like he used to. Longing mixed with the anger in his gut, made it impossible to ignore the memories that rushed into his mind. Ones he'd been fighting ever since he walked away from her.

"Anthony," she said, her voice breathless. Scared. She cleared her throat. "Hi."

He should walk away now. He didn't owe her anything, not even politeness. But he made the mistake of turning, and noticed how nervous she looked, the way she twisted her hands together at her waist.

And his feet froze to the floor.

"Hey," he said gruffly, all he could give her. All he wanted to give to the girl who'd lied to him, who'd made him look like such a fool.

She'd cut her hair, he realized with a jolt, his fingers twitching with the need to touch it, to see if it was still as soft as he remembered. Instead of falling to her shoulders, the pale, almost white strands barely reached her chin now and her thick, straight bangs skimmed her eyebrows.

She was unique, so different from all the other girls with her light hair and blue eyes, her lush curves and go-to-hell attitude. She was beautiful. Smart. Funny and sarcastic and jaded. It was the combination of her looks and her world-weary attitude—as if she'd seen and done it all and found each experience boring as hell—that made her seem older. More mature.

Except she was neither. She was sixteen.

He'd kissed her, touched her and she was just a kid, five years younger than he was, two years too young for him.

When he looked at her, when his stomach tightened with attraction, he felt like a creep. Like a loser who couldn't get a girl his own age or worse, some pedophile preying on young girls. He hadn't known the truth about her age until after they were involved. But he knew now. It should be enough, he thought desperately, her age and the fact that she lied, should be more than enough reason for him to hate her.

He didn't. Couldn't.

Anthony turned away. His movements unsteady, he grabbed his full cup with too much force and coffee sloshed over the side and burned his fingers. Swearing under his breath, he jerked his hand back.

Jessica reached for him, frowning in concern. "You okay?"

Wiping his hand on the side of his leg, he stepped back. If she touched him, he'd be lost. Wrapped up in her again, unable to get her out of his head when he'd finally, finally, stopped thinking about her every day. Stopped dreaming about her.

"I'm fine," he said, more harshly than he'd intended.

She dropped her arm. Swallowed and then licked her lips. "Uh, are you on fall break?"

"Brandon's first game is tomorrow." Anthony dug his wallet out of his back pocket. "I promised him I'd go."

"Oh, right. He's really excited."

Anthony rubbed his thumb across his wallet with

enough force to wear a hole in the soft leather. Brandon was his cousin, his family. Not hers. But she'd managed to infiltrate even that part of his life. Ross Taylor, her uncle and guardian, practically lived with Anthony's cousin Layne. As long as Layne and Ross were together, Jess would be there, at Brandon's games, at family celebrations and holidays.

"How's school?" she asked, just like everybody else who didn't know what to say to him.

He sipped his coffee, glanced over her head. "Same as always."

"Good. That's…good."

She paused, looking at him expectantly, but he wasn't about to ask her how she was, what she'd been doing lately. She picked up a candy bar and turned it in her hands.

He'd teased her about the candy bars when they'd first met. Had flirted and practically begged for her number. He didn't usually go to so much effort. If a girl wasn't interested, he moved on, no harm, no foul. But he'd seen a vulnerability in her eyes, a softness and hopefulness that intrigued him. He'd wanted to break down her walls, see who she really was behind her cynical smirk.

It'd taken time and patience but he'd done just that. He'd gotten to know her, the intelligent, wounded girl who'd so quickly stolen his heart. He'd trusted her, had told her things he'd never told anyone else. His doubts about going to law school, how pressured he felt to follow in his father's footsteps. He'd thought what they had was real but it was all some sort of joke on her part.

"Well," she said, sounding disappointed he wasn't willing to pretend everything was okay between them. That he forgave her. "I guess I'll see you around sometime."

He shrugged. Sent her a cool look as he took another

sip of his coffee, the hot liquid scalding the roof of his mouth. "Probably."

Only way he could figure to avoid it was to never set foot in Mystic Point.

It might be worth it just so he'd never have to see her again.

Keira walked up to them, her quizzical gaze going from Jess to him. "Hey, Anthony," she said, her tone friendly as always, but she linked her arm with Jess's, a clear sign of whose side she was really on.

He tipped his cup. Message received. "Good to see you, Keira."

And he walked away. As he paid for his coffee and a pack of gum, he felt Jess watching him. Waiting.

He pocketed his change, dropping a couple of coins in the process. They spun on the dirty floor, but he didn't bother picking them up, just shoved open the door and stepped out into the bright sunshine and hurried to his Jeep. Only when he was inside, the radio blaring, did he take a full breath, his lungs burning painfully.

He shouldn't feel guilty. He didn't owe her anything. Not friendship or whatever she was looking for. She'd used him. Lied to him. Made him look like an idiot. She'd caused him nothing but trouble, brought with her nothing but heartbreak. He was better off without her. Hell, even if none of that was true, he couldn't be with her—not without going against everything he'd been taught his entire life about how a man was supposed to act. Everything that he knew was right.

So he'd let her go.

But he hadn't wanted to. Despite everything, despite only being with her for a few weeks, he still felt a connection with her. Still wanted her.

And he had to learn to live with that.

WALKER STEPPED OUT into the parking lot of the police station and inhaled deeply. The briny scent of the ocean tickled his nose. Made him realize he couldn't remember the last time he'd been out on his sailboat.

He worked too much, he thought, shifting the folders in his arm, his laptop case in his other hand. If he hadn't known it as fact, his mother and sisters were all too happy to remind him. Every chance they got.

The breeze ruffled his hair as he approached his car. Setting the folders on the roof so he could dig his keys from his front pocket, he glanced up, saw Officer Evan Campbell, with his round cheeks and earnestness, standing by a cruiser. He glared at Walker, his thin arms crossed over his chest. The kid didn't look old enough to drive, was pathetically easy to read and was about as intimidating as Paisley, Walker's six-month-old niece. And yet the great state of Massachusetts had seen fit to legally entitle him to carry a firearm.

He was as obvious in his resentment of Walker as the rest of the town's police department. Hell, anytime Walker set one foot outside of the office he'd been assigned at the station, all sound and most movement ceased. It was actually a pretty cool trick, the way every person in the building went completely still, as if they weren't even going to breathe in his presence lest he somehow contaminate their air.

Suddenly feeling a hell of a lot older than thirty-six and wearier than he should, Walker took off his sunglasses, rubbed the bridge of his nose between his thumb and forefinger. He dropped his hand and held Campbell's gaze until the kid shifted and looked away. Then after a moment, walked into the station.

And all was right with the world once again.

"Do you have a minute?"

Walker didn't jump at the sound of the voice, but it was close. "Any questions or comments about your suspension can be directed at the mayor," Walker told Taylor as he unlocked his car and set his laptop on the backseat.

"This isn't about my suspension. It's about you interviewing Tori Mott without her attorney being present."

"It wasn't a formal interview."

"It was a fishing expedition."

It was, but Walker wouldn't admit it. He gathered the folders, put them on top of the laptop before facing Taylor. "Mrs. Mott agreed to speak to me without the presence of legal counsel and was free to go at any time."

Even if he had indicated otherwise. But she'd left, hadn't she? Without him stopping her.

It'd been a risk, talking to her outside of the police station without the legality of a formal interview. But he'd seen the opportunity and had taken it.

Just because he helped enforce the rules didn't mean he was above bending them a bit when it suited his purpose.

"Any judge worth their robe will toss out anything she had to say," Taylor said.

Undoubtedly. "I guess that's a chance I'm willing to take."

Taylor stepped forward, his eyes hidden by sunglasses, his mouth a hard line. But his voice remained neutral. "While you're taking chances, Captain Sullivan and I are fighting for our careers and reputations and a murderer is walking free. Maybe you'd do better to play things by the book instead of playing hotshot."

"When it comes to solving my cases, I do whatever it takes to get justice for the victims. Whether you get caught in that crossfire, are found innocent or guilty, really doesn't matter to me. All that matters is finding the truth."

Walker had the sense that Taylor was studying him behind the dark lenses of his glasses. Trying to see how far he could push, if he could push him at all.

He couldn't. At least, not without getting shoved in return.

Finally the chief nodded slightly as if coming to a decision. He held out a large mailing envelope. "Here."

Walker narrowed his eyes. "What is it?"

"A little light reading for the weekend."

Walker opened the flap, pulled out the thin sheath of papers and scanned them. They were copies of bank records. "Who is Joel Cannella?"

"Dale York. At least, that's who he was for the past eighteen years."

"What? Where did you get these?" A thought occurred to him and he squared himself to Taylor so they were toe-to-toe. The few inches he had on Taylor didn't make up for the twenty pounds Taylor had over him, but it would make any physical altercation between them interesting. "Did you take these from the station? Do you realize what the penalty is for tampering with an ongoing investigation?"

Taylor kept his hands loose at his sides, his shoulders relaxed. "I'm aware of the consequences of breaking the law. But those papers were never in the station or entered into evidence. They're something I was working on before your arrival."

"Covering your tracks, Chief?"

"Doing a little research, Detective."

Walker didn't believe it. Taylor was probably trying to make it look as if he'd been investigating Dale's death as mysterious this entire time. "I was under the impression Dale's whereabouts for the past eighteen years were unknown and now you're telling me you discovered he'd been living under the alias of Joel Cannella in—" he checked the address listed on the form "—Corpus Christi all that time?"

"No identification of any kind was found on Dale's body, in his room or car, not even a credit card. The only thing in his wallet, besides a couple of hundred dollars," Taylor continued, "was a piece of paper with a nine-digit number. I asked a friend of mine who used to work in the Crime Lab Unit of the Boston P.D. to do some digging for me. After a few false starts, he discovered the number was for Cannella's bank account. Once I had the name, I was able to track down Cannella's movements and found a safe-deposit box in a bank in Marblehead rented in his name." He inclined his head toward the envelope. "You'll find the contents in there."

Walker turned the envelope upside down. A driver's license, social security card and a credit card all bearing the name Joel Cannella slid out. The photo on the license, though, was none other than Dale York.

He squeezed the license, the hard plastic cutting into his fingers. "This should have all been logged into evidence."

"Yes."

But it hadn't been. Walker had seen everything the MPPD had about both Valerie Sullivan's murder and Dale York's death. There was no mention of any account numbers or that Dale's alias had been discovered.

"You're admitting—to the officer investigating accusations of ethics violations against you—that you withheld evidence?" Walker asked.

"I'm handing over evidence that I believe will be helpful to the officer in charge of Dale's murder investigation."

"You want to help me? Why?"

"Because it's the right thing to do. And because once I saw those toxicology reports, I would've fully investigated Mr. York's death as a murder."

"I guess we'll never know if that's the truth or not."

"No, we won't. But instead of whiling away our time trying to see which one of us can piss farther, I thought it might be in both of our best interests to get these investigations over as soon as possible."

"You mean it's in your best interest. And I don't need help with investigations." He worked alone. Part of the reason he enjoyed his job was that he wasn't stuck with a partner, didn't need every idea he had, every move he wanted to make, vetted by someone else.

And he sure didn't need Taylor getting involved. Walker already had a case with so many twists, turns and knots, he didn't think he'd ever get it all straightened out.

"I screwed up," Taylor said simply and, if Walker was reading him right, honestly. "I had no reason to suspect Mr. York died of anything other than natural causes. I had the coroner's report telling me it was a heart attack and there were no signs of foul play, nothing to indicate a struggle had taken place or that another person had even been in that motel room."

"Could've been suicide," Walker said.

"You don't believe that any more than I do."

"No, I don't. But I have to cover all the bases." Had to cover his ass. Taylor might want to consider doing the same.

"There was no goodbye note, no confession of guilt and remorse. Hell, there wasn't so much as an aspirin found on scene." Taylor's jaw tightened. "All the evidence pointed to a heart attack. But…"

"But?"

"My instincts told me otherwise."

Walker shoved the cards back into the envelope. "Those the same instincts that told you to keep pertinent evidence hidden?"

"I had no proof it was pertinent until Tuesday."

"And yet you still kept digging until you found out who Dale had become, where he'd been all these years."

"I had my reasons."

Walker widened his stance. "Reasons like wanting to bring some sort of closure, give some answers to Captain Sullivan and her family?"

Taylor took off his sunglasses and hooked them to the neck of his shirt. "You think I don't know how this looks, how tangled it is? Believe me, all I want is the truth."

"That might be hard to come by. Dale York was the main suspect in Valerie Sullivan's murder but everyone knew there wasn't enough evidence to even charge him with the crime. He was a free man and, unless a witness came forward or he confessed, he'd remain a free man. That couldn't have sat well with the family and loved ones of Valerie Sullivan. That's plenty of people with motive."

A car pulled into the lot. Taylor waited until the person had entered the building before asking, "What if Dale didn't kill Valerie?"

"Do you think York was innocent?"

"I think it's a possibility."

"That's about as big of a nonanswer as you could give while still speaking."

Respect entered Taylor's eyes but was quickly banked. "I don't like to speculate. I look at the facts and the facts pointed to Dale York being the most viable suspect."

"Most viable, but not the only suspect." Walker watched Taylor carefully. "Captain Sullivan admitted to having argued with her mother the night she disappeared."

"Captain Sullivan was only fourteen—"

"We both know that doesn't mean anything."

"She's innocent," Taylor said mildly.

Walker couldn't help but admire the chief's control. His

conviction. "Are you saying that because your instincts and the facts are telling you she's innocent? Or because you're sleeping with her?"

"I'm saying it as a cop with fifteen years' experience."

"But you're still not sure Dale York was guilty of the murder."

"I had some questions," Taylor admitted slowly. "Such as where Mr. York spent the past eighteen years, why he disappeared off the face of the earth. Why he came back if he was guilty."

Walker had those questions, too, especially the one about York returning to town. He'd told the police he'd been out of the country and when he heard that he was wanted for questioning regarding his lover's death, he'd sauntered into Mystic Point as if he'd done nothing wrong.

Walker suspected York returned to Mystic Point because he knew the police didn't have any evidence against him pertaining to Valerie Sullivan's murder. With no evidence, there was no reason for him not to cooperate with the police.

But that didn't mean he wasn't guilty.

"I don't think Dale returned to Mystic Point just to cooperate with the investigation," Taylor continued. "He knew he was safe coming back here, and we couldn't get him to break on his story that he'd gone to the quarry to meet with Valerie as planned but she never showed. He ditched his car there and took a bus out of town. So why did he leave if he didn't kill her? And what was the real reason he came back?" He nodded at the envelope. "I'm guessing something in there will lead to the answers to those questions."

"Or more questions." Nothing new there. Oftentimes when one layer of truth was peeled away, another truth was revealed. Or another lie.

"Valerie Sullivan disappeared September 20, 1994," Taylor said.

"I'm well aware of—"

"Check the date when that bank account was opened. And the amount deposited."

Walker flipped through the pages then used his finger to trace the lines until he found the date. September 19, 1994. He whistled under his breath. "Where the hell did a small-time convict like York get a half a million dollars?"

"That's what you need to figure out. Once you do, I have a feeling, you'll find out who killed him." Taylor put his sunglasses back on. "And who really killed Valerie Sullivan."

CHAPTER FIVE

TORI WIGGLED HER hips to the synthesized song playing through her headphones, did a little shoulder shake that undoubtedly looked better in her imagination than reality, but what the hell? It was hard to worry about smooth moves when Beyonce sang about girls running the world.

Amen, sister. They didn't need no stinkin' men.

If she felt the slightest twinge of guilt for the thought when her son was in his bedroom, no one had to know but her.

Doing a two-step shuffle, Tori added a package of ground beef to the hot pan on the stove. She loved her son and in general liked men just fine. They came in very handy for certain tasks including, but not limited to, rodent disposal, unclogging drains and lawn maintenance.

Yeah, yeah. She was more than capable of taking care of all of that on her own. Being raised by Layne, the original self-sufficient, hear-me-roar-while-I-burn-my-bra woman, Tori had no choice but to learn how to take care of herself.

And she did. But some tasks were better suited to the male of their species.

Hey, she may be empowered and independent and blah, blah, blah, but that didn't mean she had any desire to get within ten feet of a mouse. She didn't care how dead it was.

She stirred the meat. Tapped the spoon against the side of the pan then went back to dancing. God knew she was better off on her own. She'd gotten so tired of always wondering, worrying if she was good enough for Greg. If she was making him happy.

The answers to the above were resounding *hell nos*. Followed by the realization that if she didn't get free from Greg, from his adoration and expectations, she'd do worse, much worse, than make him unhappy. She'd break his heart. Damage him beyond repair.

Like her mother had done to her father.

Still, she'd hurt him. She'd known she would, but it had been the only way either of them could have a chance at happiness. One he grabbed mighty quick with the super sweet, super malleable Colleen.

She'd wanted Greg to be happy, Tori reminded herself adding salt to the beef, giving it a stir. For him to find a woman who could return the love he'd showered upon Tori. The love that had suffocated her. That she hadn't been able to return, no matter how badly she'd wanted to.

The song ended and a slow one started, one about love and loss and heartbreak. Not tonight, she thought, clicking Forward until she found Kelly Clarkson's "What Doesn't Kill You." Tori smiled. That's bet—

Someone tapped her shoulder and she whirled around with a shriek, held the spoon over her shoulder like a small baseball bat. She blinked but the image of Layne glowering at her remained.

Tori lowered her arm and yanked the headphones out, her heart racing, her breathing ragged. "God! You scared the crap out of me. There's this new thing, it's called knocking. You should try it. I hear it's all the rage in Europe."

"What the hell is wrong with you?" Layne asked, pacing the kitchen, her strides aggressive and pissed off. She spun around, jabbed a finger in Tori's direction and Tori considered hitting her sister upside the head with the spoon on principle. "Are you really that stubborn? Or just stupid?"

Tori's face warmed even as her fingers twitched on the spoon. She tossed it aside, lowered the heat under the pan, taking a moment to gather her control, to shore up the act she always, always maintained.

The one where she pretended she didn't care what her sister, what anyone, thought of her.

She faced Layne. "I'm not, nor have I ever been, stupid."

"I told you not to speak with Bertrand without your lawyer being there," Layne said. In a pair of faded jeans and a sky-blue T-shirt, her hair down, she looked...well... *pretty* was the word that came to mind. Softer. More approachable. Almost...human.

Instead of the robotic cop and judgmental older sister Tori knew her to be.

"First of all," Tori said as she opened a bag of tortilla chips and helped herself to one, "I don't have a lawyer."

Layne rolled her eyes. Tori wondered if maybe Brandon, who saw the back of his head more often than not lately, picked up that annoying trait from his aunt. "Uncle Ken wouldn't have recommended having Russell Wixsom represent you if he didn't think he was the best choice."

Tori nibbled on her chip. "I'm sure Russell is a fine lawyer, but I didn't hire him. You all made that decision for me. So when Detective Bertrand stopped by the café the other day and asked if we could have a little chat, I decided to agree."

"Wait. He found you at the café?"

Tori brushed off her fingers. "Is that a cop thing? Repeating everything you're told? Because it's really annoying." But Layne just looked at her. "*Found* me is a bit misleading seeing as how I wasn't hiding, but yes, he came into the café."

"When?" Layne asked so quickly, Tori raised her eyebrows.

"The day we had our little meeting in Ross's office—"

"Tell me, exactly what happened. What was said."

Tori bit back the flip retort on the tip of her tongue. Layne seemed so serious, her expression hard, her eyes searching, Tori didn't have it in her to be a bitch. Not at the moment anyway. So, while Layne grabbed a handful of chips and ate them with the salsa Tori had poured into a bowl and set on the table, Tori recounted the conversation between her and Bertrand. It hadn't been that long of a discussion, but even so, by the time Tori finished, Layne had plowed through half the salsa.

"That's it?" Layne asked. "That's all he said? You said?"

"Yep." Other than her defending her sister and Ross. But Layne didn't need to know everything.

"That son of a bitch." Layne shoved another chip into her mouth and chewed viciously. "He sought you out."

There was a loud thud, then a burst of laughter from Brandon and his best friend playing video games upstairs. Tori smiled. She never got tired of hearing her son's laugh. It was an all-too-rare occurrence lately.

"I hate to break it to you," Tori said, sprinkling taco seasoning into the meat, "but I've had men seeking me out for a number of years now."

She'd learned early that she could use her looks and people's reactions to them to her advantage.

It was the one lesson her mother had taught so very well.

"Which was why I've always told you not to give them

what they want," Layne said, sticking her head in Tori's refrigerator.

Her sister always thought that was what Tori did. Gave men what they wanted. As if she was so needy, so lacking in self-respect, she rolled over for any man just because he paid attention to her.

Why bother trying to change her mind?

"I have a hard time imagining Detective Bertrand wanting anything from me other than answers," Tori said.

He'd looked down on her. Was condescending. Arrogant.

"Don't you have any beer?" Layne asked, her head still in the fridge.

"No." Beer wasn't in the budget. Tori hip-checked her sister with enough force to push Layne into the door. The condiments rattled. "Get out of there," Tori said. "If you're thirsty, have some lemonade."

Layne straightened, the lemonade in her hand. "You never should've talked to him alone."

"So you've mentioned. But why shouldn't I answer his questions? I have nothing to hide and it was convenient. He was there. I'd just got done with my shift—"

"He was using you," Layne said flatly, pouring two glasses of lemonade and handing one to Tori before drinking deeply. "He chose you, waited until he knew you were finishing up work and then he pounced, hoping you'd be tired, that you'd be in a hurry to go and your guard was down."

No kidding. God, her sister must think she was a complete idiot. Tori pulled lettuce, tomato, cheese and avocados from the refrigerator. Slammed the door shut.

"He chose you," Layne continued, as always oblivious to how sanctimonious she sounded, how offensive, "because he sees you as an easy mark."

Tori carefully laid the tomatoes on the counter before she squeezed them into pulp. "As usual, I'm flattered and, I have to admit, a bit humbled by your high opinion of me." She handed the avocados to Layne. "Make yourself useful and cut these, please."

Layne took a large knife from the wooden block on the counter. "I'm just saying it's what I would've done. Figured out who the weak link was and go after them first, try to create dissent in the ranks, if you will."

"I'm no one's weak link," Tori said, ripping the plastic off the lettuce with way more force than necessary. No man used her. Not if she didn't want him to. "Just because I didn't study The Law doesn't mean I'm brainless. And there's no reason to create dissent in the ranks—and really, could you ever just talk like a normal woman instead of a cop?—because as we both know, we already have dissent."

"What? No, we don't." Layne whacked the knife down on an avocado's pit and twisted. "We're the same as we always were."

"Even if that was a good thing—and I'm not so sure— it's not exactly true. I mean, look at Nora. She's been avoiding us for months."

"Maybe she's just engrossed in the newness of her relationship with Griffin."

"She's keeping something from us. She can barely be around us more than half an hour. Mark my words, she has a secret."

"I think she probably just feels weird, being with Griffin. She's getting used to it and, knowing Nora, trying to ease us into the idea as well."

"Seeing as how she's obviously not going to get rid of him any time soon, I'd say she could knock off with the weirdness. Besides, there's more to it than that." Glancing at the doorway to make sure Brandon and his friend weren't there, she lowered her voice. "Do you think she knows something about what really happened to Dale?"

"Of course not. What could she know? And don't start spouting off about Griffin being a possible murder suspect," Layne ordered.

Tori, her mouth open to do just that, shrugged ill-naturedly. "You act as if it's beyond the realm of possibility."

"If Nora says Griffin was with her that night, then that's where he was."

"Maybe he snuck out while she was in an orgasmic induced coma."

"No. Nora wouldn't lie about something like that, not even to protect Griffin. She's too honest, you know that." Layne pointed an avocado at Tori. "And no more talking to Bertrand on your own."

"I don't know what you're so worried about. I certainly didn't kill Dale." A thought occurred to her. "Oh, my God. You didn't kill him, did you?"

Layne glared at her.

Tori held her hands up. "Okay, okay. I was just asking."

"Mom," Brandon said, coming into the kitchen, his best friend Ryan behind him. "Oh, hi, Aunt Layne."

"Hey, tiger. What's up?"

He lifted a shoulder, and took a chip as their cat Fang padded into the room then settled on the rug in front of the back door. "When's dinner?" he asked Tori.

"Soon. Why don't you help speed things up by setting the table?"

He went to the cupboard without complaint. Her mom-sense started tingling, telling her he was up to something. Her son didn't do anything she asked lately without complaints, groans or out-and-out defiance.

"Are you eating with us, Aunt Layne?" he asked, taking down four plates.

"I'm sure Aunt Layne and Ross have plans," Tori said.

Layne cleared her throat. "Actually Ross is at his parents' house. He wanted to explain everything that's going on to them in person."

Then Layne did the strangest thing. She looked at Tori as if asking permission. Or waiting for an invitation.

What was up with that? She and Layne didn't hang out, not on their own anyway. They did the family thing at holidays and birthdays, sometimes did dinner when Nora set it up, but that was it. They'd never been friends. Were too different to ever be close.

Brandon glanced between them. "So is that yes or no?"

Layne smiled but it looked forced. "I just stopped by to talk to your mom. I'll probably grab something at the café later."

And it hit Tori, what Layne was going through. Her job was on the line, her ethics were being questioned. She was stuck between doing what was right, what her job entailed and protecting her family. She wasn't in it alone. She had Ross and her family and they'd all stand by her for as long as she needed them.

But she was alone tonight.

"Aunt Layne's staying," Tori said, keeping her tone matter-of-fact. If Layne thought for one moment that Tori felt sorry for her, she'd lay into Tori like the wrath of God.

Brandon set the plates on the table, came back over to her for the forks. "Can Ryan spend the night?"

"What about the game tomorrow? You both need your rest."

He shook his floppy hair out of his eyes. "We'll go to bed early. Come on, Mom. Please?"

Damn it. She hated to be put in a corner like this, always felt like she had to claw her way out. Tori glanced toward the table where Layne and Ryan discussed the chances of the Patriots making it to the Superbowl this year. Brandon knew he wasn't supposed to ask if someone could stay when that friend was in the same room. It made it that much harder to say no.

"I thought we'd hang out tonight," she said softly, brushing his hair back then letting her hand linger on his shoulder. It was hard to believe he was already almost as tall as she was. Her boy, her baby with his soft cheeks, braces and wiry build. "Just you and me. We could get a couple of movies and I'll make root beer floats—"

"I want Ryan to stay," he said, stepping back.

Her stomach dropped. She didn't take his rejection, his attitude, personally. At ten months shy of becoming a teenager, he was just asserting his independence.

No, she didn't, wouldn't, take it personally. Even though he was always perfectly happy to spend time with his dad and Colleen.

Brandon was her heart. Her joy. He had Greg's light brown hair and smile, his father's way with numbers and athletic ability. But his eyes were all her. When she looked at him, she got such a rush of love so pure, so true, it still had the power to bring her to her knees.

He was the only male she'd ever loved unconditionally. Being a mother was the only thing she'd ever been any good at.

But since the divorce, every move she made, every decision, came with self-doubt and worry that her son's resentment toward her would only grow. That she'd lose him completely someday.

"I guess it's okay if Ryan stays," she said slowly. "But it's lights out at nine-thirty." Brandon opened his mouth, looking ready to argue—a look she easily recognized as she saw it on a daily basis lately—and she continued, "I mean it, Brandon. I'm not about to have Coach read me the riot act because you two didn't get enough sleep."

"Okay, nine-thirty," Brandon said as if he'd just agreed to death by hanging at that time. "Call us when dinner's ready," he added then he and Ryan went back to their video games.

"You're welcome," Tori muttered, watching his back disappear. She loved her kid, she really did, but sometimes she wanted her sweet, good-natured boy back. The one who'd thought she could do no wrong.

"You can say no to him once in a while," Layne said, carrying over the bowl of guacamole she'd made. "It's not good for kids to get their own way all the time."

"I tell him no plenty," Tori said tightly. Although, if she was honest with herself, she'd admit that ever since she and Greg separated, those times were few and far between. Good thing she tried not to be honest with herself. "It's just a sleepover. It's not like he asked permission to start a meth lab in the kitchen."

"Just because you feel guilty," Layne said quietly, "is no reason to give in to him."

Guilty. God. Tori could've laughed but was afraid she'd start bawling instead. Of course she felt guilty. She'd ripped her family apart, had hurt her son. But worse than that?

She couldn't regret it. Any of it.

Layne didn't understand her reasons for divorcing Greg. Most people didn't. After all, he was a good man, a kind, decent man who'd loved her half her life, who worked hard to provide for her and their son.

But it hadn't been enough. He hadn't been enough.

Just like her father hadn't been enough for her mother.

"No guilt here," Tori said, placing taco shells onto a cookie sheet. "Just doing what I do best. Giving a guy what he wants."

THE REF'S WHISTLE blew as Walker jogged across the back parking lot toward Mystic Point's middle school, a sprawling building set amidst scattered trees at the edge of town. On the football field, the game was halfway through the second quarter and the home team, in blue and white, was behind by three but had the ball on the other team's twenty-yard line.

People milled about, watched the game from the track that wound around the field or sat in the bleachers—home ones to his right, visitors on the other side of the field. Though it was barely eleven, the scent of charred hot dogs filled the air, reminding him he hadn't eaten today. He slowed to a walk as he circled the field, sweat stinging his eyes, his lungs burning as he took in the game.

The kids were a hodgepodge of sizes, weights and—he thought with a wince as a beautifully thrown pass hit a wide receiver on the back of the helmet—talent. He should keep going. Or, better yet, head back the two miles to his motel. He'd only meant to take a quick run, clear his head a bit before getting back to work.

He'd already sent copies of the bank records Taylor had given him to a buddy at the state crime lab to figure out where that half a million dollars had originated. He also wanted to canvass the area around the motel Dale had stayed at, where he'd died, question the employees, talk to any neighborhood residents. Or he could go over his notes again, study the reports—complete with photos of Dale's body and his motel room—that Taylor had meticulously put together.

Or try to figure out why the chief had gone to the trouble of documenting the scene of what he'd claimed to believe was a natural death.

Yeah, Walker thought, wiping sweat from his forehead with the back of his hand. He could head back. But the home team's quarterback was a pleasure to watch, even at…ten? Twelve? Who could tell? And Walker couldn't remember the last time he'd seen a football game—even a midget one.

Plus, he was hungry.

He walked up to the concession stand and ordered a bottle of water, two hot dogs and a coffee, finishing the water before his order was ready. Setting the coffee down, he squirted mustard onto the first hot dog. Was about to repeat the action on the second when his nape prickled with unease.

"Good morning, Detective Bertrand," an all-too-familiar voice said from behind him. "This is a surprise."

Unease. That's what he felt when he sensed Tori Mott was near. When he heard her husky tones, when he inhaled her spicy scent.

Unease. Attraction. Lust. And way too much interest. Last night when he was lying in bed, her image had floated through his mind. That sharp grin, those long legs, that lush body. He'd thought of her. It pissed him off.

He carefully squirted the mustard before facing her. "Mrs. Mott."

She waved that away. "Call me Tori."

"I think it'd be best if I continued to call you Mrs. Mott."

"Do you?" she asked with a grin that made him wonder what she was up to, what she was thinking. "Why? After all, we're good friends now. And you know all about me. I wouldn't be surprised if you knew all my deep, dark secrets."

He didn't. Doubted any man could ever know her, not really.

Walker bit into his hot dog. Chewed and swallowed. "You don't strike me as a woman who'd let that happen."

Now she laughed, the sound causing the couple ordering next to Walker to turn toward her, the man with a smile, the woman with a sneer. If Tori noticed, she gave no indication. She just stepped closer to Walker, lightly brushed her hand over his arm despite the light coat of sweat on his skin.

"What kind of woman do I strike you as?" she asked softly.

Wishing he hadn't left his sunglasses in his motel room, he skimmed his gaze over her. Dark, tight jeans. Black, high-heeled, over-the-knee boots. A red sweater that clung to her breasts. Her hair was tousled, her cheeks flushed and every time she moved, her long, dangling earrings—resembling layers of gold leaves—swayed, catching the sunlight.

He raised his eyes, met hers. The sounds of the announcer calling the play-by-play, the crowd's cheers and clapping faded. She was close enough to touch, to feel the warmth of her skin. All he had to do was shift, just a few inches, and he could brush his hip against hers.

He didn't move. "You want the truth?"

"Could there be anything less between us?"

She was messing with him. Provoking him.

"You strike me as a woman used to getting what she wants," he said, "and is willing to do whatever it takes to ensure she does. You always hold something back, some small piece of yourself in the name of self-preservation and you're rarely honest about who you are or what you want."

Something flashed in her eyes, something resembling pain. Embarrassment. But it passed, leaving him to wonder if he'd imagined it, because part of him, the part that wanted to take her to bed, wanted him to be wrong about her.

But the truth was what he saw in front of him. She was

just a pretty face and sexy body, a woman who excelled in giving a man what he wanted, saying what he wanted to hear, making him feel powerful. Desirable.

"It seems you do know me after all," she said, brushing at something on his shoulder—though he doubted anything was there. "So you'll call me Tori and I'll call you…"

At her raised eyebrow look he took another bite of hot dog. "Detective Bertrand."

"Now, Walker, is that any way for friends to act?"

His jaw dropped. Since there was still food in his mouth, he snapped it shut again and swallowed quickly. "You know my name." It wasn't a question. It was an accusation.

"I hadn't realized it was a secret."

It wasn't but it was one of those things that created intimacy between people when he needed to keep his distance from her, from everyone involved in this case.

Damn it, this was why he didn't like to get too involved in the community of a place while he worked on a case. It was too easy to lose his judgment.

Getting cozy with strangers, with friends and family of the people he was investigating, was never a good idea. He'd never understood how a small-town cop, like Layne Sullivan, could work in the same place where they'd been raised. How they maintained their professional detachment.

And the only thing more important than that was closing the case.

"I didn't tell you my name," he pointed out, sounding harsh, feeling like a fool trying to intimidate her in a pair of sweatpants, his T-shirt clinging to his chest. But hearing her say his name did nothing for his equilibrium or his judgment.

Looking way too satisfied, Tori clasped her hands together in front of her. "No, Rumpelstiltskin, you didn't."

A buzzer rang indicating it was halftime. Players headed toward the locker rooms. Tori stepped aside as people lined up at the concession stand.

"We'd better get out of the way," she said. "Here, I'll take that." Before he could react, hell, before he could even blink, she picked up his coffee.

He wasn't sure how long he stood there, staring at her back, her ass as she walked away. Wishing, just for a moment, that things could be different. But then he caught sight of how many men were checking her out. It was humiliating, demoralizing, to realize he was simply another of her conquests.

No. He didn't want things to be different. He wasn't about to drool over her like some besotted idiot. And the only reason he followed her around the side of the building was that she had his coffee.

Just because he searched for the truth, didn't mean he couldn't lie to himself on occasion.

"Could I have my coffee?" he asked when he reached her. She sent him a look, one he'd seen often on his own mother's face. Hell, thirty-six years old and he was still being chastised by the Mom Look. "Please," he ground out.

"Sure," she said with enough cheer to set his teeth on edge. "But I feel I should warn you, it's like drinking drain cleaner. Only not as smooth."

He took a sip. Grimaced. Drain cleaner was too generous.

"You often spend Saturday mornings at the football field?" he asked.

"Only in the fall. During the winter months I can be found at the gym watching basketball. In the spring, it's the baseball field at the park."

"I wouldn't have guessed you were a sports fan," he said before going to work on his second hot dog.

"I'm not. But I am a fan of an athlete."

Right. She had a son. Wish he would've remembered that—and the possibility that the kid would play football—before he'd decided to stick around.

Walker polished off his food then took his life in his own hands by taking another sip of coffee. "What position does your son play?"

"Quarterback," she said, tucking her hair behind her ear.

The kid with the arm. "You must be proud."

"I'm proud of him for many reasons. He loves sports, loves playing and being part of a team. I just want him to have fun." The look in her eyes made Walker nervous. "It's not like I expect him to get offered a scholarship to play at Penn State or anything."

He stilled, felt as if that last bit of food was permanently lodged in his throat.

She knew. How the hell she'd found out he could only guess. He edged closer in a way that should've put the fear of God into her eyes. Instead she stood there, her hair blowing in the breeze, her face tipped up so she could keep her eyes on his.

"You checking up on me, Mrs. Mott?" he asked, his tone low and dangerous.

She patted his hand, the one holding his coffee, her fingers soft and warm. "Now, Walker, whatever gave you that idea? Besides, as far as I know, it's not exactly a state secret that you were offered a full ride to play ball there. One you turned down for an academic scholarship at Northeastern. Didn't want to leave home?"

Hadn't wanted to have a career that relied on too many unknowns. Hadn't wanted to take the chance on getting injured, cut, or worse, playing second or third string. He preferred to rely on things he could control.

Where he was number one.

"Did Captain Sullivan do a background check on me?" he asked, irritated to have the tables turned on him.

"I have no idea."

"Then how—"

"You see, the thing is, I had some free time on my hands last night and as I sat there surfing the Net for this cute little red dress I saw in a magazine, I realized that you knew everything there was to know about me and my family." She started ticking items off on her long fingers. "My cousins' names and about my son and I'm sure you're aware that I'm divorced. It didn't seem fair that my entire life was out there on display for you while you got to hide behind some sort of mysterious cloak of anonymity." She smiled at him. A real smile, one that reached her eyes, lit her entire face. Had his breath catching. "So I looked you up on Google."

He shook his head. Tried to get his bearings but it wasn't easy, not with her standing so close, looking so triumphant and cocky.

Not when he found her so damn appealing with her windblown hair and smartass mouth and guarded eyes.

"You looked me up?" he repeated.

"Yes. You'd be surprised what information is out there on the World Wide Web. Although I hadn't expected there to be so much detail put into your Wikipedia page."

He narrowed his eyes, lowered his voice. "I do not have a Wikipedia page."

Horror filled him. Did he?

"Got ya," she said with a wink.

Walker fisted his hands. Heard conversations around him, kids yelling and racing around, but he blocked it all out, focused only on the manipulative, irritating, breath-taking woman in front of him. "I don't appreciate you running a background check on me."

She nodded as if in commiseration. "Annoying, isn't it? To have someone look into your life, your background?"

Like he did to her. To her family.

With one swift motion, he tossed the contents of his coffee aside, crushed the cup in his hand. "Listen, I'm in the middle of an investigation—"

"Please," she said, "don't go into the whole, *I'm just doing my job* spiel because I couldn't care less."

"How about I go into my invasion of privacy spiel, then?"

"What invasion? What privacy? It's on the internet for God's sake. It's not like I broke into your house and rifled through your underwear drawer. I just wanted you to think twice the next time you get it into that handsome head of yours that I'm some sort of brainless, weak link who can be used to hurt my family." She stepped closer, rose onto her toes and, laying her hand on his shoulder for balance—or just to torture him—spoke into his ear, her breath warming his skin. "Don't underestimate me," she said, her words a threat. A promise. "You have no idea what I'm capable of."

CHAPTER SIX

HER HEART POUNDING, Tori leaned back far enough to meet Walker's gaze. Heat filled his eyes, darkened them. Her fingers tightened involuntarily on his shoulders. She glanced at his mouth. He hadn't shaved and golden stubble covered his upper lip, his chin. The sun highlighted the pale strands of blond in his hair, the strands waving in messy disarray. It was strangely alluring, this less-than-perfect side of him. He was solid and smelled so good, like clean sweat and man.

And she was at her son's football game, her body swaying toward Walker like he was one of those fairy-tale princes she didn't believe in. As if she was so weak she needed a man's support to keep her upright on her own two feet.

Pressing her lips together, she fell back to her heels, let her hand drop to her side. "You enjoy the rest of your weekend, Walker," she told him, unable to work up even the pretense of a smirk.

She sauntered away but felt him watching her, that hot gaze boring a hole between her shoulder blades. So she kept her strides long and loose, her arms swinging casually by her sides, her head up.

There was no way he could tell she was trembling with fear and nerves and, God help her, attraction.

She slid her sunglasses on. Damn Walker Bertrand and his broad shoulders, blue eyes and sexy scowl.

But she'd shown him, she assured herself as she skirted around a group of giggling middle school girls. She'd proved her point.

He couldn't intimidate her. She could hold her own against him, against any man. She wasn't afraid of him.

Liar, the little voice inside her head singsonged.

Stupid voice.

"Where's your cocoa?" Layne asked when Tori returned to their spot on the track behind the team bench.

Tori looked down at her hands as if a hot chocolate would somehow magically appear. "Oh, uh, the line was too long. I'll have one at the café later."

Layne looked over Tori's shoulder at the concession stand, undoubtedly seeing that the line was no longer than usual. "You were gone awhile. Get sidetracked?"

Tori laughed humorlessly. "You could say that."

She could feel Layne frowning at her, trying to see inside her head.

You strike me as a woman used to getting what she wants—and is willing to do whatever it takes to ensure she does. You always hold something back, some small piece of yourself in the name of self-preservation and you're rarely honest about who you are or what you want.

Biting her lower lip, Tori kept her gaze on the field where the two teams were lining up for kickoff. Walker's assessment of her had been dead-on, eerily so. She wasn't ashamed of who she was, of how she acted. But for the first time, she wished she could be different. Wished he could see more in her.

Brandon's team kicked the ball and she watched her baby race down the field, held her breath when he zoned in on the ball carrier and wrapped his arms around him in a bone-crushing tackle. She didn't exhale until both boys were on their feet, jogging back toward their respective teammates.

God, she hated football. Had always hated it, even when she'd cheered for Greg and the rest of her classmates in high school. It just seemed so senseless and idiotic, boys... men...running around in their tight pants trying to flatten each other. There had to be a better way to spend free time.

She wondered if she could possibly talk Brandon into taking up tennis. Or golf.

"You okay?" Layne asked.

Tori didn't take her gaze from the field. "Just dandy."

"What number is your son?"

She didn't even bother sighing, just glanced at Walker as he stepped up to stand beside her. "Eighty-eight."

Since they didn't have enough kids for a full roster, most of the boys ended up playing both offense and defense, which was why Brandon was out there now.

"That was a good tackle," Walker said with a nod to the action on the field. "He needs to keep his head up, though."

"I'll be sure to pass that along," Tori said.

"What are you doing here?" Layne snapped at Walker. "This is harassment."

Walker barely spared Layne a glance. He was probably used to people—women—being pissed at him. "Just taking in the game, Captain. No law against that, is there?"

"If you ever try to talk to my sister or any other member of my family without proper legal counsel present," Layne said, her tone all the more dangerous for its softness, "you will regret it."

Now Walker gave Layne his full attention. He shouldn't have looked so...commanding, so daunting in his stupid, baggy sweatpants and faded T-shirt. But somehow, he still came off as if he was in charge and he'd do whatever it took to keep it that way.

"Is that a threat?" he asked.

Layne edged toward him, forcing Tori back a step, the confrontational look on her face one Tori had seen many times before. Usually directed at her. "Damn right it's a threat."

"I'd appreciate it if you didn't start a scene at my son's football game," Tori said, keeping her voice even despite the urge to yell. She faced Layne. "Didn't anyone ever teach you that you get more flies with honey than vinegar?"

"I'm not interested in collecting flies," Layne said. Then she sneered at Walker. "Unless they're smashed under a fly swatter. And I try not to remember any of the lessons Mom taught us."

Tori tossed her head, cocked her hip. "Oh, but some of them come in so handy."

Layne's mouth flattened. She took a hold of Tori's arm and tugged. "Let's sit in the bleachers."

Sit up there with Greg and Colleen and Greg's parents? So she could watch her ex-husband snuggle up with his girlfriend while pretending she didn't notice how happy his parents were, how relieved, that he wasn't with Tori anymore? That he'd finally found someone worthy of him?

She pulled away from Layne's grasp. "I'm fine right here. But you go ahead."

Layne stared at her for so long, Tori fought the urge to squirm. To not give away any of her thoughts. Because that's what Layne wanted. To see inside her head, inside her heart.

But no one got that close to her. Not her sisters. Not the man she'd been married to. No one.

Finally Layne whirled around, her ponytail hitting Tori's arm before she stalked off.

"You always do the opposite of what your sister wants?" Walker asked.

Tori stuck her hands into her pockets and wished she'd bought that cocoa. She wanted something to do with her hands. "Pretty much."

"That's quite the cheering section your son has," Walker said.

She followed his gaze to where Layne was joining their family. The Sullivans were out in full force for the game. Something in Tori warmed, loosened.

Her family wasn't perfect—far from it. But they did try to be there for each other.

Layne took the spot at the end of the bench seat next to Nora. Tori had no doubt her younger sister would've dragged Griffin along, if not for the fact he worked Saturday mornings at the garage he owned. Ross's niece, Jess, a high school junior who worked part-time at the café, sat on Nora's other side. As Tori watched, Jess leaned over toward her boyfriend, Tanner, said something that had him giving one of his slow grins.

And Tori tried really hard not to hold it against Tanner that he had the bad luck of being Griffin's half brother.

"Is that Celeste Vitello?" Walker asked. "The dark-haired woman next to your father."

Tori looked up to the stands again, saw her dad and Celeste with Uncle Ken and Aunt Astor. Their daughter, Erin, and her fiancé, Collin, sat one row up with Anthony. "How do you know that's my dad? Wait," she said drily. "Stupid question. You know everything."

Nothing. No flash of humor crossed his handsome face, no warmth entered his eyes. "Actually I know because I interviewed him yesterday." Walker sent her a pointed look. "He was very cooperative."

"I'm sure he was." Her father had nothing to hide, of

that Tori was certain. He was too decent, too honorable, to have committed murder.

"He must love watching his grandson play," Walker said, the easy, conversational tone of his voice putting her on edge. What was he up to now? "My dad gets a huge kick out of going to all of his grandkids' sporting events."

"What's this?" she asked lightly. "Changing tactics on me? Gotten tired of trying to intimidate information out of me?"

"Just making conversation."

But a flush coated his cheeks. Too bad it only made him look sexier.

"Dad's a good grandfather," she admitted grudgingly, unable to figure out any reason she couldn't have a discussion with Walker, one that didn't include accusations, suspicions and half-truths. "He tries not to miss any of Brandon's sporting events and at least once a month spends one-on-one time with him."

"You don't sound too happy about it."

There it was. The reason she needed to keep her mouth shut around him, why she should keep her distance. He saw too much, things she didn't want to give away, thoughts and emotions he had no right digging into.

"Like I said, my dad's a good grandfather." But that didn't, couldn't, make up for all those times when it'd been her event—a soccer game when she'd been in middle school, cheerleading competitions when she'd gotten older—when she'd look up into the stands searching for him, hoping that once, just once, he'd be there for her.

He never was.

It wasn't until Layne was away at school and Tori got married that he stopped spending all his life at sea and started being home more. Must be why he and Nora were so close. He'd been there for his youngest daughter in all the ways he hadn't been for Tori and Layne.

That was okay. They hadn't needed him as much as Nora had, hadn't needed a parent—not when they were so used to taking care of themselves.

On the field, Brandon's team had gotten the ball back on downs and he was set up behind his center. At the snap, he tucked the ball against his stomach and took off, making it three yards before one of the opposing players hit him hard enough to knock him off his feet. He landed with a hard thud.

Tori cringed at the sound of pads hitting pads, her son's grunt as he hit the hard earth. "Are they sure that kid is only twelve?" she muttered, eyeing the other boy's bulky frame. "He looks at least fourteen."

"Relax," Walker said, making what could have been—should have been—a lovely reassurance sound more like an order. But then he glanced down at her clenched hands and when he spoke again, his tone was softer, almost… kind. "He's fine. He'll be fine."

And for some stupid reason, she believed him.

God, she must be losing her ever-loving mind. What other explanation could there be for her trusting anything Walker said? She inhaled deeply, breathed in the crisp fall air, trying to clear her head. She had to remember why Walker was in Mystic Point. To drag up the past. To destroy her sister's career and prove that someone in her family was a murderer.

On second down, Brandon's team tried another running play, this one resulting in no gain. Third down, he took the snap and dropped back to pass—a rare occurrence at this age level but Coach Stillman had a lot of faith in Brandon's abilities.

"Go, go, go," she murmured when Brandon scrambled

left, then cut back to the right. She bit her thumb knuckle as he evaded one tackle, looked downfield then let loose with a beautiful pass. The ball spiraled, arcing in the air, then hit Ryan right in the number on his jersey and Ryan, God bless him, wrapped that ball in his arms like it was a newborn baby and ran like hell toward the end zone.

Tori bounced on her heels. The crowd went wild, cheering him on. Twenty-yard line. Ten. Five.

Touchdown!

"Yes!" Tori hopped up and down, her yell drowned out by the roar of the crowd. "Whoo hoo!"

"Nice pass," Walker said.

"Nice?" she repeated on a laugh as she turned toward him. It was then she realized she was clutching his arm. She let go as if he'd caught on fire. "That wasn't nice," she said, her voice trembling, her world tipping slightly, as if the track was shifting under her feet. She curled her fingers into her own palm. "That was a beauty."

"He been playing long?"

"Since he was ten. His father, my ex, played in high school. Varsity quarterback two years."

Walker sent her a sidelong glance. "Following in his father's footsteps?"

"God, I hope not," she blurted, then shut her eyes briefly and wished she could take the words back. They sounded so...angry. Resentful. They were too revealing. Too truthful.

"I take it your divorce wasn't amicable."

"Oh, no, it was very amicable. Friendly even." The wind blew her hair into her face and she tucked it behind her ear, kept her gaze on the game. "No hard feelings, no anger or recriminations. It was all very...civilized."

Yes, civilized. She'd said she wanted a divorce and he'd just...agreed. Simple. He hadn't asked what he could do to change her mind. Hadn't apologized for not keeping the promises he'd made when he'd proposed. He claimed he loved her, but he hadn't fought for her.

Feeling Walker's eyes on her, she faced him. "It all worked out in the end," she said, trying to assure herself as much as him. She lowered her sunglasses and sent him a heavy-lidded look over the top of the frames. "I like the freedom of being single. There are so many...possibilities out there."

But she'd underestimated him—or overestimated her acting ability. Because though his eyes remained cool, she noted sympathy in the blue depths.

And that would not do.

"Life's a buffet, is that it?" he asked softly.

Tori's stomach churned. She shoved the glasses in place. "That's exactly right. And I want to try all it has to offer. You let me know if you ever want to be added to the menu."

SHE WAS NOTHING short of a chameleon, Walker thought fifteen minutes later as he caught sight of Tori. Again.

Ever since she'd walked away from him after her son's touchdown pass, he found himself searching her out. It wasn't hard to do as she was easy to spot, usually surrounded by people. If she wasn't talking with her family, she was flirting with one of the many men who approached her.

She handled it all like a pro. Always giving the men enough attention to make them feel as if they had a shot but then sending them on their way before they got too comfortable. They all seemed happy when they left so she obviously left them with the hope they had a chance in hell. Maybe they did, but Walker didn't think so. She was playing them, playing everyone.

He wondered who the real Tori Sullivan Mott was. If she even knew.

He could've left, probably should have, but he'd seen Tori's uncle Ken Sullivan in the stands and realized he had an opportunity to ask him a few questions. Besides, Walker was obstinate enough to want to stay all because Layne Sullivan wanted him gone. And he could think of worse ways to spend a sunny Saturday morning than at a football game, his gaze drawn again and again to the beautiful Tori Mott.

She'd spent most of her time with Celeste Vitello, their heads together as they spoke. Even from a distance, he could see there was a bond between the two women. Tori seemed more at ease with the older woman than with her own sisters.

Something to tuck away for future reference.

Time wound down and the visiting team tossed a wobbling Hail Mary pass that ended up on the ground. As the home team celebrated, the bleachers started to clear out. Walker couldn't stop from looking up at the stands one last time. As if sensing his gaze on her, Tori slowly turned. He didn't need to see her eyes behind those dark glasses to know she held his gaze. Her lips curved up invitingly. Mockingly.

You let me know if you ever want to be added to the menu.

He did. He wanted her hands on him, those lush curves pressed against him like they had been earlier so he could feel her body heat, smell her enticing scent. It'd taken all of his willpower not to pull her closer, not to take that mobile, smart-ass mouth in a deep kiss.

He wanted her. And she knew it.

He wasn't used to denying himself but in this case, he saw no other choice. He was there because Ross Taylor hadn't been smart enough to put his career, his reputation, before some woman.

Walker would be damned before he made the same mistake.

Deliberately turning away from Tori, he scanned the crowd, swore under his breath when he spotted Tori's tall, blond father but not her uncle. That's what he got for letting his guard down, for letting his personal desires get the better of him. He walked swiftly along with the crowd exiting through the gate, and picked up his pace when he spotted Ken and his family across the parking lot.

"Excuse me," he called, closing in on them as he unzipped the side pocket of his sweatpants. "Ken Sullivan?"

Ken turned and gave Walker a politician's polite smile. "That's right."

Walker pulled out his badge. "Mr. Sullivan, I'm Detective Bertrand from the state attorney general's office. I'd like to ask you a few questions regarding the murder of Dale York."

"If you want to interview me," Ken said dismissively, "you can set it up through my office."

Walker had tried that. He'd called Ken's office several times for two days straight only to be told by Ken's very polite secretary that her boss was otherwise occupied but would get back to Walker as soon as possible. By Friday afternoon, Walker had had enough of pissing in the wind and had gone to the austere law offices of Sullivan, Saunders and Mazza.

Ken hadn't been there.

Walker had spent the rest of the day trying to track the man down—first at the courthouse where that same secretary—though not quite as politely as before—had informed him Ken had gone. By the time Walker had made it back to Ken's law office, the entire building was locked up tight. So Walker had gone to the fancy, two-story house outside of town but no one answered the doorbell.

He knew when he was getting the runaround. Just as he knew what to do about it.

"A formal interview won't be necessary, sir," he said smoothly, making sure his voice carried not only to Ken, but also to his family who were now gathered around a glossy black Mercedes. "I was just hoping you could clarify for me why Dale York was seen leaving your office the night of July 10."

"Ken," his wife, a pretty woman with chin-length, honey-blond hair asked, frowning in concern, "what's he talking about?"

"It's nothing, honey. Here." He crossed to her and handed her keys. "Go ahead and wait in the car. I'll only be a minute."

Ken's son stepped forward. "But, Dad—"

"Anthony, it's fine. Go with your mother. I'll be there in a minute."

Anthony and his mom hesitated but then she smiled and took her son's arm. "Come on. Let's let Dad handle this."

Ken watched them walk away then turned to Walker. "I don't appreciate you bringing this up at this time, nor in front of my family."

"I apologize for the inconvenience," Walker lied. "Maybe you were right and we should schedule an interview. Or, if it'd be more convenient for you, we could go down to the station now."

Ken looked pointedly at Walker's clothes. "Son, let me give you a piece of advice, don't try to bullshit an attorney. We know all the tricks. Now, you can't intimidate me and we both know you have no right to take me anywhere, so ask your question. My family is waiting for me."

Lawyers. Even ones who used to fight on the side of

good were sneaky. "I have a witness statement," Walker said, his tone rigid, "from one of the crew who cleans your office. She states that she saw Dale York leaving your office, your personal office, the evening of July 10. Why was he there?"

Ken spread his hands in a helpless gesture. "I have no idea."

"You have no idea why the man who allegedly killed your sister-in-law was at your office."

"Did this witness recognize Dale York?"

Walker's eyes narrowed. "She recognized Mr. York from a photo I showed her." He'd questioned not only the cleaning crew but also several employees of Ken's law firm trying to discover if anyone had seen Dale and Nora Sullivan together, had ever heard her speak about him or noticed Dale hanging around.

Instead he'd found another connection between York and a Sullivan.

"Did the witness see me that night?" Ken asked.

"No."

"Did they see me with Dale York?"

Wait a minute, who the hell was asking the questions here? And why did Walker feel as if he was on the witness stand? He pulled his shoulders back. "No," he admitted.

Ken nodded. "Then there's nothing more for us to talk about."

"Mr. Sullivan, do you have any idea what Dale York was doing at your office that night? Any idea how he got into the building?"

"Detective, there's no way Mr. York could've gotten into the building unless someone from the cleaning crew let him in. I believe you've been misinformed."

He was lying. Walker knew it. But until he could prove it, there wasn't a damn thing he could do except return to his room and do some more digging for the truth. "Thank you for your time, Mr. Sullivan."

Walker went around the end zone toward the back parking lot. He needed to check his notes and the cleaning woman's statement about seeing Dale York at Ken Sullivan's offices.

As he hurried down a set of concrete stairs, his mind replayed the conversation he'd just had. As much as he hated to admit it, there was no denying Ken had gotten the better of him.

Walker would have to make sure it never happened again.

Only a few cars remained in the back parking lot as most of the parents seemed to have parked closer to the admission box on the other side of the field. A group of boys in street clothes with various stages of helmet-hair were gathered by a set of glass doors. Laughter rang out.

"Take that back," a tall kid with brown hair yelled, his hands fisted.

"Why?" a shorter, rounder boy asked with a sneer. "It's the truth."

The tall kid stepped closer to the chubby kid, his face red with rage, his skinny body vibrating with it. "Take it back now."

Slowing down, Walker hoped like hell the conversation wasn't going to end how he thought it was going to end.

"No," the chubby kid said.

And then the tall kid punched him.

Walker squeezed the back of his neck. He really didn't have time for this.

The rest of the boys encircled the combatants, their voices raised as they yelled—encouragement or abuse or for them to stop—Walker had no clue. Still, he waited, hoping a parent or coach would show up.

No such luck.

Shit.

He stormed up to the boys. "Knock it off," he growled.

A few of the kids on the outer edge looked at him wide-eyed, nudged each other and pulled back enough for him to see that the tall kid had the other one pinned to the ground, his knees on the chubby one's shoulders as he pounded on the poor kid.

Walker stepped forward, snatched the kid by the scruff of his skinny neck and hauled him to his feet. The kid kept swinging, one of his bony elbows catching Walker below the ribs. He grunted. Gave the kid a shake that he hoped rattled his teeth.

"Boy," he said, giving him another shake because, damn, but that elbow had caught him good, "you need to settle down because you are pissing me off."

The kid stilled, his chest rising and falling rapidly. A few of the other boys helped the chubby kid to his feet. Blood dripped from the cut on his mouth. The kid's cheeks were scraped and a bruise was already forming above his eye.

Walker looked at the group as he took his badge out with his free hand. Showed it to the kids, who all stepped back in unison. The power of the badge. "Beat it," he told them. "Now."

They took off, feet slapping against the concrete.

"Get your hands off my son!"

Walker shut his eyes. Of course. He shouldn't have expected any less.

When he opened them it was to see Tori racing toward him, her hair flying, her eyes blazing. A mama grizzly in full overprotective mode. One of the boys who'd been part of the huddle hurried after her—must've run to get her while Walker was breaking up the fight.

He glanced down at the kid, saw Tori's eyes glaring at him. "You're Tori Mott's son?"

The kid's face was flushed and sweaty, his hands scraped. But in his eyes was pure defiance. Pure Tori. "Yeah."

And wasn't that freaking perfect?

CHAPTER SEVEN

TORI HURRIED down the steps, her entire focus on her son. And the man holding him by the back of the neck.

The son of a bitch.

She'd been waiting with the other parents—deliberately not thinking about Walker Bertrand—when Ryan raced up and told her that Brandon was in trouble. Close enough now to see her son's dirty face, the scratches on his skin, she stumbled. Her fingers curled into claws.

"What did you do?" she yelled at Walker, their rapt audience the only thing stopping her from ripping his throat out. She took Brandon's arm and yanked him away from Walker, examined his face. "What happened? Are you okay? What did he do?"

Brandon pulled away from her, his expression mulish. "I'm fine."

"You're not fine. You're hurt." She whirled on Walker, tried to figure out why he looked so damn put out when surely he was to blame for this. "What's the matter, Detective? You get tired of going after the adults in my family so you thought you'd abuse my kid?"

Walker didn't even have the common courtesy, the decency, to look abashed. "Maybe we could go over there," he said, indicating the far corner of the parking lot. "Discuss this."

"The only discussion we're going to have is in front

of Chief Taylor…or Meade or whoever is in charge at the police station."

Walker rolled his head from side to side, looked as if the weight of the world was on his very capable shoulders. "He was fighting."

She blinked. Frowned. "What?"

"He was fighting. I broke it up."

That didn't make sense. Brandon didn't fight. He was easygoing and fun and nice. Likable. Lovable. He was everything she wasn't. Everything she wanted him to be.

But when she cleared the righteous anger from her gaze, looked closer, she saw the truth on her son's face. The guilt and shame.

Walker inclined his head to something behind her. She didn't want to look, didn't want to see whatever Brandon had done. She wanted to protect him. Even from his own mistakes.

Just because you feel guilty is no reason to give in to him.

Her sister's voice floated through her head. Tori wished it would float right back out. It wasn't guilt that made her want to hide from this, it was fear. That whatever was going on with her little boy was all her fault.

Slowly she turned. Saw Dalton Nash, his lip bloodied, his round face bruised, his shirt ripped. "Oh, God," she breathed. "You did that?" she asked Brandon, her voice raw, her stomach cramping.

Her son, her baby, had inflicted violence on another person. Had hurt his teammate, his friend.

Tori went numb, couldn't wrap her mind around what had occurred. She stared at Brandon but it was like looking at a stranger. How could the boy she'd raised, the one who just last year was always smiling and happy, have turned into this child she didn't even know?

"Why?"

She hadn't realized she'd asked that question out loud, hadn't meant to say it or to sound so desperate. Desperate to understand. To somehow make this right, make her son be okay again.

Brandon stared at the ground.

"What happened?" The woman's screech had Tori hunching her shoulders. Dalton's parents rushed forward to crowd around their son.

"Shit," Walker said mournfully.

"Me, too," she whispered.

A muscle worked in his jaw but when he stepped past her toward the Nashes, she could've sworn she felt the brush of his fingertips against her wrist. In understanding? A show of solidarity? She had no clue; all she knew was that, brief as it was, that light touch was comforting.

She couldn't afford to find comfort in him, to take it from him. That she wanted to was enough to have her straightening her shoulders, ready to face whatever hellstorm came her and Brandon's way. She had to stand on her own, take care of this by herself. She couldn't trust Walker not to twist this to his advantage, use it against her and her family.

All the boys seemed to be talking at once, trying to explain what happened. Mrs. Nash alternated between fussing over her son and sending Brandon skin-melting glares. Mr. Nash stood with his hand on Dalton's shoulder.

Walker stuck two fingers in his mouth and gave a shrill whistle that silenced everyone.

He stepped into the middle of the crowd, tall and in charge even in jogging clothes. "You," he said, pointing to the Nash family, "and you—" This time a two-finger point at Tori and Brandon. "Don't move. The rest of you…" He swept his gaze over the crowd, which now included a few parents and Coach Stillman. "Clear out."

Coach stepped forward. "Now wait a minute—"

Walker held out his badge, cutting off the rest of Coach's words. "I'll handle this. Any team discipline you want to enforce, you can do so at a later date."

"Uh, all right," Coach Stillman said, then swept his glance around the crowd. "You heard the man. Let's give them some privacy to work this out. But, boys," he said to the fighters, "we will discuss this at tomorrow's practice."

The crowd dispersed, most of them dragging their feet and shooting curious glances over their shoulders.

"Call the police, Michael," Jennifer Nash said.

"Whoa," Tori said, moving to stand beside Brandon, to show they were a team even if her son didn't believe it. "Why do you want to involve the police?"

Jennifer folded her arms across her flat chest, the light-colored mom jeans she wore doing her wide hips no favors. "We're going to press charges."

"Press charges?" Tori asked incredulously. "What for?"

"What for?" Jennifer threw an arm out, almost hitting her son upside the head with her dramatic gesture. "Look at Dalton! Brandon should be punished for attacking him."

"We don't know what happened," Tori said, hating that her voice shook, that she was so unsure of her son's innocence. "Or who started the fight. I think we should just calm down and—"

"Of course you want us to calm down," Jennifer said, her pointy nose stuck in the air. "You want your son to get away with this…this…vicious assault."

"I want to get to the truth," Tori insisted.

Hopefully before she perpetrated a vicious assault herself. All over Jennifer Nash's gray-streaked head.

"Michael," Jennifer snapped. "Call. The. Police."

"What's the point?" he asked distractedly as he turned Dalton's head this way and that to check his injuries. "You know Tori's sister is the assistant chief and she's sleeping with Chief Taylor. Do you really think they'll do anything about this?"

Jennifer pulled her own phone from her huge purse. "Then I'll call the state police."

"I'm already here," Walker said, looking as if he'd rather be anywhere else, doing anything other than getting involved in a skirmish between a couple of preteens and their parents. He showed his badge again, this time letting Michael examine it instead of just flashing it and shoving it back into his pocket. "Now, we can go the legal route," he continued, sounding way too calm for the situation, "or we can try to resolve this on our own." Without waiting for their agreement, he faced the boys. "What happened?"

They both shrugged.

"Who started the fight?" Walker asked.

They dropped their gazes.

"From what I gather, and what little I saw of the beginning of the…disagreement…we've got two boys who are evenly matched who had a difference of opinion, one they stupidly thought to handle with their fists. That about right, boys?"

Again with the shrugs. Really? Did they practice this? Or maybe twelve-year-old boys shared one universal brain.

"Dalton," Jennifer said, bending at the waist as if she was talking to a reticent toddler, "did Brandon start the fight?"

Dalton's cheeks got even redder, his eyes glistened. He shook his head.

Tori had no idea if that was a negative answer to his mother's question or a refusal to answer.

Tori took a hold of Brandon's shoulders and forced him to look at her. "Enough of this. Tell the detective what happened, what really happened, right now."

"I don't remember," he grumbled.

"Okay," Walker said, as if it didn't matter to him one way or the other what either boy had to say. "I'll question the rest of your teammates. I'm sure one of them can tell us how, exactly, this went down."

"No," Brandon blurted, his face white.

Walker towered over her son, looking steady and implacable. "You have something you want to say?"

Brandon glared at Walker. "I did it," he ground out. "I started the fight."

Tori's thoughts spun. "What? Brandon...why?"

"I just did," he said.

"See?" Jennifer said. "He admitted it." She looked to Walker. "You heard him confess. We want to press charges."

Walker didn't even spare her a glance. "You grow up around here?" he asked Michael.

"I did."

"You play a sport? Have a group of buddies you hung out with?"

His hand still on his son's shoulder, Michael looked wary when he asked, "Why?"

"Boys fight. It's stupid and wrong and it shouldn't be tolerated, but not everything is a punishable offense by the law. Plus, kids don't usually hit someone on their team, one of their friends, unless they're provoked in some way." Walker turned his attention to Dalton. "That what happened? You guys were razzing each other and it got out of hand?"

Jennifer looked ready to shove Walker's opinion down

his throat. "No matter if they were...*razzing*...each other, it's no excuse for violence."

"Agreed," Walker said mildly, "but sometimes things are said that a man can't let go."

"Did you say something to Brandon?" Michael asked his son.

Dalton flushed so hard, Tori worried the boy was going to have heatstroke. "I don't want to talk about it," he mumbled.

"I'm guessing the coach will come up with some sort of punishment for these two," Walker said. "I can't imagine he tolerates fighting."

Both boys groaned. "He'll run us until we're dead," Dalton said, looking more worried about that prospect than being taken down to the station. Tori would never understand boys. Males were much easier to deal with when they turned into men.

"I hope he makes you sit out a few games," Michael said. "Both of you."

Walker and Michael exchanged a loaded look, one between men who were on the same wavelength. Tori wasn't sure if she wanted to join them there or let them keep their manly thoughts to themselves.

The latter. Most definitely the latter.

"I'd say between the coach's punishment and whatever you all dole out as parents, these boys will learn a valuable lesson," Walker said.

"I can guarantee that Brandon will be punished," Tori said. She just hoped she could come up with a suitable discipline—one that'd make such an impression Brandon didn't dare raise a finger to another child. "I'm really sorry about all of this."

Michael nodded but Jennifer and Dalton just walked away.

Tori's chest was tight. Anger, disappointment and fear mixed together in her stomach like toxins.

She didn't even wait for the Nash family to disappear around the corner of the building before turning to her son. "What has gotten into you?" When he just stared at the ground, she snapped, "Look at me."

He lifted his head. And she stepped back at the fury in his eyes.

"What?" he asked in that tone she hated, the one that reminded her, every day, that he was slipping further and further away from her. That he no longer looked up to her, no longer adored her. That he no longer loved her like he used to.

"What?" she repeated. "You were fighting. What were you thinking?"

He glared, his lower lip stuck out in a pout better suited for a six-year-old. "I don't know."

He was mad at her? Unbelievable.

"Fine. You want to act like a tough guy? Go ahead. But you'll be doing it from your room. You're grounded."

He shrugged. "Big deal."

"You want a big deal?" she asked, feeling hapless dealing with her son, to give him a punishment that would teach him a valuable lesson. "You're off the football team."

His eyes rounded. "That's not fair."

"Life often isn't."

"Dad won't let you do that. He'll let me play."

Brandon was right. Greg would probably want to come up with some other form of punishment. She and Greg were still a team when it came to their son. Thank God. Because when it came down to just her and Brandon, she'd been giving in too often.

Was afraid if she didn't, she'd lose him.

"What you did was wrong," she told Brandon. Glanced at Walker who witnessed how truly inept she'd become as a mother. "Very wrong. And neither I nor your father are going to let you get away without some sort of consequence. It doesn't matter what Dalton said to you, there's no excuse—"

"He said you were hot," Brandon spat, his hands fisted, his chest rising and falling heavily. "He said he wanted to screw you."

Tori went hot and then cold, her fingers going numb. "I…I'm sure he was just trying to get a rise out of you."

But she didn't sound sure. She sounded as if someone had just hit her in the stomach.

"He meant it," Brandon said, now close to tears. "They all do. They love talking about you. How you look, how you dress. The things they'd like to do to you."

Bile rose in her throat. She swallowed it. "Honey, they're just—"

"It's your fault," he said, his voice rising. "You dress like you're a teenager and you're always flirting and laughing with them. And I have to listen to them all the time about how pretty you are, how sexy. Sometimes they say it when I'm not around but it always gets back to me and sometimes, like today, they say it to my face. How you looked standing out there, jumping up and down in your tight jeans, how you hang on any man that talks to you." He sniffed but didn't let the tears in his eyes fall. When he spoke again, his voice was whisper soft. "Why can't you be a normal mom?"

Tori was shaking. She couldn't seem to stop. "That's enough," she said but her voice was weak. "Wait for me in the car."

Brandon's lower lip quivered. "I want to go to Dad's."

She could do that. He was to spend the night with his

father anyway. She could drop him off early, let Greg be the bad-guy parent, let Colleen fuss and soothe her son. It'd be easy, so frighteningly easy for her to walk away from her son when he acted this ugly toward her.

After all, she did so take after her mother.

But not in that way. Never in that way.

"Go to the car," she told him, steeling herself against the anger in his eyes, the hatred. "Now."

"No. I'm going to Dad's."

"Your mother told you to wait in the car," Walker said in his commanding tone. "Do as she says."

Humiliation swamped her, had sweat forming at the small of her back. She wanted to tell Walker to mind his own business, that she could handle this on her own, she didn't need to lean on him or anyone else to get through this.

God, but she was a liar.

Finally Brandon turned, swiped up his duffel bag and headed toward the parking lot. Her head aching, her body sore as if she'd been the one fighting, Tori watched him until he turned the corner of the school.

Walker came up behind her and she waited for one of his condemning, judgmental put-downs about how she'd handled—or mishandled—that scene with her son.

"You okay?"

At his low, rough question, tears stung her eyes. She blinked them back but couldn't force herself to face him. "No. Not really."

She walked away before any more truths could come out. She should have given him one of her snappy quips or, better yet, flirted a bit. Instead she was the one on edge, wondering how much more she could take before she lost her hold and fell off.

"Want to catch the rest of the game with me?" Ken asked, holding out a beer for Anthony. "Last I checked, the Sox were up by one, bottom of the fifth."

"Can't." Anthony let out the dishwater in the sink and dried his hands on the towel hanging on his shoulder. "I already made plans with J.J., Matt and David."

He reached for the beer but his dad retracted it. "You driving tonight?" Ken asked.

"Matt's picking me up."

"He's not drinking tonight?"

"He's the DD. Designated driver," Anthony explained.

"I know what the DD is," Ken said, finally handing the beer over. "I wasn't always middle-aged."

"You have been ever since I've known you."

"Your son's a real comedian," Ken told Astor as she came into the room.

She didn't seem to hear him as she made a beeline for the bottle of wine on the table. Anthony exchanged a raised eyebrow look with his dad as she poured a generous glass and gulped half of it down.

"Something on your mind, honey?" Ken asked, a laugh lacing his voice.

"This wedding," she said, "is going to be the death of me."

She took another long drink.

"It's not too late to hire a wedding planner," Ken said, taking the bottle from her and pouring more into her glass.

"And miss out on the joy of planning my own daughter's wedding?" she asked, as shocked as if he'd suggested she put that same daughter on the white slave trade market. "Not on your life."

Ken sat. "If I remember correctly, your mother drove you nuts while we planned our wedding."

"How could you even say such a thing?" Astor asked,

her eyes wide, her hand over her heart. "I am not driving Erin crazy. All I'm doing is offering my help, guidance and opinions on what's best for her special day."

"Just remember, you had a wedding and got everything you wanted." Ken tugged her onto his lap. She squealed, holding her wineglass out so it didn't spill. "And I got everything I wanted on the honeymoon."

Anthony choked on his beer. "Jesus. Is that necessary?"

His parents laughed and Astor hooked her free arm around Ken's neck. Leaned her head on his shoulder. "Sorry, honey. Dad and I will pretend we don't like each other if that makes you feel better."

"You can like each other fine," he muttered, "as long as it's platonic."

Ken brushed Astor's hair off her shoulder, settled his hand on the back of her neck. "We'll do our best."

But their eyes were locked on each other and they kissed. Ken murmured something into Astor's ear. She smiled and they kissed again, longer this time.

"You do realize the mental anguish I'm suffering right now, don't you?" Anthony asked.

They pulled apart. Thank God. "We'll pay for any therapy you might need," Ken promised.

"I'm holding you to that."

Not that he was really all that freaked out. His parents had always been loving and demonstrative with each other and their kids. He'd always respected their relationship, had looked up to them and knew he wanted that for himself someday. A woman who'd be his lover, his partner and his friend. Someone he could spend the rest of his life with.

Finishing his beer, he wondered if that was even possible. He'd never been in love, not really and the only time he'd thought he'd come close, it was to find out it was all a lie.

"I'm so glad you could make it home for Brandon's game," Astor said, getting to her feet and crossing to him. "You're a good man."

Anthony shrugged. "I promised him."

His mother's mouth thinned. "I hope it wasn't too… awkward with…that girl…being there."

That girl. Jessica.

Anthony lifted his bottle, but it was empty. He'd seen her. She'd been with that floppy-haired kid she'd been dating since summer. They'd kept their distance from him, only coming close once when they told Layne they were leaving.

Anthony had had to turn away.

"It's fine, Mom," he lied.

"I hope so. Your father and I are proud of the way you handled the whole situation."

He'd handled it the only way he could. Even if he forgave her for lying, she was a kid. They couldn't be together.

"Are you and Mackenzie still seeing each other?" Astor asked.

"Yeah." He and Mackenzie had gone to high school together and had hooked up a few weeks after the situation with Jess. Mackenzie was smart, beautiful and, best of all, twenty. "She couldn't come home this weekend, had some sorority deal."

"Honey," Astor said carefully, "we'll understand if you don't want to come back for any more games since that girl will be there."

"She has a name," Ken pointed out, looking over the top of his glasses as he checked something on his laptop. "And it's Jessica."

"I know her name."

"She made a mistake," Ken said. "It happens to the best of us."

"It does but she hurt my son and that's a little tougher to get past."

"I'm sure you have it in your heart to do so."

It was true. Anthony's mother was forgiving. Accepting. Tolerant.

Usually.

"I don't want you to hold a grudge against Jess because of me." He also didn't want to talk about her, to think about her, but that seemed to be out of the question. "It's over. I'm not hung up on it and neither should you be."

He wasn't hung up on Jess.

Ken slapped him on the shoulder. "That's the right attitude." He pulled Astor in close to his side. "Besides, I'm not sure our marriage would've worked all these years if your mother didn't have the ability to forgive."

She raised her eyebrows. "You can say that again."

Anthony watched them walk out of the kitchen, their arms around each other's waists. They'd probably hang out in the study, watch a movie. They'd be in the kitchen tomorrow when he woke up, his sister, too. After a leisurely Sunday brunch, he'd head back to school, his mom giving him enough food to last four people a month, even though they had actual grocery stores in Boston.

He was lucky. He knew that. Appreciated it. He had parents who loved him and, maybe just as importantly, loved each other. And while he'd been too embarrassed to talk to them about what had happened with Jess, he knew they were there for him. They always would be.

Even if he told them he was reconsidering law school.

It wasn't his passion, and he was afraid it never had been, that he'd made a huge mistake in thinking it was.

Yeah, they'd be there for him, would support him in whatever decision he made, just like always.

But they'd be disappointed in him.

So he needed to suck it up. He'd made his choice and his life was good. Hell, it was great. He did well in school, would graduate in the spring and then move on to law school. He had a beautiful, smart, classy girlfriend in Mackenzie. Life was great. Just great.

It would be perfect as soon as he stopped thinking about Jess.

TORI CROSSED HER arms as she stepped onto the sidewalk and headed toward room 114 of the Tidal Pool Motel. At the door, she rubbed her fingertips against her palms. Her stomach quivered. She felt guilty. Panicked.

Like she was cheating on her husband.

She chewed on the inside of her lip. Then knocked on the door.

She didn't have a husband. Still, she felt as if she was doing something wrong just by being there. As if she was betraying her family. Stupid, she told herself, shifting her weight from her left foot to her right, resisting the urge to knock again. She was there for a damned good reason, not to spill family secrets.

The door opened. Her eyes widened.

Oh, no.

Walker frowned at her, his faded jeans hanging low on his hips, his T-shirt proclaiming she should Trust Me, I'm a Jedi. His feet were bare. One side of his hair stuck to his head, the other stood on end. He held a paperback in his hand, his finger marking the place.

All of that she could've handled with skill and ease. But there was more. He had on glasses. Wire-rimmed.

Seeing him so deliciously mussed and enticing only reminded her that she'd been divorced for months now, that she hadn't had sex in a very long time.

Damn him.

"Mrs. Mott," he said, his voice deeper, huskier than usual. "What are you doing here?"

He got right to the point, a trait she appreciated despite that she rarely did. She preferred to keep so many things hidden.

"I'd say I was in the neighborhood but that would be a lie." She waited but he just stared down at her. "Well," she asked softly, "aren't you going to invite me in?"

He wanted to say no. She saw the refusal flash in his eyes. He didn't want her there.

And what the hell was that about? Men didn't deny her. Period.

Finally he stepped aside and she entered, making sure to oh-so-subtly brush against him.

"Nice place," she said of the cramped space. The bed-covers were rumpled, one half of the mattress covered with scattered papers and files. A military documentary flashed on the TV. His laptop was open on the nightstand next to the bed, the screen blue.

He hit the book against his thigh. "Is that why you stopped by? To see my room?"

Feeling unsure and awkward, she faced him, her high heels sticking to the nubby carpet. She took great pleasure in being able to keep other people on their toes. Keep them guessing. But with him, she was never sure where she stood.

"Actually," she said, "I wanted to thank you for breaking up the fight between the boys today. And for smoothing things over with the Nashes."

"You're welcome."

That was it? She edged closer. His expression remained

unchanged, his gaze curious and wary, watching her as if she was potentially dangerous, possibly lethal. "Let me take you out, buy you a drink and thank you properly."

He tossed the book onto the bed. "That's not necessary."

"I think it is."

"It's not a good idea," he said.

She narrowed her eyes slightly. She should've known this wouldn't be easy. Walker seemed to make everything more difficult than it had to be.

She shouldn't find it so interesting.

Luckily Tori had ways of getting what she wanted. Her peach top clung to her breasts, the bright color accentuating the remnants of her summer tan and contrasting with her dark, tight jeans. The glossy black ankle boots with the pointy heels and open toe added three inches to her height, elongated her legs and were worth every blister she'd have by the end of the night. Her makeup was perfect—smoky, lined eyes. Glossy lips.

She looked hot. Sexy.

If he didn't notice he was either blind or a liar.

"Come on," she said. "We'll go to the Yacht Pub. Dale York's old stomping grounds."

The place where Valerie had worked, where she'd flirted with the customers and had started the affair that would end her marriage. And her life.

"It's not a good idea for us to form any sort of…personal relationship."

Picking up the book he'd tossed aside, she smiled at him. "It's a drink or two. It doesn't have to mean anything more than that. Unless you're concerned it could turn into more?"

In her experience, most men couldn't resist a challenge. Certainly not someone like Walker who solved puzzles for a living.

"Not interested," he said.

She laughed but the sound came out bitter and self-deprecating. "Really? Then you're the first man I've met who isn't." Shaking her head, she dropped the book onto the corner of the bed. Her face was hot, her chest so tight it was all she could do to keep breathing. "You know what? Never mind. Forget I ever came here."

She crossed to the door when his voice stopped her.

"What are you really doing here, Tori?" he asked.

Hearing him say her name in his low, rumbling voice made her stomach flip. She turned slowly. "Isn't it obvious?"

"Not to me."

"Like I said, I came to thank you. I thought you might like to take a break from all of this—" She gestured to the papers on the bed. "Have a drink since you're new in town and obviously alone."

"Are you?" When she looked at him quizzically, he added. "Is that why you're here? Because you're alone?"

Something inside of her shifted, cracking the hard shell she kept around her heart. She was alone. Increasingly felt alone. Was afraid that was exactly what she deserved. "Look, I just…"

"You just what?"

"I thought we could hang out," she admitted.

Brandon was at his dad's and as she sat in her empty house, she'd become increasingly antsy. Anxious. Walker was right. She hadn't wanted to be alone. But coming here when she was keyed up and restless and, most frightening of all, feeling so needy and reckless, was a mistake.

She was always making mistakes.

"But since you're not interested," she continued, giving him a sharp grin, her nails digging painfully into her palms, "I'll have to go see if I can find some man who is."

CHAPTER EIGHT

TORI YANKED THE door open and Walker stepped back in time to save himself from a broken nose. Before he could grab her arm, hell, before he could even figure out why he would want to try to stop her, she was gone, her long legs eating up the distance between the motel and her car.

Good. It wasn't up to him to keep her from doing something she might regret. He was nobody's savior. Had no desire to be.

Walker leaned against the doorjamb, his ankles crossed, gooseflesh rising on his bare arms as she cranked the engine and drove away. He wasn't one of those cops who needed to save everyone, even from themselves. He did his job, found the truth, made sure justice was served and then moved on. Tori Mott and whatever had sent her to his room weren't his problems.

But he could still smell her, he thought as he shut the door. Her intoxicating, sexy scent lingered in the air, colored his intentions. He could still see her standing next to his rumpled bed and it was easy, way too easy, to imagine her in it. Imagine them in it, her golden skin a contrast against the whiteness of the scratchy sheets.

He kept remembering how crushed she'd looked when her son had yelled at her after the game. How she'd seemed almost vulnerable standing at his door.

It was all an act. Part of her illusion. There was nothing real about her. Was there?

He grabbed his keys, went outside. The cold on his bare feet reminded him he didn't have any shoes on. He went back inside, caught sight of himself in the mirror above the dresser, tried to smooth his hair down, realized it was no good. It took him fifteen minutes—twenty tops—to shower and change. By the time he pulled into the Yacht Pub's parking lot, he wondered if he'd made a mistake.

Walking into the bar he was sure of it. It was a dive, one where regulars went. Dark with ancient woodwork and scarred tables and fishing items hanging on the walls— including a huge swordfish—it smelled of stale beer. Though it was still early by Saturday night standards, there was a decent size crowd. He didn't see Tori as he walked farther into the room. She'd probably already left. Or had never been there.

He was about to turn around when he caught a flash of color from the corner of his eye, saw her on the dance floor.

And was so mesmerized by her natural rhythm, the sensual way she moved, her hips and arms swaying to the beat, it took him a minute to realize she wasn't dancing alone. Her partner was tall and lanky and all of twenty-one, twenty-two at the most. The kid couldn't take his eyes off Tori, didn't seem to mind in the least having her rubbing against him.

Ignoring the curious looks he got from the other patrons, Walker crossed to the dance floor, walked up to Tori and took a hold of her arm. "Time to go."

She startled, her eyes showing her surprise—and even though he hadn't taken long to get there, she was well past tipsy and quickly heading to drunk. But then, as if realizing what he was doing, what he'd said, she tugged free.

"I'm not ready to go." She smiled up at the kid, laid her

hand on his chest—and Walker wanted to smack the kid's sloppy, self-satisfied grin off his face. "Me and James—"

"John," the kid corrected, taking advantage of Tori's position enough to settle his own hand just above her ass.

More and more that smack seemed like a great idea.

"Whatever," she said with a wave of her hand. "We're dancing."

"Yeah?" Tired of her games, pissed that he'd ignored good sense and was even there, Walker yanked her against him. She stumbled and fell into him, one of her damned pointy heels landing on his foot. No doubt purposely. "Now you're done," he ground out, his big toe throbbing.

The kid stepped forward. "Now, wait a—"

"John," Walker said in a tone that had the kid freezing and looking uncertain. "Be smart here."

John was bright enough to realize he'd best be on his way.

"Hey," Tori called as John walked over to the bar, unable to follow him with Walker's strong grip on her arm, "where are you going?" When John ignored her and started flirting with a girl his own age, Tori glared at Walker. "That wasn't very nice."

Nice. Jesus. "Did you bring a purse?"

"To the Yacht Pub?" She tried to break free of his hold. He held tight but wished he had a pair of cuffs on him. "What am I, stupid?"

"That has yet to be determined."

He pulled her out of the bar without any problem. Guess the clientele didn't want to get involved.

"What the hell do you think you're doing?" she demanded, struggling to keep up with him in her heels, her balance unsteady.

"Saving you," he muttered.

"What?"

He sighed. Stopped and faced her. "I said I'm saving you."

"I don't need saving," she said emphatically, her words only slightly slurred. "I don't want saving."

"Well, you should. That kid was barely legal."

Even in the dim parking lot, he could see her blush. "He's twenty-five."

"My mistake," Walker said, opening the passenger door of his car. "But playtime's over. Time to go home."

She slid him an unreadable glance. "I bet you say that to all the girls."

"Only the stubborn ones."

"Lucky me."

"Yeah. Lucky you. Get in," he said, indicating the passenger seat.

"I'm perfectly capable of driving my own car."

Walker edged closer, forcing her to back up until she was trapped between the car and his body. He searched her eyes, noted the glassiness, the alcohol on her breath. "Don't make me put you through a field sobriety test."

"I only had a few shots." She frowned as if thinking caused her great pain. "And a rum and Coke. And then another shot."

"Uh-huh." No wonder she was halfway to being completely toasted. Shots had a habit of doing that. "Get in."

She hesitated and he'd had enough. He practically shoved her into the passenger seat and slammed the door shut. He slid in behind the wheel then reached over her to pull her seat belt across her lap, his knuckles brushing the side of her breast. He wrenched the belt hard enough to have it snapping loose, clicked it into place and sat back.

"What about my car?" she asked, turning to look out the window at the parking lot as he pulled away.

"Guess you'll have to get it tomorrow."

She slid down into the seat and crossed her arms. "You're a real prince, you know that?"

He had no desire to be a prince. At the moment, he was cursing himself for giving into this hidden noble streak. "How the hell did you get so much to drink when you didn't even bring your purse?"

He felt her looking at him. "Do you really think I have to buy my own drinks?"

Good point. She probably had guys lining up to ply her with liquor the moment she set foot in a bar.

And he was the one to take her home.

He strangled the steering wheel, not loosening his grip until he pulled into her driveway and shut off the engine.

"I guess it's not surprising you know where I live," Tori said, unbuckling her seat belt. "Weird, but not surprising."

"It's my job to know."

"It's still weird."

He climbed out, circled the front of the car and opened the door for her. Without a word, without even one of her seductive glances, she brushed past him and walked up the short driveway. He followed her across a covered patio and up the steps into a tidy kitchen.

She sat on a chair at the table, reached down to slip off a boot, wiggling her toes with a soft groan. Repeating the action with the second boot, she looked up at him. "Your good deed for the day is done so you can go now. Since you're not interested and all."

Oh, he was interested, all right. Attracted. Even when she was amped up and looking for a fight.

There must be something wrong with him.

"I could make coffee," he said, searching through her cupboards.

He heard the second boot hit the floor with a thud. "I don't want coffee. I want you to go."

But she sounded uncertain. And when he turned, she looked so fragile sitting there, her arms crossed, her shoulders drooping, as if one wrong word would break her. He realized he didn't want that. Didn't want her spirit broken or even cracked. He just wanted to know her, to catch even a glimpse of the woman she was beneath her high heels and makeup, beneath her cynicism and smart mouth.

"I could stay," he heard himself say.

Just like that, her expression closed. Studying him intently, she rose, crossed the room until she stood before him. "What for?"

Without her heels, the top of her head only reached his nose. "We could…talk."

"Is that what you call it?" she asked, her tone sensual. She laid her hand on his chest, like she'd done with John on the dance floor. Walker froze; even his heart seemed to stop beating. She stepped closer and he could feel her warmth, could see the flecks of gold in her eyes. "Okay," she whispered, her breath fanning his chin, her other hand sliding up his arm to settle at the back of his neck. "Let's *talk*."

She rose onto her toes, brushed her mouth against his. Want, need, unlike anything he'd ever experienced coursed through him, tightening his body, heating his blood. And he knew if he wasn't very, very careful, this woman, this irritating, fascinating, complicated woman, could bring him to his knees.

He gripped her shoulders and pushed her away from him. Dropped his hands before she could see they were unsteady.

"What is your problem?" she asked, sounding confused and exasperated. "Don't you find me attractive?"

"You're beautiful," he said gruffly. Honestly.

Her smile didn't reach her eyes. "Then there's no reason to stop."

"No reason except that you're a possible subject in a murder case—"

"We both know I didn't kill anyone."

He didn't know that, not for certain, though something told him she was innocent. But was that his gut talking or his desire for her?

"Even if I wasn't on the job," he said, "even if you had no connection to Dale York, you and I would never happen. Not when, fifteen minutes ago, you were plastered against another man, ready to take him home, to your bed." He tugged her forward, bent his knees so they were eye to eye. "Not when I'm some sort of backup lay."

Her head snapped back as if he'd slapped her, the color drained from her face. "I want you out of my house, my home," she whispered.

He should. He absolutely should because he had no right to be there, he'd had no right to drag her from that bar—even though it was in her best interest. But he'd put that injured look in her eyes, caused her pain.

He'd only been honest, but he'd hurt her. And he hadn't meant to. Hadn't known he could.

He opened his mouth, but had no idea what to say, if he should say anything.

"Leave," she said, before he could speak. "Now."

Her mouth was set, her body unyielding. She wasn't going to listen to anything he said. He would never get through to her, at least not tonight. A smart man knew when to cut his losses.

And if there was one thing Walker Bertrand was, it was smart.

"Good night, Mrs. Mott," he said. Stepping into the dark night, he swallowed past the apology stuck in his throat, the one that would only cause more problems, would make it seem as if he cared about her personally. He'd already stepped up to that line separating his job from his personal life by tracking her to that bar and driving her home.

One little nudge could push him into dangerous territory.

TORI'S HEAD POUNDED. She hadn't had that much to drink last night but she'd still ended up with a wicked hangover.

Guess that was what she'd missed out on by getting pregnant so young. When all of her high school friends had been in college and partying at bars, she'd been home with her baby and husband.

Thank God. She'd hate to think about what her life would've been like if she hadn't gotten pregnant. She liked to pretend that she'd have gone on to college, would have moved away from Mystic Point and had some fabulous career. But with age came wisdom and hers told her she probably would've stayed in this town. At least this way she had something to pin the blame on.

The back door opened and Brandon came in. She smiled. She did love her kid even if he drove her crazy sometimes. "Hey. How was your night?"

"Good," he said, not bothering to look at her, avoiding her touch as he walked past.

She opened her mouth to call him back when Greg and Colleen stepped inside.

"Tori," he said, "do you have a minute?"

"Sure," she said, determined to be pleasant and polite no matter what. "Come on in. Hi, Colleen."

See? She was all sorts of friendly.

"Good morning," Colleen said in her soft way.

They were an odd couple, Tori thought. Greg was still

as handsome as he'd been in high school with thick brown hair and green eyes. He was average height but had broad shoulders and only the slightest paunch. He wasn't as tall as Walker or as handsome.

And why she was thinking of that son of a bitch, she had no clue.

Shoving all thoughts of Walker out of her head, she concentrated on her ex. Greg was a good man. Honest and honorable and easygoing. He'd done his best to make Tori happy, to give her whatever she'd wanted. Colleen was plain and chubby but good-natured and a little on the shy side. The complete opposite of Tori.

Brandon preferred Colleen. It ate Tori up.

Greg stood by the counter, seemed nervous, which was unlike him. Then again, this was the first time he'd stood between his ex-wife and his current girlfriend in what used to be his home. He and Tori had been together for so long, at times she couldn't remember a time when he wasn't a part of her life, wasn't her partner. Her friend.

She missed him, she realized with a jolt. Not as her husband or lover, but as her friend.

"Do either of you want coffee?" she asked, trying to ignore the ache in her head, the way her stomach turned.

Greg looked to Colleen, who shook her head. "No, thanks," he said. "Listen, we need to tell you something."

"Did something happen with Brandon?" Tori asked.

After the fight yesterday, she and Greg had agreed that Brandon should be grounded for a month with no electronics of any sort, then they'd gone with him over to the Nashes to apologize to Dalton and his parents.

Tori had sat on their ugly, floral-print couch, all the while remembering what Brandon had told her Dalton had said. She'd felt ill and guilty, as if she'd somehow done something wrong, as if there was something wrong with her, something lacking in her as a mother. Those thoughts, those worries, had pushed her into going to Walker's motel room.

He'd been right. She had been lonely. Had been so tired of being alone.

Then he'd proved why being alone was so much better.

"No," Greg said. "Brandon's fine. It's…it's about us."

"Us?" No sooner was the word out of Tori's mouth than she realized he wasn't referring to them—him and her—but to him and Colleen.

He tugged on Colleen's hand and brought her forward to stand next to him. "Colleen and I are getting married."

Tori jerked her gaze from their faces to Colleen's left hand, saw the ring sparkling there. "You…" She inhaled deeply to quell the nausea in her stomach. "That's…great. Congratulations. Does Brandon know?"

Greg nodded. "We told him at breakfast."

"Oh." She swallowed, rubbed her thumbnail along the crease of the counter. She had no idea what to say. She wanted Greg to be happy, of course she did. But shouldn't he have waited a little longer?

It hadn't taken him long to replace her.

"Have you set a date?" she managed to ask, proud she sounded so mature and reasonable when she hated herself for feeling so envious and petty.

"I'd like a Christmas wedding," Colleen said, smiling shyly at Greg.

"That sounds…nice."

"Tori," Greg said, "there's something else. It's about Brandon…"

"He's not happy about the engagement?" she guessed. She could only imagine how this would affect him.

"No, just the opposite. He's really excited about it. In

fact, he..." Greg pressed his lips together, softened his voice. "Tori, he wants to live with us."

Tori stilled, could hear the pounding of her heart in her ears. All she could do was stare at Greg. Finally she blinked. "I'm sorry.... What?"

Greg looked at her with such pity, it almost undid her. Even Colleen, plain Colleen who'd probably never had a boyfriend before Greg, who was so much...less than Tori, pitied her.

"Brandon wants to live with Colleen and me," Greg said.

"Brandon lives here," Tori said, her lips barely moving. "He lives with me. We agreed he'd stay with me."

When she'd asked Greg for a separation a year ago, had asked him to move out to give them both time to figure out what they wanted, he'd agreed without hesitation. Without argument. And, after two months when she'd realized they were both better off on their own, when she'd told him she wanted a divorce, he'd gone along with it. Good ol' Greg, always giving her what she wanted.

She knew, had known for years, she was honest enough to admit to herself, that their marriage wasn't working, would never work. Greg gave too much.

Tori took. She was a taker, like her mother. And she hadn't wanted him to end up like her father.

But she'd also wanted more out of her life. Was that really so wrong? So selfish? Didn't she deserve to have everything she wanted? Why did that make her a bad person, a bad mother?

She and Greg didn't have a formal custody agreement because they'd both wanted Brandon to stay in the house where he'd always lived. They had wanted to give him that stability.

"We did agree to that," Greg said, as always patient,

"but now circumstances have changed and I think we should do what's best for Brandon."

Tori trembled with outrage, with pain. "I'm what's best for Brandon. I'm his mother."

She had always prided herself on being a good mother, one who'd given her son equal amounts love and discipline. Time, attention and freedom to explore who he was, who he wanted to be. She was nothing like her own mother who'd only been good at being fun and beautiful. Tori hadn't had enough of her mother's attention so she'd made sure Brandon hadn't lacked for hers in any way. And now that wasn't good enough?

She wasn't good enough as a mother.

"No," Tori said. "No. Brandon lives here and he'll continue to live here."

Greg looked disappointed in her, as if he was her father and not her ex-husband. "I think we need to take Brandon's wants and needs into consideration."

"Brandon wants us to not have gotten divorced," she said flatly. "He needs to know he can't always get his own way."

She hated knowing her son didn't want her, didn't want to be with her. Hated having this conversation in front of Colleen, the next Mrs. Gregory Mott. It was humiliating, not being good enough.

"This isn't about him getting his own way," Greg said while Colleen just looked uncomfortable. "This is about doing what's best for him. And if you don't agree that he can move in with us, that he can live with me full-time, we'll have to go to court."

Her teeth clenched, her hands fisted, and she nodded sharply once. "You want a fight? Fine. Because I'm not giving up my son without one."

Greg sighed and led Colleen to the door. Colleen

stepped out but Greg turned back to Tori. "I'm sorry it has to come to this."

The worst part? He meant it. He was nothing if not sincere and so good she'd often felt lacking next to him, being with him. As if she was holding him back. When he'd held her back just as much.

He shut the door quietly behind him and she stood in the kitchen, her arms crossed, her heart pounding as she listened to them drive away.

"You can't make me stay here."

She whirled around to find Brandon standing in the doorway between the kitchen and living room, his face flushed, his shoulders hunched.

"You live here," she said. "When we split up, your father and I agreed you'd live with me."

"You didn't split up," her son spat at her. "You kicked him out. You didn't want to be married anymore so you just quit."

"It's not quite as simple as that," she said, fighting not to lose her temper. "Your father and I care about each other very much but that's not enough to make a marriage work."

"It worked until last year."

God, if only life was as simple as a preteen saw it. "It wasn't enough, what Greg and I had wasn't enough for either of us." She softened her tone. "I know it's hard for you to understand now, but when you're older—"

"I'll never understand," he yelled. "And I don't want to live here. I don't want to live with you."

Temper began to simmer in her veins. "Well, let me give you a hard life lesson. You don't always get what you want."

His eyes flashed, but his bottom lip quivered. "I hate you."

He stomped off, his feet too big, his arms and legs too long.

"Yeah?" she muttered, her heart breaking. "Well, I'm not too crazy for you at the moment, either."

TUESDAY AFTERNOON, Walker sat behind Chief Taylor's desk as Tori entered the office.

As in the first time he'd seen her, he couldn't take his eyes off her. In a pair of loose, faded jeans and a sweatshirt that fell off one shoulder, her face clean of everything but the barest of makeup, she looked approachable and...real.

And she wouldn't meet his eyes.

"Something wrong, Detective?" she asked, sitting in one of the chairs he'd set up across from him. She lifted her gaze to his for the briefest of seconds. "You're staring," she said flatly.

"And here I thought that's what you wanted. Attention."

"Well, I certainly seem to have captured yours."

That was truer than he wanted to admit. Even to himself.

"You're here," Nora said to Tori as she and Layne came into the room. "You're early."

"Don't sound so shocked, baby girl. I have been known to be punctual every once in a while."

"Right, but only when it's about you." Layne took the seat farthest from Tori then looked to Walker. He didn't like the calculation in her eyes or her smirk. "Did you enjoy your first weekend in Mystic Point, Detective?"

He glanced at Tori. "Excuse me?"

"Aren't you the polite little cop?" Tori muttered.

"Just wondering if you had fun at the Yacht Pub the other night and whatever you—" she sent Tori a pointed, accusatory look "—did...after."

Tori's shoulders went rigid but she didn't defend herself, didn't tell her sister to mind her own business or to go to hell.

He wished she would.

Walker drummed his fingers on the table. "Word gets around fast here."

"That it does. Small town. Plus, when you're a cop, people love to spread tales about what's going on, especially if it involves your family or a sister who has decided to sleep with the enemy."

Nora stared at the ceiling as if God Himself had carved a message for her there. Tori said nothing.

He found himself wanting to defend her, wanting to protect her.

Hell.

"I'd think you'd be used to rumors," he said. She and her sisters had spent their entire lives being talked about, their family fodder for gossips and speculation.

"I don't think it's something you ever get used to," Layne said. "Then again, if people wouldn't make such stupid decisions, there wouldn't be as much to talk about."

"Have you ever made a mistake, Captain?" he asked, feeling Tori's eyes on him. "Ever do something you wished you could take back?"

The captain's eyes narrowed. "Yes, I've made mistakes. But I try to learn from them, not repeat them endlessly in the hope that the outcome will be different."

"If I'd wanted your opinion," Tori told her sister, her voice giving none of her thoughts away, "I would've asked for it."

"You don't ask because you know I'm not going to agree," Layne said.

Walker knew he shouldn't get involved but he didn't like hearing Layne's not-so-subtle inference that Tori was somehow less than her sisters. Less bright, less virtuous, less worthy.

Damn, but he was losing his footing with Tori. He needed to keep his emotional distance. There were too many unknown variables and too many connections, things were too intertwined for him to start to question his initial judgment of her.

Besides, he hated being wrong.

"Look," Layne said, glaring at him as if he was a bug she'd like to stomp on, "can we get on with this? You insisted we all drop what we were doing and meet you so let's hear what your big secret discovery is so we can all go on our merry ways."

"Fine by me." He was starting to doubt the wisdom of calling them. Yes, they were all involved in his investigation but that didn't mean he had to keep them abreast of every development. But he'd wanted to see their reactions when he told them what he'd found. "I thought this might interest you."

Walker handed a piece of paper to Layne, noting the emotions flicking across her face as she read the information. Confusion. Surprise. Denial.

"What the hell is this? Where did you get this?" she demanded, slamming the paper down.

Tori picked it up, frowned as she read it. "I don't get it."

"It says a large sum of money was deposited into an account Dale used after he left Mystic Point all those years ago. And that the money was traced back to Uncle Ken."

"What?" Tori scanned the paper again. "That's ridiculous. There's a mistake."

"No mistake," Walker assured them. His buddy in the Boston office had uncovered the real name behind the mysterious account. "I double-checked and had other sources verify the information. Two days before your mother disappeared, Kenneth Sullivan transferred half a million dollars from an off-shore account set up under a dummy corporation to the account of Joel Cannella. Mr. York has been living as Joel Cannella for the past eighteen years. We also found that the initial account was set up under two names, the other one being a Whitney Williams."

Layne and Tori exchanged a look, while Nora stared at her hands.

"What?" he asked.

"Whitney was our maternal grandmother's maiden name," Tori said.

"Tori," Layne warned.

"What does it matter? The truth's going to come out."

Nora made a sound like she'd been hit in the stomach.

"You okay, Miss Sullivan?" Walker asked.

She nodded, still wouldn't lift her head.

"I had your uncle brought in for questioning a few hours ago but he wasn't cooperative." Sullivan had refused to answer their questions and had told them that if they wanted to talk to him again, they could do so in the presence of his attorney. But Walker had noticed that Mr. Sullivan had seemed nervous and on edge. He was hiding something.

"There could be any number of reasons that Uncle Ken's name was on that account," Layne insisted. "He could have been set up by someone, maybe even Dale. York was a sneaky bastard."

From what Walker knew, that was true. York had been mean and violent but more than that, perhaps what made him more dangerous, was that he was also smart. Clever.

"It's possible that's the case," Walker agreed. Hell, anything was possible, though it wasn't likely. "Or maybe your uncle knew exactly what was going on."

Tori moved to the edge of her seat. "What are you saying?"

"I'm saying, it's just as possible Ken Sullivan paid Mr. York to kill your mother. From all accounts your father and his older brother are close. Maybe Ken found out about your mother's affair and figured the best way to solve that problem would be to pay York and your mother to leave town. Or to kill your mother. Or maybe your father went to him—"

"He didn't," Nora blurted, her face red, her eyes wet. She looked at Layne then Tori, desperation on her face. "He didn't. Uncle Ken didn't pay Dale to kill Mom. That's not what happened."

Walker's instincts told him she knew something but he didn't rely on instincts, he relied on facts. "Miss Sullivan, how can you be so sure?"

"I…" She stared at her sisters, her eyes bleak. Swallowed visibly. "Uncle Ken wouldn't hurt anyone." She looked to Tori. "You know he wouldn't."

"Of course he wouldn't," she said, reaching over to take her sister's hand which Nora gripped like a lifeline.

"If you know something pertinent to this case," Walker said, using his best cop voice, all hard-assed and controlled, "then you need to tell me."

Nora shook her head.

Tori scowled at him. "What could she possibly know? You're upsetting her."

But Layne was watching her youngest sister and he saw on her face the same thoughts, the same questions going through his own mind. The same suspicions.

She crouched next to Nora's chair. "Nora, if you know something, you have to tell us."

"I'm sorry," Nora said barely above a whisper. She met Tori's gaze then Layne's. "I'm so sorry."

"Hey, hey," Tori said softly, rubbing her arm, her other hand reaching for Layne. They linked their hands, fingers entwined. "It's okay. Just tell us so we can fix it."

They were a unit. A shaky one, one they probably weren't even sure they wanted or needed but he saw in them the same bond he'd seen his entire life between his own four sisters. The love and connection despite the arguments and personality conflicts. And these three women had taken care of each other, had only each other to rely on so that bond was doubly strong.

But he didn't have time for them to get their stories straight, didn't want to admire them or like them. He had a job to do.

"Miss Sullivan," he said, a snap to his tone, "tell me what you know."

"Quit yelling at her," Tori told him. He had a feeling if he'd been closer to her, she would've kicked him.

"It's okay," Nora said. "He's right. He needs to know. You all need to know the truth." She trembled and Walker could see her sisters' fear and worry for her on their faces. "I've been keeping something from you both, from everyone. The truth is…" She inhaled deeply then said in a rush, "The truth is I'm not your sister."

CHAPTER NINE

TORI SQUEEZED NORA's hand. "Honey, what are you talking about? Of course you're our sister."

"I'm not," she said hoarsely. "Not fully."

Unease prickled the base of Tori's spine. An idea, a crazy, unbelievable idea, formed in her head but she pushed it aside before it could take shape fully.

"Tell us," Layne ordered softly.

"A few days before he died, Dale came to my house," Nora said in a robotic monotone.

Layne bristled. "He came to see you again? And you didn't tell us?"

Tori shook her head at Layne. Now wasn't the time. But she, too, wondered why Nora hadn't reported Dale's visit. When Dale had come back to Mystic Point, one of the first stops he'd made was to Nora's office. He'd wanted to intimidate her, their family, by visiting the youngest. But if he sought her out maybe there was more to it than that?

"I couldn't," Nora said.

"Do you have any idea why Mr. York sought you out a second time?" Walker asked, all unemotional and detached. Of course he was—this wasn't his sister, his town and family and life.

"At first, I thought it was because of what happened at the bar, the fight between him and Griffin. I thought Dale was trying to use me to get back at Griffin. But that wasn't it. He wanted me to help him blackmail Uncle Kenny."

"What did he say exactly?" Layne asked, sounding as much like a cop as Walker did. Thank God Ross wasn't here or Tori and Nora would be outnumbered.

"He said...he said he had a proposition for me, a way for us to help each other." Nora spoke flatly, her gaze somewhere over Tori's shoulder. "He said that Mom had an affair years ago, a one-night stand. With Uncle Ken."

Layne's face went white. Tori felt cold all over. Oh, God. She held on to Nora tighter for both their sakes, felt Layne's grip on her shift and tighten, too.

"Was that all he said?" Walker asked.

Tori almost snapped at him to shut up, to go away and leave them be. She didn't want him around, didn't want him watching them with his cool eyes and judgmental attitude.

She didn't want to know anymore. Didn't want to know the truth.

"I didn't believe him at first," Nora said. "Couldn't believe that Ken would hurt Dad that way. But Dale said he had proof."

Tori let go of Layne's hand and tucked a stray piece of Nora's hair behind her ear. "Honey, you don't—"

"Yes. She does," Layne said. "It'll be okay." She looked at Tori. "No matter what, it'll be okay. We'll get through it."

Nora nodded at Layne. "He said...he said *I* was the proof."

Tori's thoughts spun. Denial whipped through her, fast and furious. No. God, no. "He was lying," Tori said, knowing she sounded desperate. "He was a liar. A criminal."

"He was both of those things," Nora said. "And I didn't believe him but he had a copy of my medical records from when I had my tonsils removed. It lists my blood type. Dale said Mom didn't know I wasn't Dad's child until she saw that form but then she realized that I had to be Ken's daughter."

"Wait," Tori said, holding up a hand. "I don't understand."

"Mom was type O and Dad's B. I checked," Nora said as if she could barely get the words out. "I went to your house," she said to Layne, "that night after you went to work. I used my key and went through the papers in the attic. I found a copy of Mom's medical records and a blood donor card of Dad's. I'm type A. I even went to a doctor a week after Dale died, just to make sure he hadn't falsified the record in some way."

"What does that mean?" Tori asked.

"Any child of your parents, any biological child, would have to have either type O or type B blood," Walker explained, like some damned biology professor.

"I'm B," Layne said, obviously as stricken as her sisters. She glanced at Tori.

"I have no idea." She'd never known her blood type. Was that something people did, something they had to know? She supposed it was in her medical records somewhere.

She wasn't sure she wanted to find out.

"I don't know if Ken is my biological father or not," Nora said, "but I know that Dad...that Tim Sullivan isn't. Dale gave me until that Monday to convince Ken to pay him or else he was going to expose not only the secret about the affair, but about me, too."

"Ken Sullivan isn't aware that you could possibly be his biological child?" Walker asked, taking notes, observing them dispassionately, as if he witnessed families being torn apart every day.

Bastard.

Nora rubbed her palms up and down her thighs. "According to Dale, the only two people who knew were Mom and him. They must have blackmailed Ken eighteen years ago, had planned on using that money to start a new life."

"That's why he came back," Layne said, almost to herself. She stood and began to pace. "He was safe. He knew we didn't have enough evidence to even bring charges against him for Mom's murder so he saw an opportunity to make more money off Uncle Ken."

"Miss Sullivan," Walker said, his voice softer than before, his expression kind. Seemed there were times when he wasn't a complete jerk. "Did Mr. York tell you how he came into possession of your medical records?"

Nora raised her hands in a helpless gesture. "He didn't say and I didn't ask. I figured Mom had given him a copy when she told him all of this."

"God, it all makes sense now," Layne said. "Mom and Dale blackmailed Ken eighteen years ago. And he paid. He paid knowing they'd planned on leaving Mystic Point."

"Or else he paid to have your mother killed," Walker pointed out.

"Stop saying that," Tori snarled. "We don't know why Uncle Ken paid."

"Eighteen years ago, Uncle Ken was heavily involved in local politics, he'd even considered running for state attorney general," Layne said thoughtfully. "He never went through with it. At the time I didn't think anything of it, and later when I overheard Dad bring it up to him, Ken said he wanted to help his local community, focus his efforts here. Any hint of scandal would've hurt him. By paying Mom and Dale, he got them out of his life forever. His secret was safe."

"Is this why you've been avoiding us?" Tori asked Nora, not caring why Ken had done what he had, not caring about anything except her baby sister. "You've been holding on to this secret."

"I couldn't tell you. I couldn't tell anyone." Nora flushed, dropped her gaze. "Except Griffin. He knows."

Before Tori could lay into her about trusting a man over her own sisters, Layne lightly touched Tori's arm. "You should've come to us," Layne said to Nora. "You shouldn't have had to go through this alone."

"I didn't want anyone to know. I still don't. Keeping this to myself has been a nightmare but you know what's going to happen when this gets out. There's more at stake than just my feelings. Ken and Astor's marriage… God, what about Erin and Anthony? How are they going to react? And Dad. He's going to be crushed. He'll never forgive Ken."

"That's not your fault," Layne said.

Nora laughed softly but it held no humor. "I know but I can't help thinking that none of this would be a problem if I hadn't been born."

"Don't you ever talk like that," Tori said, shaken to her core. "You are not to blame. This is Ken and Mom's fault. And no matter what happened twenty-seven years ago, you are and have always been a blessing."

Nora's eyes welled and damn if Tori didn't want to curl up in a ball on the floor and cry right along with her.

"You're still our baby sister," Layne said quietly. "Fully. Forever. Nothing will ever change that."

The tears in Nora's eyes spilled over. She wiped them away with her fingers. Sniffed delicately. "Thank you. You don't know what that means to me."

"I think I can guess," Layne said before facing Walker. "You need to question Ken again."

He leaned back, king of his domain. "I know my job, Captain."

"Then why aren't you forcing him to answer your questions?"

"Do you even hear yourself?" Tori asked. "You sound like a crazy person. What would you do, Layne? Arrest Uncle Ken?"

"Yes," she said so simply, Tori had no choice but to believe her. "If Dale did blackmail Ken—twice—that's a strong motive for murder."

Tori's stomach dropped. "Oh, my God. You don't believe…. Uncle Ken could never kill someone."

"Up until ten minutes ago, I wouldn't have believed he could cheat on his wife, either."

Which meant her uncle had just become the prime suspect, not only in Dale's murder but in their mother's as well.

"What are we going to do?" Tori asked. They had to take care of this, had to take care of Nora and their dad…. Oh, dear Lord, their dad. It was going to kill him when he found out the brother he loved and admired his entire life had betrayed him.

"We're going to handle it," Layne said firmly. "Just like we always do. Together."

Could they? Could her family survive it? Tori wasn't sure. Nora had already been hurt and it would only get worse. She and Ken's daughter Erin were only a few months apart in age which meant that when Ken slept with their mother, his wife was pregnant with their first child. And Nora and Erin were the best of friends. Nora had always been close to Ken and Astor, had spent more time with her uncle and aunt than either Layne or Tori.

"If there's nothing else, Detective, I'd like to take my sister home now," Layne asked tightly, as if it killed her to ask his permission.

Getting to her feet, Nora rolled her eyes. "I'm perfectly

capable of seeing myself home." She checked her watch. "Or, in this case, back to the office."

"Forget work." Layne wrapped her arm around Nora's shoulders and led her toward the door. "You're taking the rest of the day off." Layne glanced at Tori. "You coming? We can all go to my house, discuss what we're going to do about telling Dad."

"I'll be there in a few minutes."

"See that you are," Layne said, her gaze bouncing between Tori and Walker, her meaning so clear, only a blind woman could've missed it. *Stay away from Walker Bertrand. Don't trust him with your secrets. Don't believe anything he has to say.*

All of which Tori already knew.

"Something I can do for you, Mrs. Mott?" Walker asked when they were alone.

His low, smooth voice scraped against her skin like sandpaper, the sound of him calling her Mrs. Mott like a slap in the face after what he'd said and done Saturday night. She'd kissed him, had felt the rapid beat of his heart under her hand, seen the flame of desire in his eyes and he'd still rejected her. Worse than that, he'd hurt her.

She'd let him hurt her.

"Are you happy?" she asked roughly. "My family is being torn apart all because you couldn't stop digging."

He rose and circled the desk. "It's my job to dig for the truth."

Tori knew that, understood it. But that didn't make it any easier to accept. "Do you think Uncle Ken killed my mother?"

She hadn't meant to ask that, was half-afraid to know the answer. But it was too late to take it back.

"I think any opinion I might have at this time would be conjecture."

"You really are a cop through-and-through, aren't you?" she said, disgust lacing her voice.

Walker leaned against the desk. "Do you think your uncle killed your mother?"

"No." She had to keep believing that. It was the only way she'd get through this without losing her mind. "What I think is that, like all men, he was weak. Mom got to him using her face and body. He was probably so wrapped up in her he didn't even consider what his actions would do to his wife and brother."

"You blame your mother." It was a statement, not a question.

Tori answered him anyway. "She was beautiful. And selfish. When she saw something she wanted, she took it, no matter who it belonged to first."

"Seems to me Ken should shoulder his part of the blame for the affair. Then again, you don't hold men in very high esteem, do you?"

"Detective, I love men. Ask anyone."

He crossed to her. Tori's heart pounded with excitement and sexual awareness and a healthy dose of panic. She held the power in any relationship, no matter if it was a platonic friendship, professional or with her family. But Walker would fight her for that control, would try to take it from her, use it against her.

"I'm asking you," he said. "I can't figure you out."

That, at least, was a relief. She didn't want anyone, especially not a man, getting inside her head. "That's the nicest thing you've said to me."

"It wasn't meant to be. I'm not sure what's real with you and what's not. You protect yourself. But from what? What are you so afraid of?"

Tori tipped her chin up, her pulse racing because he was so close, his aftershave light and musky. Because he was trying to dig into her psyche, into her soul, and he was right. She was afraid. Always so afraid of proving everyone right.

She really was just like her mother.

WALKER WAITED. His chest hurt and he realized he was holding his breath, that he was getting somewhere with her, was seeing something real in her. But then her expression changed and she reached out and smoothed her hand down the front of his shirt, played with the top button.

"What could I possibly be afraid of?" Tori asked in that damn sexy voice, the same one he had heard in his dreams last night. Calling him. Teasing him. Saying his name.

He pulled back, both physically and mentally. But he couldn't deny he'd thought of her, had dreamed of her every night since he'd brought her home from the bar. That he wanted her.

"I hope Captain Sullivan doesn't plan on warning Ken that he's a suspect in a murder case." Although if Ken hadn't figured that out when Walker had questioned him earlier, the older man needed to put away his lawyer shingle.

"She won't. Layne doesn't do anything that gets her into trouble. Actually that's pretty much what I said the first time I met Ross, too. Seems I'm always setting you men straight on my older sister."

"Chief Taylor was worried about Captain Sullivan?"

"Worried? Nah. At the time he was just pissed off. Layne and I had a little…disagreement at the police department that concerned him."

Walker shouldn't be surprised they'd fought at the station. He'd witnessed countless fights between his sisters everywhere from birthday parties to high school basketball games to church.

"Don't look so suspicious," Tori continued. "The only person Layne will tell about our conversation in here is Ross. She's not how you think."

"And how do I think she is?"

"You think she's some sort of liar. Someone who'd break the rules but she's not. As a matter of fact, Layne's spent all of her life proving she's nothing like our mother, who broke all the rules."

"And why would she do that?" he asked, knowing Tori was vulnerable and only opening up to him because of what she'd discovered about her uncle and mother. But he wasn't about to let an opportunity pass to get to know her.

For the case, he assured himself.

But Tori shrugged. "I still can't believe Uncle Ken fell for my mother. I'd thought more of him."

"Your father fell for your mother, too." Walker couldn't understand how Tori could hold it against her uncle when her father had married her mother. Had, by all accounts, loved her above all else.

"Dad had no choice. He and Mom were high school sweethearts and when she got pregnant with Layne before graduation, they got married. I remember them arguing about it one time." Tori's tone was thoughtful, her gaze over his shoulder as if looking into the past. "She accused him of being happy she'd gotten pregnant because then he'd been able to convince her to marry him. He didn't deny it."

"He also didn't force her to marry him."

"True. But he couldn't resist her. She was so beautiful, so alive. Even after all these years I can still hear her laugh. She had a great laugh, all low and husky." Tori slid him a grin that held a sharp edge. "It made people stop in their tracks. *She* made people stop, made them take notice of her."

Tori looked so sad, so lost for a moment, his resolve to keep his distance from her waned. His good sense, the one that told him she was a heartbreaker, a cold and ruthless woman, seemed to fade when, more than ever, he needed it to stay solid and in focus.

"Layne looks just like her," Tori continued. "Sometimes, when she talks, when she smiles—and as you may have realized, my older sister doesn't smile nearly enough—it about knocks me on my butt. The resemblance."

Walker couldn't read her, not fully and that pissed him off. He had more questions than answers and that frustrated him. She intrigued him and that scared the hell out of him. "You loved her. Your mother."

"Of course. Oh, don't look so shocked, Detective. She was my mother, after all. And despite her faults and failings and weaknesses, despite her vanity, she loved us. All of us, even my father...the best she knew how. The best she could."

"That makes it all right? The things she did, the lies and the infidelity?"

"It makes it understandable. She couldn't change who she was. None of us can change who we are, how we are, on the inside."

He edged closer, couldn't stop himself, her skin, her scent, beckoning him. And that made him a fool, one of the many men who fell at her feet. "From all accounts, your mother wasn't the nurturing type."

"No, she was the fun type. The 'let's have a party' type. She cared more about taking care of herself than her kids."

"You and Layne took care of Nora."

"Layne took care of all of us. Me, Nora, Dad. She always carried the weight of the world on her shoulders."

Tori shifted, glanced out the window. "Layne loves nothing more than being the boss."

But her words lacked heat; instead they sounded respectful. And Walker knew there was more to the story than Tori let on. He'd seen how she'd been with Nora, how Nora had leaned on both of her sisters, not just Layne.

"I don't think you're giving yourself enough credit," he said. "Nora looks up to both her sisters, that much was clear back there. Do you want to know what I think?"

She smirked. "Not particularly."

"I think you're not as hard, as cold, as you want people to believe. You love your son and your sisters, told Nora she was a blessing."

"She is. She's the best of us."

"What does that make you?"

Tori grinned but it was so sad, it made his chest hurt. "Just like our mother."

His mother had been crying.

That was what Anthony noticed when he walked into the kitchen and saw his parents and sister. Erin hurried over to hug him. "Thanks for coming so soon," she whispered.

"What's going on?" he asked, mimicking her soft tone. Their mom wiped the spotless counter. Their father sat at the table, his face pale, his fingers twisting and untwisting the tablecloth.

"I don't know. All I know is what I told you over the phone."

What she'd told him was that there was an emergency and he needed to come home tonight, now. Luckily traffic was light and he'd made it back to Mystic Point in record time.

"Hey," he said to his parents, feeling as if he had to

somehow take care of Erin even though she was his older sister. "You two okay?"

"Could you…could you and your sister sit down?" his dad asked, indicating the empty chairs at the table.

Anthony and Erin exchanged a look then crossed to the table and sat.

"Astor?" Ken said to his wife.

She flinched, exhaled heavily then set the dishcloth down and in stilted steps, walked to the table. Sat next to her husband.

"You're scaring me," Erin said. "What is it?"

Anthony gently squeezed her hand. He was scared, too, but he'd never admit it.

Ken looked at Astor but she stared straight ahead, her shoulders rigid, her face a mask of pain. As always, they were side by side. A unit. A team.

Side by side. That's how Anthony pictured them, thought of them. Not his mom, Astor Sullivan. Not his father, Ken. They were Mom and Dad. And they needed his help, needed him to be strong.

"Whatever it is," he said, "we'll get through it together."

They had to. His parents had always been there for him and Erin and he knew he and his sister would be there for them no matter what.

"There's no easy way to start this conversation," Ken said, looking weary and much older than his years, his face drawn. He rubbed a hand over his eyes. "No easy way to say this so I'm just going to say it. Years ago, before you both were born, I had an affair."

"What?" Erin asked while all Anthony heard was a roaring in his head. He looked at his mother, his lovely, wonderful mother. She seemed broken.

"It was a mistake, a huge mistake, one I've regretted

ever since," Ken said, sounding guilty. As he should. He should drown in his guilt.

Erin sat back, her face white. "I don't understand." She looked at their mom. "Did you know?"

"No." Astor cleared her throat. "Your father told me this afternoon."

"Okay," Erin said with a heavy breath. "It happened a long time ago, right? And like Dad said, it was a mistake. You can get past this."

Her voice wobbled, her eyes filled. Anthony knew how she felt. He'd never imagined his father hurting his mother this way, never imagined them not being together.

At the moment he couldn't picture them at all. Could only see his family being ripped apart.

"I'm afraid it's not that simple," Astor said.

"No, not simple." Erin leaned forward and covered her mother's hand with one of her own. "It'll take time.... Maybe you could attend marital counseling or talk to Pastor Rick—"

"Tell them," Astor said to Ken, sounding so unlike herself, sounding demanding and angry and hurt. "Tell our children the rest."

Anthony didn't want to hear the rest. Already he felt disgusted and angry. He knew too much about his parents' marriage. By admitting the affair his father had dragged him and Erin somewhere they had no right to be.

Ken rubbed his forefinger up and down his coffee cup. "Like I said, it happened a long time ago. I was an idiot. Your mother and I had a fight...I can't even remember about what...and I left, went out to get some air and I ended up at the Yacht Pub, thought I'd have a few drinks, calm down." He cleared his throat. "But I had too much to drink—"

"Are you trying to excuse this?" Anthony asked, incensed.

"Not excuse it, no," Ken said, his mouth a thin line, "just telling you the truth. I had too much to drink and I made a mistake. I cheated on your mother, the only woman I've ever loved. I broke our marriage vows and have now lost your trust and faith in me. I betrayed your mother and my brother."

"Oh, Daddy," Erin said, her words ragged. "No."

Anthony couldn't catch his breath. Beside him, Erin cried softly but he couldn't reach over to comfort her. All he could do was stare across the table at his parents. The kitchen table had always been the place for family discussions, over a meal or not. Family meetings, his mother had called them. When Erin had told him he needed to come home, that their parents had to talk to both of them right away, he'd been terrified. Had thought for certain some-one had died or was sick.

Not sick, he thought numbly, trying to process what his parents had just told him, not dead. And he couldn't help but think that somehow, this was even worse.

"You slept with Aunt Val?" Anthony asked, so disgusted he could barely look at his father, his anger threatening to overtake him.

He didn't remember her, had only been three when she'd disappeared but he'd heard about her his entire life, knew his family had lived with the repercussions of her life and disappearance.

"I regretted it immediately," Ken said almost desperately.

Of course he was desperate, Anthony thought. He should be. "Does Uncle Tim know? And the girls?"

His cousins, all of whom he loved like sisters.

"The girls know but I've asked them to let me tell Tim."

Anthony sneered. "Big of you."

Ken's face lost color but Anthony refused to feel sorry for his words, for how angry he was.

"I'm taking responsibility for my mistake," Ken said. "And part of that is to admit the truth, the whole truth. Dale York and Valerie blackmailed me eighteen years ago, threatened to tell Tim and your mother about the affair if I didn't give them half a million dollars. They wanted to leave town, to start a new life together."

"You knew Aunt Val was leaving her husband and daughters and you didn't say anything?" Anthony asked incredulously.

"I couldn't, I was too afraid of my secret coming out so I paid them. All these years I thought he and Val had done what they'd set out to do—start new lives with new identities. When Val's remains were found, I was certain Dale killed her and took the money, but I had no proof and couldn't admit what I knew without incriminating myself. I was selfish and wrong. And when Dale returned to Mystic Point two months ago, he wanted more money to keep my secret. I told him no. I knew I had to come clean."

"But you didn't," Erin said.

"Until now." The back of Anthony's neck itched with apprehension. "You're telling us now. Why?"

"Dale spoke with Nora," Ken said. Something in his tone, in the way he seemed to have aged ten years, warned Anthony what his father was about to tell him would destroy them all. "He told her about the affair. I had no idea." Ken gazed beseechingly at him. "You have to believe me, I had no idea…"

Why would Dale talk to Nora unless… Anthony slowly got to his feet, a sick feeling in his stomach. "You didn't know what?"

But his father hung his head, his shoulders shaking.

"When did you sleep with Aunt Val?" Anthony slammed his hands onto the table causing his mother and sister to jump. "When? How long ago?"

"Twenty-seven years ago." Ken raised his head, and for the first time that Anthony could remember, he saw his father cry. "I'm Nora's father."

Everything inside Anthony froze. His father, the man he'd trusted, had looked up to and practically worshipped was nothing but a liar and a cheat. Ken had taught him right from wrong, had lectured Anthony his entire life about honesty and integrity and taking responsibility for his own actions. But it was all bullshit.

And for that, Anthony would never forgive him.

CHAPTER TEN

"YOU SHOWING UP when I'm finishing work is becoming a habit," Tori said Friday as she opened the café's door to find Walker on the other side.

She was less than thrilled to have him show up at the end of a double shift, one that had been nothing but torture. Thank God it was late enough that everyone else had gone home.

"A good habit or bad one?" Walker asked in that way that told her he didn't really care which one it was. He was there for a reason and what she thought or felt didn't concern him.

"I haven't decided yet. I need more time to make a... well-informed decision." She knew her flirtatious tone would bug him. Good. He bugged her, kept her guessing so why shouldn't she give him a little payback for it? For not being like other men?

That seemed to give him pause and Tori knew that even though he was the one who'd come to her, he was thinking everything through, his thoughts and actions. Wondering if he'd made a mistake by showing up there.

She could respect that about him. She liked to think things through, too. Liked weighing her options before making any decision.

"This is the closest I can get to a homemade meal," Walker said, peering over the top of her head at the dining room. Most of the chairs had been set on top of tables so the cleaning crew could mop the floors.

"Well, homemade meals are hard to come by, especially this late. It's a shame we're closed."

"Sign on the door says you're open until ten."

"Kitchen closes at nine and when all the customers are gone, we shut— Hey," she said when he brushed past her, forcing her to step back.

Tori told herself she didn't care one way or the other what he did; he could go or he could stay. She was still in control.

She held the door open. "Look, the past few days have been really crappy." She'd tried to ignore the gossip, the knowing looks she'd received from customers, had pretended it hadn't bothered her when her coworkers suddenly stopped talking whenever she approached them. "And I'm not in the best of moods," she continued, gesturing for him to walk his sexy ass right back out the door again, "so maybe you could be a nice guy, just this once, and not give me a hard time."

"I hadn't realized it was so late." He frowned, looked around again. "I was working. Lost track of time."

She made a tsking sound. "Luckily the fast food places are open late."

"I've had my fill of fast food."

Not her problem, she told herself as she let the door shut. She set another chair onto a table. She was tired. Irritable. She didn't want company, but wasn't sure she could handle being alone. Had never liked being alone, had always wanted to be surrounded by people. Unlike Layne who'd needed that time and space with her own thoughts.

Tori was afraid she wouldn't like what she found if she dug too deep into her psyche, if she delved too far into her soul, into what she really was inside.

But Walker was watching her in that steady, patient way that made her feel keyed up and on edge and out of control. As if he held some power over her when it should be the other way around.

"You here alone?" he asked, which, coming from any other guy, she would've taken as a pickup line or, worse, aggression. But she wasn't scared of Walker. Not physically, anyway.

"I told Celeste I'd close up."

"I thought you worked days."

What was with all the questions? The man really was an interrogator, always probing, trying to see inside people's heads. "Brandon's at his father's so I offered to work tonight to give Celeste a break."

Celeste deserved it. She'd been rock solid through it all, there for Tim after Ken had confessed his sin to his younger brother. An intermediary the night Tori and her sisters gathered with their father at Layne's house—the home they grew up in—for dinner.

Tori's throat tightened just thinking about it. The beginning of the evening had been tense and awkward with the huge, unspoken question hanging over all of them.

How would Tim treat Nora, his youngest, his joy, now that he knew she wasn't his biological child?

Tori had been certain he'd turn his back on her, had been ready to jump to her sister's aid, to help her through her heartbreak. But their father had taken a hold of Nora's hands and, in front of everyone, had looked into Nora's eyes and told her in no uncertain terms that she was his daughter. His. Always.

Nora had said only one word: Daddy. Then she'd thrown her arms around Tim's neck and as they'd embraced, something inside Tori had warmed. She'd been relieved, sure, but more than that she'd been proud. For the first time she'd been proud to have such a good man for a father.

For the first time, she'd started to forgive him for being so much less than perfect.

The truth may set you free but from Tori's perspective, it usually hurt first. Enough that she would rather avoid it and stick with subterfuge.

But they were surviving it. Their family was cracked, but they weren't broken. Not yet.

"What are you doing?" Tori asked when Walker picked up a chair and set it on a table.

"Helping you."

"Why?" He wanted something from her and, unlike most men, it wasn't her body. Probably was going to try to use his quick mind to trick her into answering more of his questions about her family.

"Because it's late," he said as if she'd scrubbed her brain with bleach, "and you're alone."

"You want something from me," she said. "Just tell me what it is so I can get on with my life."

"Why do you think I want something from you?"

She laughed. "Honey, all men want something from me, the same something."

"You don't trust anyone, do you?" he asked softly.

Tori cocked her hip to the side. "Let's see… My father spent more time on the sea than with his own kids. My mom cheated on her husband—once with her brother-in-law—and left us to start some grand new life. My uncle, a pillar of town, slept with his brother's wife and got her pregnant and paid her and her other lover off. My own sisters think I'm incapable of anything other than waiting tables and flirting." She slammed a chair down. "Why on earth wouldn't I trust people?"

She didn't need help. Didn't want it. Didn't want to

count on someone else to be there for her because that made her weak, left her vulnerable to the whims and feelings of others.

It was too risky.

"You want something to eat?" she snapped, knowing it would be the fastest, easiest way to get rid of him. "Fine. But you'll eat what I cook so don't even think of placing an order from the menu."

"Deal," he said so quickly she blinked.

Guess the man was really hungry.

"Come on," she said, grumpy and tired. Her feet hurt. Her legs and back ached. All she wanted was to go home and soak in a nice, hot, scented tub where she could plan what to do now that Greg was marrying someone else. That her son didn't want to be with her.

Where she could plan her escape.

Not waiting to see if Walker followed, Tori walked across the dining room, pushed open the swinging door that led to the kitchen. She went to the refrigerator and checked the supplies, pulled out the makings for her favorite sandwich.

"Did Brandon get in trouble with his coach for the fight?" Walker asked as he came up beside her.

She almost didn't answer, but he had helped her kid that day so she bit back her impatience. "Both boys did. They're each suspended one game and had to run extra laps all week at practice. They're also both on probation and if they mess up even once, they're off the team."

"Tough coach," Walker said.

"He is but it's a fair punishment." She heated the grill and took out two bagels, sliced them.

"Most parents would be upset their darlings got punished," he said. "My sister Kelly took on the entire school board because my niece got into trouble one day at school and had to stand in the corner."

Tori added four slices of bacon to the grill. "Brandon has to realize there are consequences to his actions—both good and bad."

"I agree that's a good lesson for kids to learn. I think Kelly sees her kids as too close an extension of herself and if they get into trouble or make a mistake, she takes it personally."

"Yeah, well, that's hard not to do. Our children *are* extensions of us and it can be frustrating. Brandon is stubborn, it's a trait he gets from me and maybe that's why it bugs me so much." She flipped the bacon. "He wants to live with his father," she heard herself admit.

Walker crossed his arms and leaned back. "You share custody now?"

"Sort of. Brandon stays with me during the week and spends most weekends with Greg. He's getting married."

"Seems a little young for such a big step."

For the first time all week, Tori smiled. "Not Brandon. Greg."

"How do you feel about that?"

She cracked four eggs onto the grill and sprinkled them with salt and pepper. "Well, Dr. Freud, I feel fine about it." *Sort of.* "I was the one who wanted the divorce," she said, knowing she sounded defensive and bitter. "He wants her, that's fine. But my son should be with me."

Should want to be with me.

"You're jealous," Walker said.

Tori whirled on him, the spatula in her hand. "Jealous? Of Colleen? Have you seen her?"

"I'm not talking about what she looks like. I'm talking about the fact that your son likes her."

Her hand shook so she lowered it. "I just don't think

Brandon should get his own way just because he's mad at me for the divorce."

"Fair enough."

"Damn right it's fair enough."

SHE WAS HURTING, Walker realized. Tough, cynical Tori Mott was heartbroken over her son.

It made her seem more human. Vulnerable and softer than when she was flirting and trying to get men to fall at her feet. It made her more enticing.

She wanted her son to choose her.

He watched as she assembled his sandwiches—bacon and avocado slices on the bagel topped with two eggs. "Like you said," Walker told her, feeling inadequate and clumsy in how to address her problems with her son, "Brandon's a kid. He's pissed. He'll get over it."

She handed him a sandwich and cut the other one in half. "I've been telling myself that for a year now and he's still mad. He gets angrier with me every day." She swallowed, stared at the food in her hands. "He hates me. My own son hates me. God, when he was little he used to look at me like I was the most important thing in the world. His sun, you know?"

Walker took a bite of his sandwich, swallowed. "Kids grow up. They realize their parents aren't infallible."

"I knew that from the time I was little. But when you have a child of your own, you don't realize how big of a love you're capable of. I sure didn't."

"You were barely a kid yourself."

"Eighteen, the same age as my mother when she had Layne." Tori smiled sadly. "I was so scared, had no idea what I was doing or getting myself into. All I knew was that I'd followed my mother's footsteps—gotten pregnant by a good guy, my high school sweetheart just like she had, got married and dropped out of school. Layne was so angry with me, so disappointed. She'd wanted me to go to college."

"You sound as if that's a crazy idea."

"Of course it is. I'm not known for my brains," she said with a wink. "Besides, I knew what my future held. Marriage. Maybe another kid or two. My life spent waiting tables right here in this town. I gave up my dreams as soon as I held Brandon for the first time. Looking at him, feeling his warm body, the slight weight of him in my arms, I felt…complete. And I couldn't understand how my mother never felt the same when she looked at her babies. How she could turn her back on her own children. I vowed that day to be the best mother I could for my son, to give him everything I didn't have. But it wasn't enough."

"If you knew how upset Brandon would be by the divorce, why did you go through with it?" he couldn't help but ask. Walker knew he was skating on thin ice, being alone with her again, the setting somehow intimate despite the size of the kitchen. Her cooking for him, talking to him so openly, was a problem.

One he had to be wary of.

"Part of your investigation?" she asked with one of those unreadable looks.

"Just curious." More curious about her than he had any right to be. "Your ex-husband seems like a decent guy."

"That aptly describes him. Greg is decent and kind. He was the captain of the football team and I was head cheerleader. We were completely cliché and totally clueless about life. He loved me and I…I wanted desperately for someone to love me more than anything. And he did. No matter what I threw at him, no matter what kind of drama I stirred up or fights or arguments I started, no matter how much I flirted with his buddies he was always there. Steady, you know?"

"Sounds like most high school relationships."

"I was a brat. Worse than that, I was a bitch. Selfish and vain. I outgrew it, for the most part. Becoming responsible for someone else forces you to grow up, to see outside yourself. Or it should. But a year ago, as we were in bed, Greg leaned over and kissed me good-night—like he did every night—and told me he loved me. Like he had every night." Using the spatula, she scraped the food from the grill, her movements rougher than Walker thought they should be for the job at hand.

She lifted her head, met Walker's eyes. "I couldn't say it back. I wanted to, but it wouldn't come out and I realized that for all those years, I'd been lying—to Greg and Brandon and to myself. I cared about Greg, I considered him my best friend but I didn't love him the way he deserved. The way he loved me. And it wasn't fair to any of us. I told him I wanted a trial separation. He didn't argue, didn't fight, just agreed. The next day we told Brandon together and Greg moved out."

"And now you're single, and men all throughout town are thanking God."

Tori grinned. "Now you're catching on. So many men, so little time."

But he didn't buy it. Not like he used to. There was more to her than she let on, more than a need for adoration, for attention. She loved her son and her sisters, that much was clear. She put on an act, put up a front to protect herself but from what?

"Now that your stomach's full, why don't you hit the road so I can finish up here?"

He needed to do just that, needed to move on. To finish his investigation and get back to his real life. He couldn't

afford to get tied up, to get entangled in the lives of anyone in Mystic Point.

But he wasn't any closer to finding out who poisoned
Dale York than he'd been when he first came to town. Al-
though thanks to the truth about Ken Sullivan's affair with
Val coming to light, his suspect list was growing.

And included many of Tori's relatives—her father and
uncle, her sisters. Not to mention Walker was still investigating Layne and Ross for misconduct.

No, there was no good reason to get involved with Tori,
for him to start believing there could be something between them, and a million reasons why he shouldn't think
about her, shouldn't dream about her.

She was caustic and guarded and fake.

She was beautiful and smart and more caring than even
she realized.

Hell.

He edged closer. She didn't back up, didn't move closer,
just watched him, that coy half smile of hers playing on
her lips. "Did you want something, Detective?" she asked,
all cocky and confident and challenging.

"Yeah," he said gruffly, sliding his hand along her
neck around to hold her head. Tugged her hair so her head
tipped back. Her eyes flashed and widened, her hands went
to his chest, lay there, not pushing or pulling, just heating
his skin. "I want something."

ANTICIPATION BUILT until Tori was light-headed, her knees
weak. Walker's grip on her hair was tight but instead of
finding it painful, she thought the bite of it exciting. Beneath her hands, his heart beat steadily. He was all solid
muscle and warmth and she wanted to lean into him,
wanted to soak up his heat and his strength and take,
take, take.

She always took.

But she couldn't feel guilty about it, not when he was lowering his head slowly toward her. Her fingers curled into the softness of his T-shirt, dug into his skin. Still he took his time and she wanted to scream with frustration. Wanted to yank his mouth to hers.

Wanted to push him away because she had a feeling, an instinctive knowledge, that once he kissed her, she wouldn't be the same.

His other hand went to her lower back, dragged her toward him until she was pressed against the hard planes of his chest, his thighs. He kissed her, his mouth firm. This was no hesitant kiss, no soft brushing of his lips against hers. It was ravenous and heated and, if she wasn't mistaken, angry.

She'd never been kissed like this before, where she felt the hunger build inside her, a fire threatening to consume her. Where she wanted to let the flames take her.

Sliding her hands up, she linked her fingers behind his neck and kissed him back.

Walker groaned into her mouth, whirled them around until she was pressed between his hard body and the cold edge of the stainless steel counter. Without breaking the kiss, he set his hands on her hips and lifted her onto the counter, the ease with which he did so causing her stomach to tumble.

She slid her fingers into his hair, held his head. He deepened the kiss, stroked his tongue into her mouth. He skimmed his hands up her side, settled them on her rib cage, his thumbs brushing the sides of her breasts.

Tori wanted to keep kissing him. Wanted him to pull her onto the floor, the counter, a table, anywhere, and touch her, all of her. She wanted, more than her next breath, this hard, enigmatic man's hands on her, to feel him moving inside her. She ached, her core heating, her panties growing damp.

She wanted to beg.

And she never begged. Men begged her. She couldn't want a man that much, couldn't give up that control.

She broke the kiss, leaned back. Though she was breathing hard, her blood feeling thick and slow in her veins, she wouldn't let him see. Couldn't let him know how he affected her. If he knew, he'd use it against her.

So she slowly slid her tongue over her lower lip, capturing the taste of him, and smiled. "Well," she said, not needing to fake her husky tone, "seems you're not so different from other men after all."

Walker's eyes hardened and cooled, a muscle worked in his jaw and she wished she could take her words back. Wished she could be sweet and trusting and naive and gullible.

Wished she could open her heart, just a little, just for a little while.

"Bullshit," he said, his voice low and gravelly and sexy. He shifted, sliding his hands over so that he brushed against the underside of her breasts. Her breath caught. He noticed. His eyes darkened, filled with pure male satisfaction. "But I'm guessing that's why you want me. And," he continued as he slowly, ever so slowly, took his hands away and stepped back, "why I scare the hell out of you."

He walked away before she could deny it with a smart-ass reply.

Before she could admit he was right.

HE WAS FREEZING. Anthony hunched his shoulders as the wind picked up. He hadn't brought a jacket, hadn't planned on being outside in jeans and a T-shirt when he'd been driving around aimlessly. All he'd known was that he couldn't go home…couldn't go back to Boston when his mom and sister needed him here.

But it was hard. Everyone in town had heard about his father's affair with his brother's wife. Anthony's family was being talked about, his mother humiliated, his sister crushed.

And him? He was pissed. So angry he couldn't be in the same room as his father, couldn't even look at him.

A car drove by and Anthony ducked down out of the line of sight. Hanging out on the porch of the police chief's house at 11:00 p.m. probably wasn't the smartest move he'd ever made but that's where he'd ended up. Had driven by it a dozen times before he'd found himself parking his Jeep two blocks down and walking back toward the house.

He should go, he thought, his stomach seizing with panic. If the chief knew he was out here…well…Anthony wasn't sure what Ross would do but one thing he knew for sure, Ross would tell Layne and then Anthony would never hear the end of it. He rose only to crouch back down when headlights flashed and a vehicle pulled into the driveway.

Huddled into the shadows, Anthony watched as a kid with brown hair got out. A minivan, Anthony thought with a shake of his head. Poor bastard.

The kid walked around the front of the vehicle and then he was walking back toward the side door with Jessica by his side. They were holding hands, Jessica's pale hair flashing in the dark. At the last minute, they veered to the left. They were coming onto the porch.

Shit.

Anthony moved farther back, his breathing ragged, his heart racing. But they didn't notice, only had eyes for each other. Jess said something softly that had the kid smiling, then they were at the door and she turned to him. Kissed him.

Anthony looked away, his chest burning.

"Good night," Jess said, sounding breathless.

"Night," the kid said, his voice deeper than Anthony would've guessed for someone his age. "I'll call you when I get home."

"Okay."

She stood in front of the door while the kid jogged down the steps. She watched him back up, waved at him as he drove past the house. When she turned to open the door, Anthony stepped forward. "Jess."

She squeaked and whirled around, her hand over her heart. Her eyes widened. "Anthony? God! What are you doing here?"

"Sorry," he said, feeling like an idiot, like some weirdo stalker. He shoved his hands into his front pockets. "Sorry," he repeated. "I didn't mean to scare you, I just…"

He just what? Thought he'd wait for her to finish making out with some other guy?

Jesus, he really was losing it. He felt edgy and out of control and he didn't know what to do, how to handle it.

"Sorry," he said yet again. "I shouldn't be here." He backed up, almost fell down the steps, caught his balance before stepping down.

"Wait. Don't go." She reached out for him only to pull back before she could touch him. "Are you okay?"

To his everlasting horror, his eyes pricked with tears. He hadn't cried in years, not since he was a kid. But he wasn't a kid anymore; he was twenty-one, a man in every sense of the word. Instead of answering her question, he looked behind him, down the road where the kid had driven away.

"You still with that guy?" he asked, then winced because, hey, she'd only been making out with him not two minutes ago. "That Tyler?"

"Tanner," she corrected, looking at him curiously. And

yeah, he'd known the kid's name. His cousin—shit, his half sister—Nora was dating his older brother. "Yes. How about you? Are you still with that brunette?"

Mackenzie. "No."

He'd broken up with her the night his father had admitted the truth. He hadn't wanted to tell anyone, hadn't wanted to explain why he wasn't coming back to school, not for a while anyway.

Hadn't liked her enough to want to make it work.

Jess sat down on the step as if it was the most natural thing in the world for her ex-boyfriend to visit her out of the blue, late at night. She slid over and he hesitated, then finally dropped down beside her.

He kept his distance, though, didn't want to get too close, didn't want to touch her.

"How's school?" he asked, unable to think of anything else to say, unable to say what was really on his mind.

"Good. I…" She rubbed her palms up and down her thighs. Up and down. "I'm taking some college prep courses. I'm going to be a nurse," she blurted, then looked at him as if daring him to make a hurtful comment about it.

"That's great. Really."

"How about you?" Jess asked, and he could feel her watching him with her big blue eyes. "How are your classes?"

He shrugged. "I'm taking a break," he heard himself say, though he hadn't really decided until that very moment to go through with the idea that had been whirling around in his head ever since he'd come home. "I'm going to take the rest of the semester off."

She tucked her hair behind her ear. "Really? What do your parents think of that?"

"I don't care," he said, knowing he sounded like a bratty kid.

"So, what are you going to do? While you're off, I mean."

He had no idea. He couldn't work at his dad's law firm, couldn't be around his father that much. "I'll get a job. I'll probably find something here in town." Though he had no idea what. He could probably work at the café. Celeste would hire him.

Anthony and Jess sat in silence for a few minutes and for the first time since he'd found out about his father's affair, since he'd discovered Nora was his sister and not just his favorite cousin, he felt like he could breathe. The sky was clear, the air crisp and, yeah, still cold. But his thoughts weren't racing, and he didn't feel as if he had the weight of the world on his shoulders, didn't feel suffocated with anger and bitterness.

"I hurt my cousin's feelings," he said. "Nora. Except, I guess she's not my cousin, but my sister. She and Griffin came to dinner—it was the first time she'd been to the house since…since the truth about Dad and Aunt Val…"

Jess brushed her fingers over the back of his hand. "I know," she said softly.

He nodded, curled his fingers into his palms so he wouldn't reach for her. "Mom and Dad were trying so hard to act like everything was normal except nothing's normal. Dad's sleeping in the guest room and Mom cries all the time and Erin walks around like a zombie. I just… I couldn't take it. I walked out. Just got up and left, right in the middle of dinner." He swallowed but bitterness still coated his throat. "Nora came after me but I couldn't even look at her. I love her, have loved her my entire life but the only thing I could think about was how, if she hadn't been born, my family wouldn't be torn apart."

He looked at Jess, saw the sympathy in her eyes and was filled with shame. He didn't deserve her sympathy.

"I'm sorry," she said. "I'm really sorry about what's going on in your family. Layne's upset about it, too. She tries to pretend that everything's all right but I can tell it's not."

"Did you ever forgive your mom?" he asked.

Jess smiled sadly. "It's hard to forgive someone who keeps making the same mistakes, the same decisions again and again. I realized a long time ago that my mom would always put the drugs ahead of me, that there was nothing more important to her than the next high. After a while, I just stopped waiting and hoping for her to change."

"What if she gets clean and stays clean this time and finds you and apologizes. What if she wants a second chance?"

"I don't know," she said thoughtfully, a frown marring her pretty face. "I mean, I'd be thrilled if she finally got clean but I'm not sure I'd trust it, you know? Some people don't deserve a second chance. Some people don't deserve forgiveness."

Anthony realized with another flush of shame that he hadn't thought Jess deserved forgiveness, either, not from him. She'd lied to him. But more than that, worse than that, she'd hurt him. He hadn't been able to give her a second chance, couldn't have even if he'd wanted to. But he could've given her his forgiveness.

"I'm sure Nora understands what you're going through," Jess said, surprising him by laying her hand on his arm. Her fingers were warm against his chilled skin.

He knew she was right. Nora had a big heart. She'd never hold a grudge, never be as cruel as he'd been.

The door opened and Anthony stiffened, glanced back

at Ross as he stood in the doorway, the light behind him casting the chief's face in shadow.

"Anthony," Ross said, surprise in his tone and Anthony knew Ross was taking in the scene before him. His niece, his underage niece, sitting in the almost-dark with a twenty-one-year-old, her hand on his arm, their hips touching.

Anthony jumped to his feet, shoved his hands into his pockets as Jess slowly got to her feet. The last time he and Jess had been caught alone, they'd been making out in his parents' hot tub. That was when Anthony had learned the truth, that the girl he was falling for was only sixteen years old.

"You shouldn't be here," Ross said, not unkindly, which sucked even worse than if he'd yelled at Anthony.

Anthony looked at Jess, felt as if, for the second time in his life, he was losing something important, something he'd never be able to get back.

"Yeah," he finally said, wishing things were different, that he was younger or she older, that being with her didn't feel so right even when he knew it was wrong. "I know."

He walked away.

CHAPTER ELEVEN

"Do you have a minute?" Celeste asked Tori Sunday afternoon after the café had closed.

Since weekends were especially busy at the café, Tori liked to pitch in with the cooking on either a Saturday or Sunday a few times a month. Not having the tips a busy weekend morning brought in ate into her wages but Celeste needed her.

"Sure." In truth, Tori wasn't in any hurry to get home. Brandon was still at Greg's and she knew when she went to pick him up, she'd have to face her ex-husband and Colleen…that they'd have to discuss the very real possibility of a custody hearing. And once she did have her son with her again, he'd likely be more sullen and angry than he'd been this past year.

Yeah, she'd much rather avoid all that for as long as possible. And who would've ever thought that she'd dread seeing her own child? That she'd feel such anxiety, such stomach-turning nerves just from the idea of picking him up? From not knowing if he was going to be her sweet-natured little boy or the bratty kid he'd morphed into?

"Let's talk in my office," Celeste said.

"Okay, just let me grab a soda first. You want anything?"

"No, thanks."

Tori went down the hall toward the drink station purposely not looking into the kitchen where she and Walker had shared that…moment.

A heated, wonderful, completely unexpected moment.

But that's all it was, she assured herself as she dispensed ice into a cup and then filled it with diet soda. It was just a brief second in time, a once-in-a-lifetime encounter. She had no desire to get involved with a man, with any man, let alone one who was investigating her sister, who suspected half her family of murder and other wrongdoings.

She stuck a straw in the glass, took a long sip as she made her way back toward Celeste's office. When she had asked Greg for the divorce, she had decided not to rely on a man to take care of her, not ever again. She needed to take care of herself and her son on her own. Needed to stop believing a man would make her dreams come true, that he'd somehow make her problems disappear.

That if a man loved her, it'd make up for all that was lacking within herself.

When Tori reached the office, Celeste was already there staring out at the rain through the window, her back to Tori. She turned and Tori paused in the act of taking another sip. It hit her that Celeste was getting older. Oh, she still looked great, still took care of herself physically, but the truth was there in the lines on the older woman's face, in the silver in her dark hair.

It gave Tori a pang to realize, to think that life was moving, as it always did, at amazing speeds and yet she was still here, still stuck. Always stuck.

"What's happened now?" Tori asked as she sat in the chair in front of the desk. "You look serious which means some new or bigger havoc has been wrought."

Smiling, Celeste came around the front of the desk to

lean against the corner. "Nothing like that. I think our family's had enough havoc, don't you?"

Though Tori's father and Celeste had never married, though he'd never even asked her, Celeste was a part of their family. Had been one for as long as Tori could remember, first as Val's best friend and now as her father's partner.

"Just because we've had our fill doesn't mean the hammer's not going to come down again. On our heads," Tori said.

Celeste's smile widened. "You sound just like your mother."

Tori's shoulders snapped back. "No need for insults."

"It wasn't an insult," Celeste said softly. "Your mother wasn't all bad, you know. I realize it's…easier to think she was, to only remember her flaws, but she was so much more." Celeste met her eyes. "And I know you remember that about her."

She did, but she didn't want to. It was easier to keep the pain at bay if she concentrated on Valerie's flaws, on how much she'd hurt them all. "Mom left us. She walked away, she made that choice."

Celeste sighed and ran the back of her hand across her forehead. "She was selfish and vain, no doubt about it. She was…looking for something. For someone to fill something inside her. Ever since we were kids she was searching…. It was as if she was empty."

Tori was afraid she had that same emptiness, that same neediness, could become just as tragic a figure if she let her guard down, if she didn't always protect her heart.

"But your mother wasn't just beautiful," Celeste continued. "Though that's the only thing people saw. She was smart, smarter than she gave herself credit for. And she was funny. My God, no one could make me laugh like your mother. She just…lit up a room. You remind me of her."

Tori squirmed. Hearing that from Celeste warmed her even as she wanted to deny it. "Layne looks more like her than I do."

"She does, but that's not what I mean. You have her sense of humor, the way you look at life, so cautiously even while you try to take the world by storm, that's all Valerie. How you read people, size them up. But you're more than that. She didn't have your ability to think through all the consequences before making a decision and she never worked as hard as you do. She always counted on her co-workers to pick up the slack for her, relied on her looks to get her by, but you rely on your brains, and on your hard work. I've known you ever since you were born, have loved you and your sisters all your lives and while I'm proud of them, I'm most proud of you."

The words hit Tori with enough force to knock the wind from her. She couldn't remember a time when someone had been proud of her. But she couldn't trust the warmth in her heart, the hope and joy that Celeste's words brought. "I got pregnant at seventeen," she said flatly, "got married at eighteen and divorced before I was thirty. I have a GED and not a diploma, never went to college and have worked my entire life as a waitress. What's to be proud of?"

"You took responsibility for your mistakes," Celeste pointed out, calmly, rationally. "You love Brandon and you tried, for years you tried to make your marriage work. For that, you should be commended. You work hard, harder than any of my other employees. You're always here, can always be counted on to solve problems or to pitch in when I need an extra pair of hands."

"I'm happy to help out," Tori said. "You know I'd do anything for you."

Celeste was one of only a few people she could ever say that to and mean it.

Celeste reached out and squeezed Tori's hand. "I do know that. And you know that while I adore your sisters, you hold a special place in my heart."

Tears clogged the back of Tori's throat. She cleared it. "Thanks. Right back at you."

Celeste slapped both hands onto her thighs. "Right. Well, before things get even mushier in here, I have a proposition for you."

"I still don't want to be manager," Tori said quickly.

Two years ago, the manager of the restaurant moved away leaving the position open. Celeste wanted Tori to take over but Tori hadn't wanted that much responsibility, was worried she'd somehow mess up or disappoint Celeste.

"That's good because I don't want you to be the new manager, either." She handed Tori a paper. "I want you to be my partner."

Tori's vision blurred but from what she could see, Celeste had had a contract drawn up, one that gave Tori the opportunity to buy into the café.

"I...I don't understand," Tori said, her thoughts scattered, her heart racing.

"It's simple. With everything that's happened the past few months, it made me realize I need to focus on what's important. Really important. And that's the people I love. I've always hoped that you'd take over the restaurant when I retire, but the other night I wondered, why wait? You could become a partner now, we'll run it together until I retire and then the café will be yours." Her expression softened. "I can't think of anyone else I'd rather have take over. There's no one else I'd trust as much to keep the place running and successful, who'll love it as much as I have."

Tori couldn't think through the panic suffusing her.

"I... How... I don't have any money," she blurted. "There's no way I could do this."

"I've already spoken with the bank manager, he seems to think you could qualify for a small business loan, and your father and I would be more than happy to pitch in as well."

"You've talked to Dad about this?"

"Of course. He thinks it's a wonderful idea."

Tori blinked. "He does?"

God, had he and Celeste lost their minds? Tori couldn't handle a job this big. Couldn't handle the financial responsibility of owning a restaurant. Why on earth would her dad think she could?

Maybe it was his way to make up for how he'd always held her at arm's length. Oh, she suspected he loved her, but he'd spent so much time at sea, away from them, that Tori had learned to get by without his attention.

Besides, he'd given most of his love and devotion to Val which hadn't left much for his daughters.

"Don't make any decision right now," Celeste said as if she could read the terror and nerves going on inside Tori. "Take as much time as you need but please, think about it."

Think about it? Think about putting herself into financial debt, into taking on that risk now that she was alone, supporting herself and her son for the first time in her life?

No. Make that hell, no. Taking that risk was way too scary. The chances of her failing were too high.

And if she accepted Celeste's offer, she'd be even more entrenched in Mystic Point. She'd never get free.

THE GODDAMN RAIN was driving Walker batty.

It'd rained practically nonstop for four days and the heavy, gray mood seemed to hang in the air, permeated people's attitudes and personalities.

Or maybe Walker was just pissed that both of his investigations were going nowhere fast. That Jack Pomeroy had called him at six that morning to chew on his ass for fifteen minutes.

Seemed the D.A. had gotten wind of Walker's rescue mission at the Yacht Pub and had taken it upon himself to warn Walker about the consequences of getting involved with a possible suspect.

Consequences similar to what Ross Taylor was facing due to his involvement with a Sullivan.

"Did you ever see the chief and assistant chief in a compromising position?" Walker asked Officer Campbell—for the fourth time—in what he considered a highly reasonable tone as he stared down the younger man. God, the kid was young, maybe early twenties. Even in uniform, his hair buzzed short, he looked like a teenager.

Campbell, his shoulders back, a mutinous expression on his face, shifted in the hard seat. "I don't think that—"

"I'm not asking you to think," Walker said mildly. "All I want is a yes or no answer."

"No."

Walker leaned back, studied the officer. He was finishing his interviews with the men in the Mystic Point police department, which so far had been less than fruitful. One thing he'd learned: the officers under their command were loyal to Taylor and Sullivan.

He wasn't sure if that was a good thing or not.

It sure as hell wasn't helping his case any. He needed the truth, whether good or bad, not nonanswers and attitude.

"Can I go back to work now?" Campbell asked, his face flushed, his arms crossed.

Walker had to stop himself from hauling the kid up by the scruff of his neck and tossing his ass out himself. "Yeah. You're dismissed."

Campbell walked out, making sure to slam the door behind him. Walker sat back and stretched. The room was windowless, the air stale. He'd conducted the first few interviews in his temporary office but when he'd had no cooperation, he'd switched tactics, moved to the interview room, but maybe treating the officers as suspects had backfired.

Live and learn.

He walked out into the squad room to find Chief Taylor waiting for him.

"Thank you for coming down," Walker said, ignoring how all conversation ceased when he stepped into the room.

"No problem. I'm glad to help in any way I can." Though he was in civilian clothes—khakis and a striped, button-down shirt—there was no mistaking Taylor's authority when he sent a pointed look around the room. "If everyone cooperates, answers questions honestly, the sooner things can go back to normal around here." Now he met Walker's eyes. "Isn't that right, Detective?"

Impressed despite himself, Walker rocked back on his heels. "That sounds about right."

Walker gestured for Taylor to go ahead of him down the hall to his old office. Inside, Walker poured himself a cup of coffee, offered one to Taylor who shook his head.

"Something I can do for you, Detective?" Taylor asked.

"Yes." Walker sipped his coffee, added sugar then sipped again. "But first I have to know, was that little show out there for me?"

"I don't perform," Taylor said. "What you see is what you get. Whether you like it or not."

Walker wasn't sure he believed that but the more he was around Taylor the more he respected him. Which made his job that much harder. "So you really want your men to cooperate?"

"Of course. The captain and I haven't done anything wrong."

"Getting involved with a subordinate officer could be construed as wrong."

Taylor studied him. "Seems to me, it's up to a review board to judge my actions. Not you."

True. And, yes, Walker was being judgmental, but only because he had the right. As a cop, it was up to him to make sure other cops toed the line, that they didn't take advantage of their position of power.

He was skating that line, Walker realized, and it pissed him off. He was getting personally involved with someone connected to this case. He couldn't deny it, not when he and Tori had had personal conversations, not when she'd cooked for him.

Touching her, kissing her, couldn't be construed as anything other than personal.

He dreamed of her. She slipped into his head when his guard was down, slid into his subconscious at night when exhaustion took over, after he'd spent hours tossing and turning trying to fight her invasion of his mind. But he could and did control his actions, his decisions.

He hadn't returned to the café since the other night, had subsisted on fast food and takeout and the occasional trip to other restaurants—the Chinese place, a pizza parlor.

Walker hadn't sought her out. Had no reason to. There was nothing she could tell him that would help his investigation, either of his investigations, he amended.

But maybe the man standing before him could.

He'd questioned Ken Sullivan twice now but was no closer to proving anything. Ken had admitted he'd paid off Dale and Valerie but that he'd refused to pay Dale this last go-round. Walker couldn't even say for sure that Dale was murdered; it was possible—though not probable—that he ingested the poison on his own.

They had two deaths eighteen years apart, two possible murders. Walker knew in his gut they were connected. More than that, his head told him they were. It only made sense that whoever killed Dale did so out of revenge for Valerie's death.

Or to keep him quiet about the truth.

And he couldn't rule out anyone as a suspect. Not even Tori.

"Any new leads in the investigation of York's death?" Taylor asked.

"I'm not at liberty to say."

"But if you were…"

"If I was…I'd say no." He hated being stuck, hated that the truth was out there but he couldn't see it. And he was getting desperate enough to ask Ross Taylor for help or, at least, his thoughts. "I still think Ken Sullivan's our man. He had motive, means and opportunity."

While his wife vouched that he was home the night Dale was killed, she also admitted she went to bed early and didn't remember him coming in. Ken could've left the house without her knowing.

"I have a hard time picturing Ken poisoning a man," Taylor said, sitting in one of the chairs.

"Maybe," Walker conceded, "but he might be the type to pay to have someone else do his dirty work." He drummed his fingers on the desk. "Who do you think is the most likely suspect, if not Ken?"

Taylor nodded, as if he knew how hard it was for Walker to even ask that question. "You've been concentrating on Ken and Tim Sullivan. Captain Sullivan and her sisters—"

"They're the most likely suspects."

"True. But sometimes, it's the person you least suspect who's guilty. If it was me," Taylor said slowly, "I'd widen my net to include everyone who may have had a motive—and not just for killing Dale, but for wanting Valerie Sullivan dead as well."

Taylor's cell phone buzzed. He took it out of his pocket. "Do you mind?" he asked Walker.

"Go ahead." He had enough to keep his mind occupied for a few minutes.

"Hello?" Taylor said, then listened as he got to his feet. "Where?" Pause. "How badly injured?" Another pause. "She'll be fine," he said in the same tone Walker used when talking down panicked relatives. "I'll be there in five minutes." He shut off his phone. "Sorry, I have to go."

"Everything okay?"

"One of Layne's sisters was in an accident on Old Beach Road."

Walker's stomach dropped, his blood ran cold. "Which sister is it?"

But Taylor was already heading out the door. Walker caught up with him by Donna's desk, grasped Taylor's shoulder and whirled him around. "Damn it, who is it?"

Several officers stepped forward but Ross shook his head at them. Met Walker's eyes as if he knew how bad Walker had it, how close he was coming to completely falling over a very steep cliff.

"It was Tori."

HER ENTIRE BODY hurt. Even her eyelids, which refused to open despite what felt like a Herculean effort. Her head pounded, each breath caused a sharp pain in her chest and her throat was raw and dry.

And someone was shaking her, causing all of her pain to coalesce into an unending torment, her stomach to turn.

Oh, she really, really wished they'd stop.

Tori just wanted to slip back into oblivion. It beckoned, the darkness, the silence and numbness, right at the edge of her consciousness. Whoever was trying to wake her could wait.

"Mom."

The voice, whisper-soft and so achingly familiar floated into her mind.

"Mom, wake up. Please."

Her baby. Her son. He was scared, she could hear it in his voice. Terrified. He wanted her.

He needed her.

Struggling, she pried her eyelids open. Blinked against the harsh glare, pain searing her head. She couldn't get her mind to work clearly, she kept seeing images—a wet road, a sharp corner, then the feeling of flying and a jarring, bone-rattling landing. Panic flowed through her as memory returned. She'd been in an accident. She remembered bits and pieces. The fear and pain, the shock. Someone holding her hand, telling her she was going to be okay, the flashing lights as the EMTs arrived, the siren blaring on the ambulance. She must've passed out because the next thing she remembered, she was lying on a stretcher in the back of the ambulance, swaying as it raced toward the hospital.

And now she was here. Hurt, but alive.

Tori turned her head slightly but her vision blurred so she shut her eyes again. Opened them and focused on Brandon's features until they sharpened.

There he was. His hair floppy and mussed, his face streaked with tear marks. His eyes worried and way too serious.

"You're awake," he said, like an epiphany. Like a prayer.

"It's okay," she said, but her voice came out a word-less croak.

"Here," Layne said, her usual brusque tone soft. She held a cup with a straw to Tori's mouth. "Drink."

Tori sucked in water. It was deliciously cool and sooth-ing. She leaned back, noticed Nora standing behind Bran-don, her hands on his shoulders, a worried look on her face.

But Tori looked at her son. Tried to smile as she reached for him. "It's okay. I'm right here."

It was a refrain she'd used many, many times when he'd been a baby and had needed soothing. She'd held him, sometimes walking until her legs ached and her arms became numb from his weight. Sometimes in the rock-ing chair as she rocked and rocked and rocked, her head heavy from fatigue. She would repeat over and over again that everything would be all right. That she was there and would never leave him.

Not like her mother had left her.

Brandon grabbed her hand, linked his fingers with hers, and her breath caught, a new sort of pain flowing through her, bittersweet and all too real. Her son's hand was as big as hers and a bit sweaty. She couldn't remember the last time he'd allowed her to hold his hand, hadn't real-ized how good it would feel to have that connection to her child again.

She met his eyes. *I've got you. I'm holding on. I'll never let go.*

She'd never let him go.

Layne came into Tori's line of vision. Her face drawn, her expression unreadable. She nudged Brandon lightly. "Why don't you run out, tell your dad and Colleen that your mom's awake?"

He looked like he was about to refuse but then he glanced at his aunt's face and nodded. "Yeah. Okay."

"Here," Layne said, giving him some cash. "Grab yourself a snack and could you bring me back a cola?"

"Sure." He stood and stuck the money into his pocket. Looked at Tori, worry still clear in his eyes. "You'll still be awake when I get back?"

She tried to smile, wanted to reassure him, her little man, who looked so scared. "I'll be awake. I promise."

Layne walked him out, her arm around his shoulder as she spoke softly to him. Nora fussed with Tori's pillow, helped her sit up.

She must've been out longer than she'd thought if Brandon and her sisters were here. And Greg and Colleen, she realized, remembering what Layne had said about them being in the waiting room. Thank God they were here for Brandon.

"More water?" Nora asked, holding the cup. Tori nodded and drank then leaned back with a groan. "Should I call the nurse?" Nora asked. "Get you some pain medicine?"

"No. Thanks. It might make me drowsy. I'll wait until after Brandon comes back. How did he get here?"

"Greg picked him up from school."

Tori looked out the window but it was still as gray and overcast as it'd been earlier. "What time is it?"

"Nearly five," Nora said, sitting gingerly on the side of the bed. "We all came as soon as we heard. Layne was already here when I arrived—"

"She always has to be first."

Nora smiled but it wobbled around the edges. "True. Greg and Colleen came with Brandon and Dad and Celeste are out there, too, with Ross and Jess. Layne called Aunt Astor... told her what was going on. We, uh, thought it would be best if they didn't come down until a few of us had cleared out."

Probably a good idea seeing as how their dad had told his brother he never wanted to see him again.

"The nurses didn't want too many people in here at once," Nora continued, straightening the bedcovers, "and Dad figured you'd want us to be here so…" She shrugged.

Their dad had been right. Seeing her son's face, her sisters being there when she woke up, meant more to her than she'd ever be able to say.

The door opened and Layne returned and stood at the end of the bed. "The EMTs didn't have much information. Can you tell us what happened?"

"I…" Frowning, she touched her forehead gently, felt a lump. "I was on my way home and I…I glanced down, just for a moment, to switch songs on the iPod…"

It all came back to her with sickening clarity. She'd been returning home from Boston, had been in a hurry so she wouldn't be late picking Brandon up from practice.

"I looked up, took the curve too fast. When the car went off the side of the road, I…I overcorrected." She could still taste her panic, could still feel the cold fear that had raced through her. "I spun…. God, I thought I'd never stop but then it did and the next thing I knew, the car was flying through the air and then it slammed to a stop." Her seat belt had dug into her, the air bag had deployed but she'd been wrenched to the side, hitting her head against the door. "The next thing I remember I was on the ground and the EMTs were there."

"You were lucky," Nora said, her hand on Tori's knee. "The doctor said other than a mild concussion and some scrapes and bruises, you're fine. He doesn't think you have any internal injuries but he still wants to keep you here overnight for observation."

Tori sighed. As much as she'd like to argue, as much as she wished she could go home, the thought of moving, let alone of walking out of the room, held no appeal. She'd much rather stay right in this bed with its easy access to pain meds.

"Thank God your air bag deployed," Layne said, sounding shaky. Worried.

"Hey," Tori said softly, holding her hand out. Layne hesitated but then entwined her fingers with Tori's. "I'm okay."

Layne nodded. "I know, it's just…"

"It was scary," Nora finished for her.

Tori squeezed Layne's hand then let go. "I'm sorry."

"Not your fault," Layne said, trying to smile. "And that's the first time I've ever said that."

Tori laughed, her breath catching at the pain. "Don't make me laugh. It hurts."

"Sorry," Layne said. She cleared her throat. "What were you doing on Old Beach Road anyway?"

Pretending to pick a piece of lint off the sheet, Tori kept her gaze averted. "I…I went into Boston. To do some shopping."

Not quite the truth, just not a complete lie. The truth was, Celeste's offer of a partnership had frightened Tori so much, she'd realized she had to make some hard choices. Immediately. Starting with what she wanted to do with her life.

What she wanted was to start a new life, just her and Brandon, in Boston.

Brandon came in carrying a plastic container of nachos in one hand, a soda in the other.

"So glad to see the healthy eating options here at Mystic Point General Hospital," Tori said. "What? Didn't they have any ice cream and jelly beans?"

"Dad said I could get whatever I wanted," Brandon said, looking defiant.

And that was the kid she knew and loved.

She sighed. "It's fine. I'm teasing."

He crossed to her, sat on the other side of the bed. "What are you guys fighting about?" Brandon asked, sipping his soda.

"Who says we were fighting?" Layne asked.

Brandon lifted a shoulder. "You're always fighting."

Tori exchanged a look with her sisters. "Well, today is one for the record books then."

"That's right," Layne said, ruffling his hair. "No fighting today." She looked at Tori. "You okay? You need anything?"

Tori laid her hand on her son's back, inordinately pleased when he didn't jerk away. "I'm good."

She had everything she needed right here. Her son by her side. Her sisters' love and concern. What more could she ask for?

"I'll stop by in the morning, see how you are." Layne leaned down and gave Tori a gentle hug, held on for a moment longer than necessary. Tori didn't mind. "You need to be dropped off?" Layne asked Nora as she straightened.

Nora shook her head but got to her feet. "Griffin's going to get me, but thanks." She leaned over and kissed Tori's cheek. "I'm glad you're okay. Love you."

Tori smiled. "Love you, too."

"I'll send Dad and Celeste in if you're up for more company," Nora said from the doorway.

Tori glanced at her son. "Sure. But could you maybe give me five minutes first?"

Nora nodded and left.

"Look," Tori said to Brandon when they were alone, "the doctor wants me to stay here for the night."

"Are you okay?" he asked.

"I'm fine. It's just a precaution. So you can spend the night at your dad's. I'm sure I'll be home by the time you get home from school tomorrow."

He slid her a look. "Maybe I shouldn't go to school tomorrow. Just in case you take a turn for the worse."

"Well, that's a cheery thought. And a nice ploy to get out of going to school, but no, sorry. You'll have to suffer through another day of sixth grade just like all the other twelve-year-old schmucks."

He popped a chip into his mouth. "It was worth a try."

And then he smiled, something he did so rarely now that tears pricked her eyes. "Yeah. It was." She cleared her throat. "Listen, I know it was scary, seeing me all banged up like this, especially before I woke up—"

"I wasn't scared," he said quickly.

"Yeah? Well, I was scared. You know that my mom left when I was your age, right?"

Brandon nodded, sipped his soda. "You thought she left but she was really killed."

"She left. When I was twelve and there was nothing I could do about it. And I want you to know that I will never leave you. Not on purpose. Not ever. No matter what. Okay?"

He studied her, his eyes, so like her own, were guarded and watchful and she hoped she hadn't done that to him, hoped she hadn't made him hard and cynical like she was. She wanted him to be open and caring and giving and trusting, like his father. Wanted him to be so much better than she was.

"Okay," he finally said. He set the empty container on the table next to the bed and picked at the faded knees of his jeans. "I'm glad you're here."

Her heart simply swelled. "Me, too. I love you, bud."

"Love you, too," he said, allowing her to hold him, his skinny arms going around her neck.

He smelled of sweat and the laundry detergent she used. He felt solid and warm and little in her arms. Brandon was everything to her and she'd almost left him alone, almost left him without a mother.

But she hadn't, she reminded herself, kissing the top of his head. She was here, where she belonged. And Brandon loved her. He wasn't mad at her anymore. Everything was going to be all right. They were going to be together. No matter what.

CHAPTER TWELVE

HE HADN'T DROPPED everything to go and see her, to see for himself that Taylor hadn't lied or sugarcoated how badly she was injured, Walker thought as he stalked down the quiet hospital corridor. He hadn't called to check on her, hadn't pestered the nursing staff or tracked down her doctor. He'd stayed at the police station, had gone through the motions of reading reports, conducting interviews. He'd worked. Done his job.

And hadn't stopped thinking about her. Not once.

But it wasn't up to him to think about Tori, to wonder if she really was okay, to worry about her. He'd headed back to his room, determined to put her out of his mind. And instead, had found himself pulling into the hospital parking lot. Now he was roaming the halls like an idiot.

The nurses had tried to stop him since it was past visiting hours so he'd flashed his badge and kept going.

Some days he really loved being a cop.

He found her room, saw the light from a TV flashing and went in.

She raised her eyebrows at him. "Detective Bertrand. This is a surprise."

"For me, too," he said, realizing it was true, that he wasn't even sure why he was there.

"It's really sort of sweet of you to check up on me this way," she said, her voice huskier than usual, those guarded eyes of her always watchful. She smiled. "Were you worried about me?"

"Don't," he said gruffly, knowing he sounded irritated but, hell, he was irritated. He shouldn't be there, had no reason to be, no right to want to check on her, to make sure she was all right.

No right to care about her.

Tori blinked but it was too well rehearsed to be taken as a true innocent expression. "Don't what?"

"Don't bother with the sexy routine. You're not quite capable of pulling it off at the moment."

Her cheeks turned pink and she seemed offended, crossing her arms over the light blanket. "Who says it's a routine?"

"Me."

An act that fascinated him even as it rubbed him the wrong way. He stood at the end of the bed, his hands stuffed into his pockets. She was alive and up to her usual tricks, but she'd been hurt. She had scrapes on her neck and her face, that beautiful, entrancing face was bruised and she had a bump the size of an egg on her forehead. Her hair was brushed but it hung lankly. She seemed small and vulnerable in the bed.

"You okay?" he asked, though she seemed to be just fine.

"Alive and kicking."

"No internal injuries? Concussion?"

She sighed. "Everything on the inside seems to be working fine and yes, I have a mild concussion. Which is why they're making me stay here the night." There was a clear pout in her voice.

"Better than spending the night at the morgue."

"You have such a way with words, Detective. Thank you for that cheerful thought."

He removed his hands from his pockets but then didn't know what to do with them. "Just laying out the facts."

"You cops love your facts, don't you?"

"I like to know what I'm dealing with," Walker said slowly, choosing his words carefully as he met her eyes. He liked to know who he was dealing with. His ability to read people helped him catch the bad guys; his focus on his cases made him one of the best at what he did.

He glanced around the room. She didn't seem to want to take over the conversation and he couldn't speak, not when his thoughts, his feelings, were all twisted up inside of him. Not when he was afraid he'd say something he'd regret, admit to something best left hidden.

She had flowers on the wide windowsill, several bouquets, it turned out. Balloons. A few stuffed animals, though why people gave a grown woman a stuffed animal was beyond him.

He should've brought flowers. Had considered it briefly as he'd passed the hospital's gift shop window display but in the end dismissed the idea.

He didn't want to be among her many admirers.

Walker cleared his throat. It was warm in there, he thought, tugging at his collar. Finally she sighed.

"Go ahead." When he just looked at her, she added, "Tell me how irresponsible I was to drive so fast on wet roads. I was careless and reckless, et cetera, et cetera…"

"I didn't come here to lecture you."

"No? Then why did you come?"

"Damn if I know."

Her lips twitched and, for a moment, he was terrified she was going to start crying but then her mouth curved up into a smile, a genuine smile that had his breath catching.

"What a surprise. Walker Bertrand not knowing something. I'm actually relieved. It seems as if most of the time

I'm the only person in the world who doesn't know what she's doing, doesn't know what she wants."

He walked closer so that he stood over her. "Oh, I think you know what I want," he said lowly.

Her throat worked. It felt good, being able to take her by surprise when she was the one always in control, always trying to keep people guessing.

She shifted and her face paled, her lips thinned.

He helped her sit up, knew it pained her and he hated that she was hurting.

"I'd better get going," he said abruptly, not liking where his thoughts were heading, not liking how much he wanted to stay.

"Oh. Well…" She cleared her throat. "Thanks for stopping by."

He nodded and then, because he couldn't resist, he touched her, just the ends of her hair, a gentle brush of his fingers. He curled his hands into fists. "I'm glad you're okay."

He made it to the door before her voice stopped him. "I thought I was going to die." He turned, saw her fingers plucking at the blanket. "I thought…God, I really am following in my mother's footsteps. Dead before I really had a chance to live. To make my dreams come true."

"You're not your mother," Walker said as he crossed to the bed.

"Out of the three of us, I'm the closest to her in personality. From the time I was little, I was aware of the similarities between us. So, I embraced them. I knew she wasn't perfect, but I understood her, I still understand her."

"You understand her how?"

Tori lifted a shoulder. "I understand that she was unhappy. Layne hated her—she hated her so much for so long, even before she left. She hated that she couldn't, wouldn't, be the type of mother Layne thought she should be. She held on to that hate, maybe still holds on to it even knowing what really happened to her. Nora is more forgiving. She likes to believe Mom would've come back, that we would've had this happy little family once Mom realized she'd made a huge mistake."

"You don't agree?"

"I knew Mom would never come back," she said matter-of-factly. "For eighteen years we all had our fears. Layne feared Mom would come back to wreak more havoc on our lives, on our father's life. Nora feared Mom wouldn't come back, that she'd never know what she was missing out on by not being a part of her daughters' lives."

Tori sighed, stared over his shoulder.

"What were you afraid of?" he asked quietly when she remained silent.

He didn't think she was going to answer or would, more than likely, give him one of her seductive smiles, one of those come-hither looks and laugh, say she wasn't afraid of anything. If she'd done either of those, he told himself, he'd be able to walk away. Could finally get her out of his head once and for all.

Would be able to convince himself she wasn't worth his time, his thoughts or the conflicting feelings she brought out in him.

"I was afraid I'd end up just like her," Tori admitted softly. "That inside, I was the same as she was. I was afraid I'd be stuck in this town in a marriage I didn't want, always wishing for something better. Layne was angry she left. Nora thought she'd never come back," Tori repeated. "And I just wished she'd taken me with her."

TORI CRINGED. Why had she admitted that? She preferred to keep the truth hidden. It was safer that way. No one could use it against you. No one could hurt you if they didn't know who you really were, what you really wanted.

Walker was getting the better of her. He confused her, intrigued her. Attracted her.

She hadn't heard or seen him since Saturday night and it killed her that she'd wanted to. That she'd wanted him to come to her, to track her down.

Wanted him to seek her out, to pursue her like other men did. Except, she was afraid that, unlike the other guys, she'd let him catch her.

She waited for Walker to give her one of his cool looks, to tell her in no uncertain terms that she wasn't worth his or anyone else's time. But he surprised her yet again.

She wasn't sure she liked being surprised.

"You think you should feel guilty because you don't hate your mother?" he asked. "You were a kid when she left."

"I loved her. Don't get me wrong, I saw her clearly. Just as clearly as Layne did but I didn't hate her for it, I didn't long for her to be different. I saw her and I accepted her and I still loved her. She was like this...light...this beacon. Whenever she entered a room, everyone paid attention. Everyone."

"Seems to me, the problem with all that attention is that some of it's going to be negative."

Tori nodded. "It was. That was another lesson she taught me. Some people were going to hate you, resent you for being what they're not. For being too afraid to go after what they want."

He nudged the side of her thigh. Startled, she scooted over and he sat on the edge of the bed. "What did she want?"

"More," Tori said simply. "A hell of a lot more than small-town life where everyone knew her every move and tried to pry open all her secrets. More than marriage to a man she didn't love, not enough."

He laid his hand on her knee and even through the thin material of the blanket, his skin was warm, his touch reassuring. "More than having three daughters?"

A painful lump formed in Tori's throat. "She loved us. She just didn't love us enough. Didn't love us more than she loved herself."

"And you think you take after her in that way? That you don't love Brandon enough?"

"I shouldn't have taken my eyes off the road, not even for a second. He was scared. I scared him."

"It was an accident, a mistake," Walker pointed out. "It happens."

"I seem to make more than my fair share."

"Guess everyone excels at something."

"At least I'm number one at something. I used to think I was a good mother. That if there was one thing in this world I was really excellent at, it was being Brandon's mom. And now I don't even have that."

Walker leaned back, his shirt pulling tight against his flat abs, his broad chest. "Just because a kid doesn't like how you're doing things, doesn't mean you're a bad parent. Most of the times I was pissed at my parents it was because they wouldn't let me do something I shouldn't have been doing anyway."

She agreed with him but ever since the divorce, she'd had to deal with Brandon's bad attitude and she hated never knowing what kind of mood her son was going to be in. What she was going to do or say that would put him into a full pout, make him sullen and bitter. She was tired of being the bad guy.

"I was so scared when I was pregnant. Scared and angry. Resentful. I'd messed up, yes, but I didn't deserve to be saddled with a kid at eighteen, did I? To be stuck with one man for the rest of my life. I had plans. Big, huge, grand plans and with one missed period, with one positive pregnancy test, all those plans were ruined."

"You considered terminating the pregnancy?"

Shame filled her, made her sick to her stomach. "I considered it, yes, but I knew I couldn't go through with it. I told Greg and he proposed. God, we were so young." Tori could still picture Greg's face. He'd been shocked but had quickly told her he'd take care of her and the baby, that they'd get married and everything would work out. "Too young to have any idea what we were getting into. We got married the day after he graduated."

"What made you decide to get married instead of having the baby and making those grand plans a reality on your own?"

Uncertainty. And the bone-deep fear that she couldn't survive on her own. "Greg proposed. He loved me."

And she'd known it was okay because she hadn't loved him back, not the same way. Not desperately, not enough to lose herself or to risk being made a fool. Not like her father had loved her mother.

But she was stronger now. Smarter. She was making things happen and though today hadn't quite ended the way she'd planned, she'd taken the first step toward a new life.

"I'd convinced myself marriage was the best decision," she continued. "That I could be happy being his wife, being a mother in Mystic Point, that it'd be enough for me."

But she hadn't counted on wanting more for herself. On how disappointed she would be when she realized that the only person you could truly depend upon was yourself.

"When Brandon was born, I was terrified to have the responsibility of this little life on my hands. To realize it was up to me to care for him, twenty-four hours a day, to care *about* him every minute for the rest of my life. To worry and wonder if he was safe. Healthy. Happy. It was so scary…so suffocating. I wasn't sure I wanted it," she admitted hoarsely. "If I wanted him."

"You were just a kid," Walker said.

"I was old enough to have sex," Tori said flatly. "Old enough to know the consequences of having sex and not caring about those consequences. Not enough. I took care of him, fed and bathed him and changed his diapers. For the first two weeks of his life, I didn't know how to connect with him."

She took a sip of the ginger ale in her cup to soothe her dry throat. "I'd made the decision to get married and to keep my baby. But I wasn't ready to love him, wasn't sure I'd ever be ready. But then, one night, Greg went out with his buddies before they all took off for college and it was just me and Brandon. And he wouldn't stop crying. The sound seemed to amplify my doubts and fears, seemed to vibrate through my body. He was so stiff, so pissed off. I had no idea what was wrong with him, what to do."

Walker stretched his legs out, leaned back slightly so that his elbow nudged her calf. "Babies cry. Parents learn how to handle it."

"I didn't want to learn, didn't want to handle it. I was angry at Greg for deserting me. I knew he was out having a good time while I was stuck in our apartment with a screaming baby. I couldn't call anyone. Greg's parents hated me, blamed me for ruining their son's life, and I knew Layne would only lecture me on how I needed to learn to take responsibility for my actions. For my mistakes." Tears pricked Tori's eyes. She blinked them back. "That's what I thought of my son, even after he was born. A mistake. My biggest one. I felt trapped and helpless. I couldn't do anything right. I couldn't even make my own baby stop crying."

She swallowed, tucked her hair behind her ear. "Then I said his name and he sort of hiccupped, went quiet, for the barest of seconds so I said it again. I talked to him, told him everything would be all right, though I wasn't sure I believed it. But he stopped crying and just…looked up at me. Like I was the most important thing in his life. I was so worried, so scared I was going to screw up, worried I'd screw *him* up." She forced herself to meet Walker's eyes and admitted what she'd held in her heart for twelve years, what she'd never admitted to anyone before. "It's still my greatest fear. That I won't be enough for him. That I'll make a mistake and damage him."

"Is that how you feel?" Walker asked softly. "Damaged because of the mistakes your mother made? Because she left you?"

"No. But I pity her for not having that love for her children. Because after that night, this love for Brandon filled me and I knew I'd do anything and everything to make sure he was always safe. Always healthy and happy."

She'd been relieved, so very relieved to have those feelings. To finally love someone, fiercely, fully.

"You're not your mother," Walker said, taking her face gently in his hands so she had no choice but to meet his eyes. "You're Tori Sullivan Mott. You would never leave your child."

"But I almost did. I almost left him and what would've happened to him then? He was so angry with me. How would he feel if I'd died and the last words he'd said to me were in anger?"

"Tori," Walker said in slight exasperation, "Brandon knows you love him. You tell him and you show him. He's a kid. They get angry, they say things they don't mean."

She sighed. Leaned back, her head starting to ache again. "You're right."

He raised an eyebrow. "Glad you finally realize that."

She couldn't help it. She smiled. "I can't believe you actually made a joke."

"Who's joking?" he asked in his gruff way, but the corners of his mouth twitched. He stood. "It's getting late."

It was. She was tired. But she didn't want to be alone. Not yet. "Would you... Do you think you could stay? Just for a few more minutes?"

He seemed ready to decline, to make up some excuse. But then he exhaled heavily and sat back down. "I could stay."

BRANDON WAS HOVERING.

Tori had been released from the hospital yesterday to much fanfare—well, as much fanfare as one single mom could expect. She'd been discharged before lunch and had spent the rest of the day surrounded by her loved ones. Brandon, of course, had stayed by her side, as if reassuring himself she really was okay. Greg and Colleen had come, and Colleen had even offered to bring her and Brandon dinner.

That woman really was too good to be true.

Luckily her sisters had been there and had told Colleen her offer—while sweet—wasn't necessary. They'd ordered in Chinese since neither Layne nor Nora cooked. Or at least, cooked often, or, to be honest, particularly well.

Celeste had come with Tori's father and they'd stayed most of the day, not leaving until Uncle Ken and Aunt Astor arrived, which put quite the strain on the day. Tori worried the rift between them would remain for the rest of their lives. And poor Nora was smack-dab in the middle of it. Fortunately her baby sister was handling it well but Tori reminded herself to speak to Layne about ways they could help mend their father and uncle's relationship.

Even Anthony had showed up but had only stayed a few minutes when he saw that Jess and her boyfriend, Tanner, were playing a board game with Brandon.

Yes, Tori certainly was lucky to have so many people concerned about her welfare, so many people who loved her. She hadn't had five minutes to herself since she got home.

She wondered if she could somehow sneak back into the hospital. Just so she could get a few hours of rest in peace.

Her body hurt and the ache in her head seemed to be constant; she wasn't sure it'd ever go away. And Brandon kept asking if she was okay. If she wanted more soda or a sandwich or a pudding snack or anything else.

Peace and quiet seemed a harsh answer to that last question when her boy was so worried about her, was being so solicitous.

The movie they'd been watching—the movie Brandon had been watching as she'd dozed on and off because she couldn't stand one more viewing of *Transformers* without wanting to do some serious damage to Shia LeBeouf—was only half over when someone rang the doorbell.

Brandon paused the movie and answered the door as Tori struggled to sit up on the end of her couch.

A moment later, Brandon reappeared in the living room. "That guy's here to see you."

Tori looked behind her son but the foyer remained empty. "What guy?"

He lifted a shoulder in a move she knew was reminiscent of her own ill-natured shrug. "That cop guy who was at my football game."

Tori's heart stopped only to resume beating triple-time. Which was stupid. She did not get gaga over guys, over any guy. Not even her husband. She kept her cool, kept her wits and, most importantly, kept her heart and emotions to herself.

If you gave someone your heart, they'd stomp on it.

"Well, did you tell him to come in?" Tori asked in exasperation as her son stood there, the sun streaming through the windows to highlight his hair.

"You always told me not to let strangers into the house," Brandon said petulantly.

And, of course, this one time he listened to her while she was certain every other bit of motherly wisdom she'd tried to teach him over the past year had gone in one ear, been turned into incoherent mush, and then slid out the other the ear.

"He's not a stranger," Tori said. "Let the man in."

Brandon rolled his eyes then stomped back to the door and opened it. "She says you can come in," Tori heard her son mutter.

So pleasant, those preteens.

And then, there he was, Walker, in her house again, all big and broad shouldered and capable. If her stomach flipped, if she felt just the slightest unease, if some sort of anticipation skimmed along her nerve endings, no one had to know but her.

"Detective. Hello," she said. "What brings you by?"

"I was in the neighborhood," he said so solemnly she couldn't tell if he was serious or not, "and thought I'd see how you were doing."

She shifted and cursed herself for pulling her hair back with a soft headband instead of washing it. Wished she had on some cover-up or at least mascara and lip gloss. A woman needed her armor, after all, when faced with such a worthy opponent.

"As you can see, I'm in good hands here," she said,

gesturing to her son, who sat down and pointedly ignored them while he resumed his movie.

Walker glanced around, seemed so out of place in her house, so nervous, which somehow made her own nervousness ease. "Good," he said, shoving his hands into his pockets. "That's good."

"What's for dinner?" Brandon blurted.

Tori raised her eyebrows at him. "You just ate a peanut butter and jelly sandwich half an hour ago."

"I'm hungry."

"What else is new? Isn't there any leftover Chinese in the fridge?"

"I ate it for breakfast."

She'd slept in, hadn't taken her pain meds or anything to help her sleep because she'd been worried about being out of it when Brandon was around but still, being back in her own bed after being surrounded by well-meaning people all day, she'd slept like a log.

"Oh. We could order pizza or—"

"I'll fix something," Walker said, taking another step into the living room.

Tori frowned. "What?" she and Brandon both said at the same time.

"I'll fix dinner. What do you want?"

"That's not necessary," Tori said. "Really. It's just as easy for us to order—"

"I make excellent spaghetti and meatballs," Walker said. "You like pasta?" he asked Brandon.

Her son glowered. "It's okay," he muttered.

"I'll run to the store, get what I need," Walker said, already palming his car keys. "Anything else you want me to pick up?"

Tori was too stunned by both the males in the room to do more than shake her head.

Walker inclined his head and then left. She turned to Brandon.

"You love spaghetti and meatballs," she reminded him. "You love all Italian food. I should know as I've made some version of pasta every year for your birthday, the first and last days of school as well as New Year's because that's all you ever request."

"I like your pasta. His will probably suck."

"His will probably be jarred sauce which you've eaten before and survived. And it's awfully hard to screw up spaghetti—you boil water, cook the noodles and drain them. You've done it yourself."

"Why did he come here?" Brandon asked, his face flush, his tone accusatory.

And here we go again, she thought. Back to normal. Too bad, she was so enjoying having her sweet son back, if only for a few days.

"You heard Walker. He stopped by to see how I'm doing," she said with what she considered a huge amount of patience considering what she'd been through the past two days.

He snorted and sent her such a disbelieving look, her heart broke, just a little, to realize that part of him came from her. That inability to trust, to always be on his guard. "Is he your boyfriend?"

She laughed, a small burst of air. "What? No. I've only known him a few weeks, Brandon. We've never even been on a date."

But they had been alone together, the night at his room then here at her house. At the café when he'd kissed her. The other night at her hospital room when he'd listened so patiently to her.

"So if he's not your boyfriend, why's he cooking us dinner? What does he want?"

And there was no way she could tell him that deep inside, she was afraid, no…she was positive…she knew exactly what Walker wanted. What all men wanted from her.

That deep inside she was so afraid sex was the only thing she was good for.

"He wants to cook us dinner," she said. "What's the matter? Don't you like him?"

And how weird was having this conversation? She'd been on more than a few dates since her divorce was final. Men were always asking her out, always had, even when she was married. But, unlike her mother, she'd been faithful to Greg.

She took great pride in that.

Tori had never figured on having to introduce Brandon to any of the men she went out with because she kept her relationships simple and without strings. She never went out with the same man more than three times, always kept things light. She didn't want to be involved with another man, didn't want to count on another man to take care of her when the two men she'd counted on had let her down.

"He's okay," Brandon said after a moment. "I mean, he didn't arrest me after the fight and he stopped Mr. and Mrs. Nash from trying to get me into more trouble."

"See? He's not so bad."

"But he's trying to get Aunt Layne into trouble."

"Aunt Layne will be okay because she didn't do anything wrong." She hoped.

He sighed. "Fine. He can cook for us but that doesn't mean I have to like him."

"No," she said slowly, "but he's going through the trouble of fixing us a meal so you'll be polite, do you understand?"

Brandon rolled his eyes.

"Is that some sort of new way you crazy kids have of

saying 'Yes, Mom, whatever you say, Mom, you're the most awesomest, coolest mom ever, Mom'?"

His lips twitched. "There's no such word as *awesomest*."

"There should be. And my face should be listed under the definition of it in the dictionary."

"You're so weird," he said, but he settled back down close to her.

She put her arm around his shoulder, ridiculously pleased when he snuggled close to her side. She smoothed his hair back. "Don't I know it."

CHAPTER THIRTEEN

THE KID WANTED to chop Walker into tiny pieces and feed him down the garbage disposal.

Or at least, kick him out of his house.

Brandon had been unfailingly polite ever since Walker returned—if you called being laconic polite. He said "yes, please" and "no, thank you" in a way that Walker knew he was really saying, "Eat dirt and die!"

Brandon's dislike for him was obvious and heartfelt. The kid wore his resentment on his sleeve, his anger on his face. He didn't want Walker near his mother, watched him warily as if Walker was a jungle cat and was about to pounce at a moment's notice.

Brandon loved his mom. He may not like her at times, may wish she was different and may, most times, be mad as hell at her but he loved her. It was good to see, especially after everything Tori had admitted to Walker the other night at the hospital.

"You sure you know what you're doing?" Tori asked, standing in the doorway in a pair of baggy sweats and a sweatshirt that fell off her shoulders showing the wide strap of a tank top. Her hair was pulled back from her face by a wide band and her face was clean of makeup, the scratches already fading. Her complexion was still pale and her mouth was tight with pain when she moved too quickly.

She was beautiful.

She made his breath catch. Made him want.

He shouldn't be there, should never have given in to the urge to check on her, but once he had and he'd seen that she needed help, that she'd needed him, he hadn't been able to walk away.

He should've let them order pizza.

"I'm sure," he said, more gruffly than necessary as he sprinkled breadcrumbs on top of the ground beef he'd put into a bowl. "I've been making this since I was Brandon's age." He faced the kid who was sitting at the table sulking because Tori had insisted he stay in the kitchen with them instead of finishing his movie. "You know how to cook anything?"

"Mom cooks," Brandon said.

"What if she's not home and you get hungry?" Walker asked, putting the rest of the ingredients into the bowl.

"I can make sandwiches and stuff. Besides," he said with an impressive sneer, "cooking's for girls."

From the corner of his eye, Walker saw Tori stiffen, probably ready to lay into her son, but Walker gave her a slight shake of his head. She frowned but kept her mouth shut.

"I'd say cooking's for anyone who likes to eat. Or at least, eat food that tastes good." Walker washed his hands. "Besides, it's nice not to have to rely on someone to cook for you, to do everything for you."

As he guessed, that resonated with the kid. Christ, he was so much like his mother, so determined not to let anyone close to him, to depend on anyone. "I guess I could learn to make a few things," Brandon said, as if someone was pulling the words out of him.

"It's good to have a couple of standby meals," Walker agreed, stirring his sauce then tapping the spoon on the side of the pot. "I started cooking when I played ball in high school. Both my parents worked and my sisters were all older and out of the house either working or at college, so if I wanted to eat I had to learn to make it myself. And as much as I loved peanut butter sandwiches, I got tired of eating six of them every day."

"Six?" Tori asked, her lips curling up in that feline grin that was so enticing. "Holy sticky mouth, Batman."

Brandon rolled his eyes at his mom's lame joke but Walker noticed he hid a grin as he ducked his head.

"You burn a lot of calories playing ball," Walker said. "By the time I'd come home from practice, I was starving. But what really cinched it for me was when I was in high school and my coach told us all that the best way to get ready for a hard practice or game was to make sure we had the right fuel." He used a soup spoon to taste his sauce, added more salt. "Which was when I asked my grandmother to teach me how to make her marinara sauce. Carbs are a good thing to eat before a game so I started making pasta dinner for the team."

For the first time, Brandon seemed interested and intrigued with what Walker was saying instead of glaring at him. "Could we do that, Mom?" he asked, getting to his feet. "We could have the guys over before the game next week."

"Not right before," Walker cautioned. "Since your games are early, you might want to consider making it a post-game, victory dinner type deal."

"Yeah, we could do that," Brandon said. "Can we, Mom?"

"You expect me to feed thirty boys?" She slid Walker a glance that said she wasn't as thrilled with the idea as her son. "Where would they sit?"

"Boys are easy," Walker said, knowing now that the idea had taken root in Brandon's head it'd be hard to get out again. "They can sit on the floor. But you can't expect your mom to cook for that many guys every week, not after she puts in so many hours at the café."

Brandon frowned. "You want me to cook."

Smart kid. "Trust me, it's a handy skill. And it impresses girls."

This time, it was Tori who rolled her eyes.

"Come on," Walker continued. "I'm going to share with you the secret to my grandmother's recipe. I'll even let you write it down if you promise never to share it with anyone. Ever."

Brandon still seemed skeptical. "Yeah. Maybe."

Walker nodded. "Okay, wash up and you can chop the onion."

Tori stepped forward as if ready to throw her body between her son and any and all sharp instruments. "I don't know if that's a good idea."

Walker sent Brandon a conspiratorial look. "Women. They don't understand us men have ingrained knife skills." He nudged Brandon. "Stick with me and later I'll show you how to juggle a meat cleaver and two machetes, then we'll practice running with scissors."

"Fabulous," Tori said drily. "It's a mother's dream come true."

Brandon came back to Walker's side and Walker showed him how to hold the knife. Brandon curled his fingers under and cut the onion in half. "Good," Walker said, "now, see these lines? Make slices into the onion following those lines, then we'll just chop them into pieces."

"Be careful," Tori said, staring over her son's shoulder.

"Mom," Brandon said, obviously completely humiliated by his overprotective mother. "I've got this."

She crossed her arms. "Sure you do. Remind me you

said that when we're in the E.R. getting your fingers stitched back on."

"Nice imagery," Walker said.

"Just doing my duty as a mother to instill caution into my son."

Luckily Brandon—and all his fingers—survived his first lesson in onion and garlic chopping. Walker had him add them to the ground meat mixture along with seasonings. "Okay, now you mix it up."

Brandon eyed the bowl warily. "How?"

"With your hands."

"Gross," Brandon said, but dove in with the same enthusiasm he'd had on the football field. "You played football?" he asked Walker.

"Since I was ten."

"Walker could've played at college," Tori said, sitting at the table now that she must've deemed it safe for her to be a few feet away from her son.

"Yeah? Which college?"

"Penn State."

Brandon's eyes widened. "No way. You got picked to play for Penn State? Why didn't you?"

"I decided to take my life in a different direction."

"Man, that was stupid."

"Brandon," Tori said.

But Walker laughed. "A lot of people agreed with you."

"Do you miss it?" Tori asked. "Do you ever regret it?"

"I missed it for years, being a part of a team, leading that team, but now I lead a different kind of team and I make a difference, a real one. Do I regret it?" He stopped, thought about it. He didn't believe in regrets, not in life. You made a mistake, you paid the consequences and moved on, moved past it. "No, I don't regret it."

But he had a feeling if he wasn't careful, there was one

mistake he could make in Mystic Point that he'd never be able to get past. One that could jeopardize his career... could seriously skew his judgment when it came to this case.

He wanted Tori. He couldn't deny it, not when he was there, cooking with her son, unable to stop looking at her. Wanting to touch her. Kiss her.

Take her, again and again until they were both breathless and satiated. Until he'd rid his thoughts of her, purged her from his system for good.

But he couldn't take that step, wasn't ready to take that chance, to risk everything he'd worked so hard for. Wasn't sure any woman was worth what he could possibly lose.

Not even Tori.

AFTER DINNER, Brandon tried to get Tori to ease up on his no-video-games-no-computer-you're-grounded restriction, but she'd held firm. Just because Walker was there and had cooked them a really excellent—surprisingly excellent—dinner and had managed to bring Brandon out of his sullen shell didn't mean she was going to forget her son was being punished.

When he'd discovered he couldn't play video games, he'd acted as if his life was ruined and he was destined to die of boredom within the next two hours. She'd suggested he read a book, which had brought on a fit of gagging and grimacing the likes of which she'd never seen. And then, once again, Walker had saved the day—or at least, her patience.

He'd taught Brandon how to play poker.

So with the sun set, the three of them sat around the cleared-off table, the dishwasher humming, her kitchen clean and, despite Brandon having three helpings of dinner, plenty of leftovers packed up and in the fridge. Brandon studied his cards, frowning. It hadn't taken her long to figure out he thought frowning was a noncommittal expression.

"You in?" Walker asked him.

"Just a minute," Brandon murmured, narrowing his eyes first at Walker and then at her, as if he'd recently been granted X-ray vision and could see through their cards. "Yeah," he said slowly, sliding two green M&Ms into the pile. "I'm in."

"How about you?" Walker asked, holding her gaze, and something arced between them, that damn connection she needed to ignore, to deny. "You in?"

And she had the strangest feeling he was asking about more than a poker game.

"Too risky for me," she said, setting her cards face down.

Instead of seeming disappointed, understanding entered Walker's eyes. As if he knew exactly what she meant and couldn't agree more—but was willing to ignore his good sense for her.

She wasn't sure if the idea thrilled and flattered her, or scared her to death.

"Looks like it's just you and me," Walker said to Brandon. He laid his cards down. "Three tens."

Brandon scowled and showed his cards, a pair of queens.

"And that was the last hand," Tori said, her body sore from sitting on the hard chair, but there was no way she would've missed out on the past few hours. "You need to get to bed. You have practice tomorrow."

"Okay," Brandon said. He stood and seemed unsure. "Uh, thanks. For dinner and everything," he told Walker.

"No problem." Walker gathered Brandon's cards. "You

did a good job for your first time playing poker, but you've got a tell."

"What?"

"A tell, it's something, a movement or expression or gesture, that people do that tells the other players if you're bluffing or if you're holding good cards. You scratch the side of your nose."

"Nu-uh," Brandon said, eyes wide.

"Sorry, kid, but it's true. Work on that and you'll be cleaning up at the poker tables by the time you're legally allowed to play."

"Great," Tori said. "Now I don't have to worry about adding any more to that pesky college fund." She kissed Brandon's cheek. "Good night."

"Night," he said but he didn't move. Finally he faced Walker. "You're leaving soon, right?"

"Brandon," Tori said on a groan. "Could you get any more obvious? Or rude?"

"It's not rude to make sure your mother is taken care of, to protect her," Walker said, though he kept his eyes on Brandon. "Yes. I'm leaving soon. Good night, Brandon."

Her son's cheeks were red but he met Walker's gaze, her little boy, trying so hard to be the man of the house when it was up to her to protect him, to take care of him. "All right. See you."

Brandon walked out of the room and Tori sighed. "Sorry about that."

"Don't apologize. He was only looking out for you."

"Yes, but it's my job to look out for him, not the other way around."

They stood and she walked him to the door. The night was warm, the sky a blanket of stars. She went with him out onto the porch. "Thanks for dinner and for being patient with Brandon."

"I had a good time," he said, and she could almost believe him, except it wasn't in her nature to trust a man, to trust anyone other than her family. Besides, what guy wanted to hang out with her in her house where there was nothing sexy about the evening, no chance of anything happening?

"You're good at that," she said, watching him through slitted eyes.

"I'm good at many things, as I've already demonstrated," he said easily. "So I'm afraid you'll have to be more specific."

"Good at coming to the rescue. At saving the day. Saving people."

"You make it sound like a bad thing."

"I'm not sure." She didn't want to be saved, didn't want to change for anyone, not even her son, but some days she wondered if she'd ever be happy, ever be truly accepted for who she really was inside. "I do appreciate how good you were with Brandon."

"Well, usually I just kick kids in the head a few times until they stop bugging me, but I figured this one time I'd try a new tact."

Her face warmed. "I didn't mean it like that."

"He's a good kid. Reminds me a lot of my eldest nephew. His father left my sister a few years ago and he's very protective of his mom and younger brother. He was pissed when she started dating but he came around eventually."

"I don't need my son's permission to date," Tori said with a smile.

"No, I'm sure you don't. But it'd probably be nice if he didn't fight you on it, either."

"It didn't bother him when Greg started seeing Colleen," she pointed out, unable to hide the bitterness from her voice. "I really don't see why I should let his attitude dictate my actions, especially when he's so enamored with his soon-to-be stepmother."

"Because he's a kid and you're the adult and that's the way it is. It's not fair. But if being a parent was easy, there wouldn't be as many kids in the foster system, wouldn't be so many kids who were neglected or abused or spoiled to the point that no one can stand them."

She leaned against the door. "I hadn't realized cops were also therapists."

His smile flashed in the night and her breath caught. "You'd be surprised at my insight."

No, she wouldn't be. Tori knew he already saw too much, expected too much of her, thought there was more to her than what she showed the world.

He was wrong. She was all flash and sparkle, sex appeal and fantasy. That was all she wanted to be.

She closed the distance between them. Smiled at him as she laid her hands on his chest. Was reassured and relieved when his heart jumped under her fingers. But he didn't pull her to him, just watched her. Waited.

"I don't need your insight," she said, making her tone husky. Sent him a look from under her lashes. "And you don't really want to psychoanalyze me."

"You've got that right," he growled, his eyes hooded. "That's the last thing I want to do to you."

Trapping her hands with his own, he kissed her, a heated, hungry kiss that made her forget everything. That her son was inside, that this was her game, one she played better than anyone else, one that she always won. All she could do was feel the scrape of his whiskers against her lip, the taste of him, like the coffee he'd had after dinner. His fingers on hers, steady and warm, the rasp of his tongue against hers.

And she wanted. For the first time, she wasn't just the object of someone else's desire. She desired. She craved. His touch, his taste, his body next to hers, inside hers.

The wanting was enticing. More so than she'd ever dreamed. But it was also dangerous. Because wanting too much made you vulnerable, made you dependent on someone else's will, their decision.

Tori broke the kiss, hated that her heart was racing, that her thoughts were sluggish, her will so weak.

Hated that he stared down at her as if he knew exactly what power he held over her.

And was no happier about it than she was.

"I don't want to want you," he told her in a low, raspy tone that only amplified the desire in her veins.

"I know," she said softly.

And with the taste of him lingering on her lips, desire for him heating her blood, she stepped inside and closed the door.

"WHERE ARE you going?"

At the sound of his mother's voice, Anthony stopped, his hand on the door handle. "Out."

"Out?" she repeated, coming up behind him. "Out where?"

His fingers tightened. "Just out."

"Anthony—"

"Damn it," he yelled, whirling around so that her eyes widened and she took a step back. "I'm an adult, a grown man and I'm going out."

Though she seemed taken aback, she recovered quickly. Nothing kept his mom down for long; she was too well-bred for that. Not even a lying, cheating husband could put a chink in her armor, could faze her.

"You may be an adult—" though she didn't sound so

sure about that last part "—but I'm still your mother and I will not tolerate you speaking to me with disrespect. Do you understand?"

His hands shook, anger built. "You won't tolerate me speaking to you that way but you'll let Dad lie to you, cheat on you? You'll tolerate that?"

She went white and he regretted his words. But he couldn't take them back, not when he felt as if they were choking him, not when he felt as if he didn't even know his parents anymore.

As if he didn't know himself. What he was capable of. He couldn't stop thinking of how he was like his father. He'd hurt Jess, had taken advantage of her. He'd do it again if she wasn't with Tanner, if she'd give him another chance. He still wanted her.

Christ, there was something wrong with him. Something rotten, poisonous inside of him.

Like father, like son.

"My marriage is not up for discussion," his mother said sharply. "This is about you and your appalling behavior lately."

"My behavior's been appalling?" He shook his head in disgust. "How can you stay with him? How can you even look at him knowing what he did? He screwed his brother's wife."

"That's enough, Anthony." But her voice shook. Her throat worked as she swallowed.

It wasn't enough. It would never be enough. He had to get it out before it exploded inside of him. Before it destroyed him. "He got her pregnant. He's Nora's father. I can barely even look at her now. How can you stay after that?"

"None of this is Nora's fault. Don't you ever, ever put the blame on her. We raised you better than that."

They had and it shamed him to admit he had this re-sentiment toward his favorite cousin. He loved her, always had. She'd babysat him, had been another sister to him.

The joke was she truly was his sister.

"What's going on?" Ken asked as he came in from the study. "I can hear you two across the house."

Astor's mouth was thin, her shoulders back. "Nothing."

"It's not nothing. It's you," he snapped at his father. "You walking around here like you're some sort of king that nothing and nobody can touch. You think you can betray the people you're supposed to love and we're all supposed to just forgive you."

His father looked stricken. "Why don't we all go sit down?" he asked in that calm, unruffled way. "Talk this through?"

"I don't want to talk about it," Anthony said. "It won't change anything. It won't change what you did."

"Nothing can change what I did," Ken said wearily. "All I can do is apologize. But if we work together, we can get past this."

Anthony shook his head, filled with disgust for his father, for the man he thought he was, the man he'd looked up to his entire life. "That's just it. I can't get past it."

He met his mother's eyes. She stood next to her husband, but they didn't touch, weren't a strong unit like they were before the truth came out. And as much as Anthony wanted to pretend that everything would someday return to normal, would go back to being the way it was before, he couldn't.

"How can you pretend it never happened?" he asked his mom.

"I'm not pretending anything," Astor insisted. "But whether or not your father and I stay together is between Ken and me. We've been through good times and bad times, we've raised two incredible children together, have been incredibly blessed."

"He ruined it," Anthony said. "All of it."

Her expression softened and she reached for him. He didn't back up, let her take a hold of his hand. She felt small and delicate to him, not the strong woman he'd always seen her as and that, too, was his father's fault. He'd made her weak and vulnerable. He'd hurt her.

"Your father made a mistake." She looked at Ken. "One I'm working really hard to forgive."

"How can you?" Anthony asked, his voice barely a whisper.

"Because I love him. I've lived with him, loved him, for all these years of marriage. And that, more than anything, more than any mistake, matters more to me."

Disappointed and angrier than he'd ever been in his life, Anthony stepped back so that her hand fell away. Then he did something he'd never done in his entire life.

He turned his back on his parents.

CHAPTER FOURTEEN

THE ANSWER WAS there, Walker knew, right in front of him, but for some reason, he couldn't see it.

Rubbing his burning eyes, he picked up a picture, this one of Dale's body as it'd been found. Walker wasn't sure why Taylor had gone to the trouble of documenting the scene when he'd had no reason to suspect foul play had been involved, but Walker was glad he did. He studied the photo—Dale's body on the bed, his mouth and eyes open in death. A lamp, a bottle of whiskey and a half-full glass on the bedside table. He flipped through the other pictures. No sign of struggle, nothing out of place.

Nothing to prove that Dale had been murdered.

Walker crossed to the minifridge and pulled out a bottle of water. Took a long drink. Lowering the bottle, he frowned at the contents on the counter. Ice bucket. Coffee, sugar and powdered creamer packets, coffeemaker, two coffee mugs, two glasses...

Two glasses.

He practically leaped across the room, tore through the pictures again, then did another, slower search. One glass. There had only been one drinking glass in Dale's room when his body had been found. Walker thought back to every hotel and motel room he'd ever stayed in. There were always two glasses.

He picked up his phone only to set it down again. Who would he call? What would he say? Even if he could prove there had been two glasses in Dale's room, he had no proof that someone had been with Dale the night he died. That someone had murdered Dale and taken the glass.

He was back to square one.

Someone knocked on the door. Pulling his wallet from his back pocket, he opened it but it wasn't the pizza he'd ordered. It was Tori, looking like some walking fantasy in snug dark jeans and a low-cut top the color of plums.

Damn, but he'd always liked plums.

He leaned back. "This is a surprise." He just wished he knew if it was a good one or one that was going to bite him in the ass.

"Is it?" she murmured as she sashayed into the room, making it seem smaller, more intimate than it was. "Somehow I doubt that."

"Late for a visit."

"I guess that depends on the reason for the visit." She sat in the chair at the desk, crossing her legs, much as she had the first time he'd seen her when it'd felt as if he'd been kicked in the stomach.

He hadn't been able to catch his breath since.

Tori leaned forward, scanning the pictures he had scattered across the desk. He quickly gathered them together, shoved them into the folder.

She smiled. "Working on the case? Gathering all the facts to prove my sister is a dirty cop? Or maybe you've discovered my other sister is really some murdering mastermind?"

She was acting different. Oh, she looked the same, beautiful as always but that sexy grin seemed strained, her gaze wary and, if he wasn't mistaken, nervous. Maybe even sad.

There were so many facets to her, so many nuances. He'd always considered himself the type of man who pre-

ferred things black or white but with her, he found he liked
knowing there were many things yet to be discovered.

And that's why he'd kept his distance these past few
days. Because when he was around her, he forgot about
the job. Lost sight of why he was there. Lost sight of who
he was.

"Actually," he said, tidying up the mess he'd made on
his bed, "I was just finishing up."

"Am I allowed to ask how the case is going?"

"You're allowed to ask anything you want." He put the
reports into his briefcase and snapped it shut. "It's whether
or not you get an answer that's the question."

She swung her leg idly. "Will I get an answer?"

"I guess that depends on why you're asking."

He wanted her to be straight with him, to admit the
truth and show a part of herself that she kept hidden from
everyone else. Wanted her to share something real with
him. Was afraid if she did, he wouldn't be able to pretend
his initial view of her hadn't changed.

"I'm curious as to what you're going to tell the D.A.
about my sister," she admitted. "But I'm also wondering
how close you are to being done."

"Eager to get rid of me?"

"No." Her gaze dropped, her throat worked. "And that's
the problem."

Her voice was quiet. Unsure. It about did him in.

"I'll tell the D.A. the truth," he said roughly, but damn
it, she had no right to come here, to mess with his mind,
to tempt him when all he could think about was her.

She rose gracefully to her feet and sort of glided over
to him, not stopping until she was a mere hairbreadth
from him. He could smell her perfume, feel the warmth
of her body.

"What if I asked you to make sure that report was favorable to my sister? Would you do that one little thing for me if I asked, really..." She laid her hands on his chest. "Really..." Slid them up to link behind his neck and stretched that glorious body of hers against his. Lowered her voice so that it was a breathy purr. "Really nicely?"

Disappointment flowed through him, the strength of it, the depth surprising and staggering. He placed his hands on her waist, tortured himself by sliding his hands up her sides, dragging the material of her top up. She was warm, the shirt was soft but he knew her skin was softer and that thought was even more torturous.

"If you put it that way," he said, not having to feign the hoarseness in his voice, "then I'd definitely fail this little test you've got going on."

She settled back, would've stepped back, he knew, if he hadn't tightened his hold on her. "I don't know what you're talking about."

"Sure you do." Watching the emotions flicker across her expression was fascinating. She was fascinating the way she tried to hide her true self all the time when that was the most interesting part about her. "This is one of those tests you like to give people, make sure they're worthy of you or that they'll stand by you or do exactly what you want. Except even when they pass, you don't believe it, don't believe in them."

"I prefer to believe in what I see," she said tightly as she slid her hands out from around his neck to fist at her sides.

She was so adamant, so goddamn beautiful even as she lied to herself. Lied to him. He wasn't sure he could trust her, not with anything, especially not with his heart, but that was okay. He wouldn't give it to her. Not fully.

"Now you're lying to yourself," he said, surprised to find himself enjoying how her eyes narrowed, her body stiffened against his. But she still didn't pull away because that would be a sign of weakness and the all-powerful Tori Mott never backed down from a man, from a challenge. "You only trust what you can control, not what you see. You don't trust what's right here, right in front of you," he continued softly. "I think the real reason you don't go after what you want isn't because you're afraid you won't get it. But that you will."

Now she moved, stepping away from him. "Oh, believe me, I like getting what I want. I like it just fine." She tossed her head and struck a provocative pose, one he couldn't help but think was contrived. "And you have some nerve, judging me, Detective, when you don't go after what you want, either."

She was baiting him. He knew it, recognized it easily, just as he recognized his reaction to it. He wanted to prove her wrong, wanted to show her he was the type of man who didn't sit back waiting for life to happen to him.

But that was what she was counting on. And he couldn't do it.

"What are you doing here?" he asked softly. "The truth, Tori."

Her mouth thinned but her expression turned sultry and she sent him one of those looks she liked from underneath her lashes. "You know why."

He shook his head. "I want you to tell me."

She laughed but it was harsh. "Now who's playing games?"

"It's not a game. It's not a test. That's what you do because you're afraid to trust in what you see. So, I'll ask you one more time. Why are you here?"

Silence filled the room, heavy and loaded. And he knew she wouldn't tell him, wouldn't open up to him that much, not enough. Not fully. And that's what he wanted. All of her. Even if it was for just one night.

Someone knocked on the door. The pizza. He went to open the door.

TORI FELT LIKE an idiot. She mentally rolled her eyes. Make that *was* an idiot.

She stood in the middle of Walker's hotel room. Goose-flesh rose on her arms and she rubbed her skin but it did little to warm her. To soothe her. Not even the warmth of her humiliation could do that, she thought as Walker spoke with the pizza delivery guy, exchanged money for the food.

From the way the pizza guy's face lit up, Walker had added a big tip. A generous one.

Guess he had a little bit of nice guy in him after all.

He wanted her to rip herself open for him, to bare her soul. She couldn't. Once people saw who you really were, they turned their backs on you. They realized you weren't good enough, weren't smart or kind enough.

Walker shut the door and carried the pizza and the paper plates that the delivery guy had given him to the small, round table in the corner. "I'd invite you to stay for a slice," Walker said, "but I think it'd be best if I didn't."

Tori's jaw dropped. She blinked. "What?"

He straightened, watched her with that patient look in his eyes, the one that said he'd wait for her but she knew that would change. No one waited. Not for her.

"I think you should go," he said, his impassive tone so much more hurtful than if he'd been cold.

Her throat constricted. "You're...you're kicking me out?"

She couldn't wrap her mind around it. He was a man, wasn't he? He was definitely interested. She wouldn't be here if she hadn't been positive of that. Even now she saw it in his eyes. The attraction.

"Do you know how many men in this town would love to be in your shoes right now?" she couldn't stop herself from asking. "How many men want me?"

They all wanted her. It was her blessing. Her curse. It was who she was, all she knew. It gave her a sense of control over her life.

Walker set a slice of pepperoni pizza onto a plate. "They don't want you," he said as calmly as if they were discussing Tom Brady's quarterback rating. "They want your body, that face of yours. They want you to remain voiceless and nameless. They want to use you, sleep with you then set you aside like they would any other plaything." He bit into his pizza and shrugged. Swallowed. "If we were to be together, I'd want more."

Fear coated her mouth. She knew that. God, didn't she know that? It was what terrified her. "I don't have more in me to give."

"I think you do," he said, not sounding too happy about it. "I think you have more in you than you could ever imagine."

Tears pricked her eyes. She ducked her head and blinked them back. Damn him. Damn him! Why did he have to do this to her? Why couldn't he be like every other guy and just take what she had to offer without wanting, without expecting more? Couldn't he see he was wrong about her? She couldn't trust what she saw when she looked at him, couldn't believe he was everything he seemed. No one was. Everyone had their secrets. She couldn't share hers.

She sneered. "Well, I guess it's your loss, then."

"I guess it is."

But she wondered if she wasn't the one losing.

She stalked to the door, opened it. Hesitated, gave him

time, plenty of time to call her back, to rush over and stop her. To make the decision for both of them, to make it easier on her. But there was only silence behind her.

Her fingers tightened on the door handle and she stepped outside, found herself whirling around, facing him. "I told Brandon he could live with his father. That I wouldn't fight for custody of him if that's what he wanted."

"When?"

"Tonight." She twisted her fingers together. "A few hours ago when I dropped him off at Greg and Colleen's."

Walker approached her, his steps slow, his gaze intense. "That must've been difficult."

Difficult? It'd broken her heart. "I wanted him to say he'd changed his mind. I wanted him to choose me," she whispered.

"He loves you."

She nodded. "He does. I guess…I guess that's going to have to be enough."

"What you did, letting him go, that was very brave."

"I don't feel brave. I feel…empty. Alone. And I…I thought maybe you could help. With that last part."

Shutting his eyes, he exhaled heavily. "Tori, I—"

"I've never been with another man except Greg."

Her words, blurted out in a desperate rush, hung in the air between them. One of her secrets, one of many, out in the open for him to see. To judge. One he could use against her.

"What?" he asked, sounding as if the word was strangling him.

She swallowed, lifted her chin. "Greg was my first. And I haven't been with anyone else."

"Shut the door."

Tori looked down, realized she was holding the door

open. She shut it, her heart racing as Walker came closer, and closer.

"You've only been with one man?" he asked, not sounding so much disbelieving as everyone in town probably would be, but more intrigued. Curious.

She tried to play it cool. "We met when we were sixteen," she pointed out. "Dated for a year before we went all the way."

"And when you were older?"

"I was faithful during my marriage." She'd had no desire to be otherwise. Had known she could've cheated, could've been with any number of the men who'd flirted with her but she'd had no interest. She'd respected Greg, had cared for him enough not to betray him that way, not to hurt him.

In that way, she was her mother's complete opposite.

Walker shook his head, standing so close now she had to tip her head back to maintain eye contact. "I meant after. Since the divorce."

Though she wanted to hide behind her usual sexy persona, wanted to be flippant and flirtatious, she didn't, couldn't. Not with Walker. Not tonight. She forced herself to meet his eyes. "There's been no man I've wanted to be with. Until now." Her palms grew damp. "Until you."

His eyes darkened, his expression turned fierce and possessive. She wasn't someone who could ever belong to a man, couldn't give herself fully to someone. But she could give her body to Walker tonight.

He edged closer, trapping her between the door and his solid body. Leaned toward her, his hands on her waist. "Tell me what you want," he demanded in a gruff tone.

She licked her dry lips, saw his gaze follow the movement. "You," she told him clearly. Confidently. No demure whisper, no purr of sensual words. Just the truth. "I want you, Walker."

He nodded once as if satisfied and then he kissed her, a hungry, demanding kiss, one so heated it felt as if her bones were melting. The hunger in him, the heat, ignited an answering flame inside her and she kissed him back just as hard, just as eagerly.

His hands skimmed over her as if unable to decide what to touch first, as if trying to smooth over every inch of her. Tori held his head, her hands above his ears. His hair was soft, his kiss a bit rough. He stroked his tongue inside her mouth and she sucked on it, causing him to groan low in his throat.

He scooped her up in his arms, his hands under her ass. She wrapped her legs around his waist as he straightened, flipped the lock and then kissed her again as he carried her to the bed, set her down with enough force that she bounced. She laughed but the sound died when his hands, sure and hot, went to the button of her jeans.

Her stomach contracted, her breath held as he undid them, dragged the zipper down then shimmied them off, his knuckles brushing against her skin. He tossed them to the carpet, trailed his palms up her sides, dragging her shirt up her rib cage, pulling it over her head.

He stared down at her, his eyes glittering, his chest rising and falling rapidly with his breathing. "You're perfect," he said, skimming his gaze from the top of her head to her feet.

She wasn't. Not on the inside where it counted, where it mattered. She was too hard, too cynical. She reached for him, feeling exposed and vulnerable in just her bra and panties, her knees bent. He came to her, lay next to her and touched her. Her face—her eyebrows and nose and eyelids and cheeks and mouth and chin. Traced his finger down the line of her throat, up under her jaw to her ear.

Tori squirmed, tried to kiss him but he leaned back. "I want to touch you," he told her in that serious tone of his. "You deserve to be touched, to be worshipped."

Her throat clogged. She didn't want to be worshipped. There was too much pressure in being up on that pedestal even as she craved the anonymity that came with being thought of as some sort of goddess. She'd spent so much of her life needing to be desired as if that alone would be enough to make up for what was lacking inside her.

But she couldn't stop Walker, not when what he was doing felt so good, so right. His hands were warm, his fingertips rough as they smoothed across her collarbone. He dipped his head, flicked the tip of his tongue across her skin, placed warm, openmouthed kisses along the upper edge of her breasts. Tugged her bra down. Her hands fisted into the bedspread as he gently pinched her nipples then took one into his mouth and sucked hard.

Her hips lifted off the bed as she moaned. She squeezed her eyes shut against the sensations rolling through her, dangerous sensations that continued to build as he hooked his fingers under the edge of her panties and slid them down her legs. He caressed her lower belly, traced his finger around her belly button then moved down to touch her legs, inner thighs.

"So beautiful," he murmured. She'd been called beautiful before, had been told it many times during her life. But this was the first time it meant anything. Made her heart warm.

Walker slid his hand up her inner thigh, settled between her legs, his fingers sure as he stroked her. He kissed her cheeks, then her mouth. Trailed his lips down her neck to her breast again as his fingers moved faster. Harder. Pressure built. Tori arched her back, seeking that release. He shifted so that he was kneeling over her. Her eyes opened and the look on his face alone was almost enough to send her over that edge. He continued stroking her as he slid one finger inside her. Her inner muscles contracted.

"You going to come for me?" he asked, his voice a low murmur. An enticement. "Oh, yeah," he breathed as he added another finger, stretching her. "You're going to come for me."

She couldn't resist his hands, his words. When he bent and gently bit her nipple, she flew apart and cried out his name.

WALKER CONTINUED TO work Tori's body until she was spent; only then did he quickly take off his clothes and grab a condom from the case in his duffel bag. He was pleased and humbled when she reached for him, her body, that glorious body as wonderful as he'd imagined—even more so. Her skin flush, her eyes glazed with passion because of him. For him. And knowing she'd only ever been with one man before, it excited him, possibly more than it should have but he'd been telling the truth when he'd said he wanted to worship her. He wanted to take it slow and make it last for as long as he could.

Wanted to make it special for her.

But when he went into her arms she kissed him. A hot, hungry kiss, her hands smoothing across his shoulders, down his chest. Her touch drove him mad, her taste inflamed him. He returned it with a fervor he'd never experienced before. He quickly sheathed himself, seized her hips with both hands and shifted her to him, rubbed his tip against her entrance. Waited until she looked at him, until their eyes locked. And then he entered her.

It was good, so damn good. She was hot and tight and

everything he'd dreamed of. She arched her back with a sound that drove him insane, drove him to plunge into her again and again, harder and faster. She gripped his arms, her nails digging into his skin. Sweat coated their bodies, the scent of sex filled his nostrils.

He watched her, hoping he could hold out long enough for her to come again, not sure that was possible when she was gasping underneath him, her body meeting each of his thrusts, her mouth open, her head tipped back slightly. He lifted her hips even more so he could go deeper and she convulsed and tightened around him, her body milking him even as she came.

He quickly followed her over that edge, tumbling after her with a guttural cry.

Walker wasn't sure how much time had passed. He'd collapsed on top of Tori, felt the hard beating of her heart against his chest, felt her heavy breathing. Knowing he was probably squishing her, he tried to roll to the side but she held on to him.

"I don't want to crush you," he said next to her ear.

She squeezed him. "Not," she said, sounding sleepy and satisfied. "I like it. I like feeling your weight pressing down on me, your skin against mine."

He smiled. Kissed her forehead. The tip of her nose. His heart tumbling when her lips curved in a satisfied, sweet smile.

"I hope I wasn't too rough," he said, unable to keep the emotion out of his voice. He just hoped she didn't hear it. "I meant to take my time."

Her eyes fluttered open and she smiled at him, a full, real smile that caused his stomach to tighten, his self-resolve not to fall for her to weaken. "I thought things were a bit rushed," she said lightly.

He grinned and flipped them over so that she straddled him. "Oh, yeah? Seems to me I wasn't the only one in a rush."

"No, you weren't the only one," she admitted, the silky skin of her thighs rubbing against his hips. "But I hadn't realized that wasn't your A game."

"Hey, now, I didn't say anything about it being a sub-standard effort."

"No, no," she said, a thoughtful frown marring her forehead, "it was definitely a good effort."

He raised his eyebrows. "Good?" He lifted his hips so she could feel his growing erection. "Is that a challenge?"

"Depends," she purred. "Are you up for it?"

He slowly tugged her toward him. "I think I can manage."

CHAPTER FIFTEEN

SITTING ON TOP of a picnic table in the café's empty parking lot, Anthony stared at the back door, hoping she'd come out. Hoping just as hard she wouldn't.

But then the door opened and there she was. Jessica. Her hair a pale beacon in the night. She lifted her cell phone as if to call or text someone and he stood, raised his hand. Even from this distance he could see the frown marring her face but she lowered her phone and walked toward him.

"Anthony," she said, her eyes wary as she took him in, noticed the six-pack on the table, three left, "what are you doing here?"

"I was just driving around," he lied, wiping his damp palms down the front of his jeans, "and thought I'd see if you need a ride home."

She raised her eyebrows. "You're drinking and driving?"

Shit. He should've left the beer in the Jeep. "I just had a couple." Just enough to take the edge off, to make it that much easier to forget how he'd spoken to his parents, how he'd hurt his mother's feelings. Just enough to make him brave enough to come here, to face Jessica.

She studied him as if she could see through all his bullshit. Which she probably could. She was savvy and smart and more mature than most girls his own age. Of course, now he realized that she'd had to grow up quickly because of her drug-addicted mother, that she hadn't had an easy life, that it had made her hard and cynical. Made it difficult for her to trust others, even with the truth of who she was.

The door opened again and one of the older waitresses came out. Jess shifted and dragged him into the shadows as the lights at the café went off. He froze. She was close enough he could smell her perfume. Feel her warm, soft hand on his arm. The waitress crossed the parking lot, got into her car and drove off, leaving them alone.

The night was warm and still, the sky dotted with stars and Jess was next to him. It was a mistake, a big one, being here with her, but he didn't care anymore. His father had made a worse mistake, had done something so wrong Anthony would never forgive him so why couldn't he be with Jess? Why did he have to play by the rules when his father didn't?

Jess eased away from him, stepping out of the shadows so that the lights from the parking lot illuminated her profile. "I don't think you should be driving," she said, biting her lower lip.

"No, you're right," he said quickly, knowing he had to do something, say something quick to convince her to stay. To not walk away from him. "I won't. Is your uncle coming to get you?"

"I was about to call him but then I saw you…" She shrugged, seemed unsure and nervous. He didn't want to scare her.

"Do you want to sit down?" he asked, retaking his place on the table. "Talk for a little bit?"

He held his breath but she gave one of those shrugs again. Her phone buzzed and she checked it. Probably a message from that kid she was dating. But she didn't take it. Instead she shut it off and sat next to Anthony.

"You want a beer?" he asked.

"You can get in trouble giving a minor alcohol," she said, staring at him as if he'd lost his mind. Who knew? Maybe he had.

He nudged her gently. "Come on, we both know you drink."

She'd admitted that much truth to him. Their last night together things had gotten pretty heated between them and she'd put the brakes on. Had admitted she'd been with a lot of guys, had partied.

"I don't drink anymore," she said firmly.

He twisted the top off another beer, took a long drink. "Playing it straight and narrow, huh?"

"Just trying to change my ways. Be a better person." He could feel her studying him, felt her bare thigh brush against his outer leg when she shifted. "Why are you here, Anthony?" she asked quietly.

He faced her, his heart pounding, his throat dry. "I miss you," he blurted, the truth he'd denied to even himself since he'd found out her real age. It was humiliating. She was a kid...just a kid and he hadn't been able to stop thinking about her. To stop wishing things were different.

"We weren't together that long," she pointed out, though her voice shook. "You should've moved on by now."

"Don't you think I know that?" he asked. "Don't you think I want to move on? God, Jess, I think about you all the time. I feel like some sort of pervert. I mean, you're only sixteen." He shook his head in disgust. "If you were twenty-six and I was thirty-one it wouldn't even matter."

But it did matter. And he hated that he felt like some sleazeball predator who lusted after young girls because that wasn't it at all. It was Jess. Only Jess. Christ, the next thing he knew he'd be caught on *Dateline* or something.

"It doesn't matter," Jess said, though he knew she felt

the same about him. Had seen how she looked at him when she thought he wasn't watching, how hurt she'd been when he'd been with Mackenzie. "I'm with Tanner now."

"But you're not," Anthony pointed out, turning to her. "Right now, you're here with me. Not him."

He kissed her. She stilled for a moment, and then she kissed him back. It was hesitant but it was enough to give him hope and he deepened the kiss, eased her back until she was lying on the table, her legs hanging over the edge. He kissed her again and again, his hands roaming over her hip, the curve of her breast. Kissing her, touching her, he didn't have to think about what his father had done, didn't have to worry about if being with Jess was wrong or right.

It felt right. It felt all too right.

He slid his hand up her shirt, cupped her breast, and she squirmed beneath him. It took him a moment to realize she wasn't squirming because she liked it but that she was also pushing against his chest, trying to break the kiss. For a moment, one brief, terrifying moment, he ignored her. Thought about not stopping. About taking what he wanted.

His breathing ragged, his hands shaking, he jack-knifed to a sitting position. "What's the problem?" he asked more harshly than he intended but damn it, now he felt guilty.

"I told you," she said, her own voice unsteady as she straightened her shirt, "I'm with Tanner now. He's my boyfriend."

Anthony sneered. He felt pissed off and mean and out of control. "Yeah? Well, your boyfriend doesn't have to know," he said, reaching for her again.

She slapped his hands. "Don't be a dick."

"Look, what's the problem? It's not like you're a virgin. You've slept with plenty of guys. What's one more?"

Even in the darkness he could see her face lose color,

see the hurt in her eyes. He felt sick to his stomach, disgusted with himself.

Jess wrapped her arms around herself. "I used to think you were something special," she said quietly. "I used to think, to dream that maybe, when I was older, we'd get back together. But you're nothing but a spoiled brat. You know what you need, Anthony?"

"Yeah. I need to get laid. Not a lecture."

"You think you have it so rough? You think that what your dad did a hundred years ago gives you the right to act like an asshole? To treat me like a whore?"

Her voice wobbled and the beer he had drank churned in his stomach. Shame filled him. "Jess, I—"

"Don't. Just...don't. I know it's been a rough couple of weeks for you and I would've been happy to have been there for you as a friend," she said, stressing the last word. "As someone who cared about you, who wanted to help you. You think you're the only person to go through something crappy? Sometimes life sucks. But you get through it. And I've learned it's how you get through it that shows what kind of person you are." She shook her head at him. "You're nothing but a spoiled, egotistical kid. Grow up."

And she walked away, calling her uncle to come and get her, leaving Anthony alone with his beer and his regrets.

WALKER ENTERED THE café, the folder he'd put together in his hand. He was still having problems processing what the contents in it meant.

For the first time, he hoped...prayed...he was wrong.

He spied Tori immediately, talking with an elderly gentleman. She must've sensed Walker's eyes on her because she tensed and slowly turned, then said one more thing to her customer and crossed toward Walker.

"Good afternoon, Detective," she said, as if he was just

another man for her to flirt with, to manipulate. "You're a little late for lunch but I'm sure we can find something delicious for you. Booth or table?"

But he wasn't going to let her play that game with him, not when he could see the nerves in her eyes, could tell she wasn't as in control of her emotions as she wanted him to believe.

"I woke up alone."

He scowled. He hadn't meant to say that, hadn't meant to get personal at all.

She blinked, glanced around as if to make sure no one had overheard him. "Yes, well, I wake up alone every day. Now, a table or a booth?"

He'd reached for her. Had wanted to make love to her again but she was gone.

Walker had been furious. She'd left without a word after they'd spent the night together, after they'd made love three times, each one better than the last. They'd eaten cold pizza, had laughed and talked and touched and kissed.

So he'd tried to push her out of his mind and gotten back to the job at hand. He'd gone through Dale's police interview again, had double-checked timelines, studied the photos, including the personal ones Tim Sullivan had given him.

And he'd found the truth.

"Look," Tori said, "some of us have work to get to so if you're not here to eat, I suggest you find somewhere else to be. We have a no loitering policy."

He wanted to drag her out of there, make her tell him what was going on in that head of hers. Force her to stop playing her games. But she was right. He had a job to do.

"I need to speak with Miss Vitello," he said, already brushing past Tori. "Is she in the kitchen?"

"Hey," Tori said, hurrying after him. She caught him

as he went into the tiny alcove that separated the dining room from the kitchen. She held his arm. "You can't go back there. Employees only. And why do you need to talk with Celeste?" Her eyes narrowed. "Is this about the case?"

"I'm not at liberty to discuss the details," he said, knowing those details were going to tear Tori's world apart. "But it's imperative I speak with Miss Vitello so either you go get her or I will."

"Fine," she snapped. "Wait here."

He didn't, he followed her into the kitchen. It smelled good and was a lot messier than it'd been when Tori had made him that sandwich. A large, bald man was chopping something at the counter and Celeste was at the grill.

Tori whirled on him. "I told you to wait out there."

He barely spared her a glance. "Miss Vitello," he said as Celeste glanced curiously from him to Tori and back to him again. "I need to speak to you. Privately."

Frowning, she set her spatula down. "Of course. Joe," she called to the bald man. "Can you take over for a few minutes?"

"Sure thing," Joe said.

"We can speak in my office," Celeste said as she led him out. "Can I get you anything to drink? Some coffee?"

"No, thank you."

Tori was hot on their heels. "What's going on?"

Walker stopped and faced her while Celeste disappeared into a room at the end of the hall. "This doesn't concern you."

"If it's about the case against my family, it damn well does concern me."

"I just need to get a few things clarified from Miss Vitello."

"Well, then you can do that while I'm in the room." And she stormed ahead of him.

"…just fine," Celeste was saying as he stepped into the small office. Both women looked at him and Celeste patted Tori's hand. "Go on. Take a seat."

"I don't think that's a good idea," Walker said tightly.

"Please," Celeste, sitting behind the desk, said. "Let her stay."

He shouldn't, but he had a feeling Tori needed to hear this firsthand.

It was probably the only way she'd believe it.

He nodded once. Tori took the chair beside him. He remained standing and he handed Celeste the item he'd received that morning.

"Miss Vitello, do you recognize this?"

"What is that?" Tori asked as Celeste studied the email he'd printed.

Celeste sat back, her face white. "Where did you get this?" she asked, her voice strangled.

"From your computer."

"You searched her computer?" Tori gripped the arms of the chair. "Are you allowed to do that?"

Telling himself he wasn't insulted she'd question his ability to do his job, he nodded sharply. "I assure you all of the proper search warrants were obtained." He kept his eyes on Celeste as he added, "Mr. Sullivan was in the residence the entire time."

Celeste swayed but then steadied herself. "Tim knows?"

"That at the beginning of June, one day after Valerie Sullivan's remains were found you ordered potassium cyanide from a website?" Walker asked. "Yes."

Tori glanced between him and her boss. "Wait…what? You bought cyanide? Why would…" Her eyes widened and she slowly shook her head. "No. Oh, no."

"Miss Vitello," Walker said, "did you kill Dale York?"

"Don't answer that," Tori said quickly, digging into her

pocket for her cell phone. "Don't say anything. I'll call Uncle Ken and—"

"No," Celeste said, sounding weary and somewhat... relieved. "Tori...don't. He can't help me. Not now. I need to do this. I need to tell the truth." She raised her chin and met Walker's eyes. "Yes. I killed Dale York. After Erin and Collin's engagement party, I waited until Tim was asleep and then I snuck out. I went to Dale's room. I didn't think he'd let me in but he'd always considered himself quite the ladies' man," she said, her mouth turned down in disgust. "I...flirted with him. Talked him into inviting me in for a drink. He was so cocky, so sure he was smarter than everyone else, that I was no threat to him."

"You put the cyanide into his whiskey," Walker said.

Her hands were clasped together on top of the desk, her knuckles white. "I almost didn't. Wasn't sure I could but when he went to the bathroom, I...I saw myself adding it to his glass, it was like my hand belonged to someone else." She licked her lips. "I waited until he came back, watched him drink it, my brain had...shut off. After he drank, he just...collapsed...and I left."

"But not before taking your glass—and your fingerprints—with you."

"I was scared," she said. "Out of my mind. I was so afraid he'd hurt someone in my family again, like he did to Val. What I did, I did to protect my family."

He noticed Tori flinch but he couldn't comfort her, he had to keep his head in the game. "And yet you ordered the poison weeks before Mr. York's return to Mystic Point. Before you were even aware that he was still alive."

She shut her eyes, slid her hands to her lap. "I didn't buy it to kill him," she whispered. "I bought it to...to..."

"To kill yourself," Walker said.

Tori spun on him. "That's ridiculous," she snapped.

"You ordered that cyanide because your secret was about to come out," Walker continued to Celeste relentlessly. "Dale didn't kill Valerie Sullivan. He was innocent and he knew there wasn't enough evidence to charge him. He was safe. So he came back to make some more money off Ken using Valerie's affair with Ken, and Nora's paternity, as leverage."

Tori shook her head. "What are you talking about? Of course Dale killed my mother. Everyone knows that."

"He was telling the truth about getting to the quarry only to find Val wasn't there. But her car was so he took it. He probably figured she'd backed out of their deal and that it would be easier to ditch her car than his. He started his new life, spent all these years thinking Valerie was still alive. When he found she wasn't, he may have even suspected Ken Sullivan was the murderer. Something else he could blackmail your uncle with."

Tori's eyes widened. "You think Uncle Ken—"

"No," Walker said emphatically as he pulled a photo out of the folder. "I don't think he's guilty, either. This—" he shook the picture "—tells me who really killed Valerie." He faced the woman behind the desk. "Isn't that right, Miss Vitello?"

A ROARING SOUND filled Tori's head, made it difficult for her to think, to process what Walker was saying. What he was implying.

He handed Tori the picture. It was one she'd seen before, one of her father, her mother and Celeste. Valerie was laughing, her head thrown back while Tim stared at her, his love for her clear on his handsome face.

But it was Celeste's image that Tori couldn't tear her eyes from. Celeste who had her arm linked with Val's,

who was staring at Tim with such…longing. Almost…
obsession.

Walker took the photo from her numb fingers and
handed it to Celeste. Tori's throat felt like it was on fire
and she couldn't stop staring at the other woman. Couldn't
help but see the guilt in her dear friend's dark eyes.

"Celeste?" she asked, unable to hide the shakiness of
her voice, the plea. "What's he talking about?"

Walker stepped forward. "Dale didn't kill—"

"No," Tori snapped at him. "No. I want to hear it from
her." She walked up to the desk, met the eyes of the woman
who'd been more of a mother to her than Valerie, the
woman who'd been like another grandmother to her son.
The woman who'd given her a job and helped her when
she'd been a scared, pregnant teenager, who'd held her
hand when she'd told her father and sisters she was pregnant. The woman her father had lived with, had loved, the
woman who'd been a steady presence in her life.

"I want to hear it from you," Tori told Celeste. "Tell
me."

Celeste nodded, her eyes filled with tears. "Dale didn't
kill Val," Celeste whispered, her voice ragged. "I did."

Tori wheeled back as if she'd been pushed. Walker was
there to help guide her into a chair, to lower her head when
she gasped for air. He murmured at her, told her to take it
easy, to just focus on her breathing, his large hand warm
and steady on her back.

She didn't want to breathe, didn't want to focus. Not
when that meant she'd have to accept what Celeste had
just said.

"No," Tori said, her head still bent, her voice ragged.
"No." She raised her head. "You didn't…you couldn't…"

Celeste was crying, the tears streaming silently down

her face. She looked older. Broken. "I'm sorry. I'm so sorry."

"Let's go down to the station," Walker said in his calm cop's voice. "We'll take your state—"

"I didn't mean to," Celeste said, her eyes pleading, but Tori's heart was cold, frozen. "I didn't mean to hurt her."

From the corner of her eye, she saw Walker start a small tape recorder and at that moment, she hated him. Hated him for doing his job, for being so calm and unemotional when she wanted to run, to hide from this truth. From what she knew was going to be a confession, one she didn't want to hear. Wasn't sure she could survive.

"You spoke with Valerie Sullivan the night she disappeared?" Walker asked. "You saw her?"

Celeste didn't take her eyes off Tori and for the life of her, Tori couldn't look away. "I saw her," Celeste said. "She stopped by my apartment, told me she was leaving town with Dale and that she wanted to say goodbye. I was…shocked."

"You didn't know she was having an affair with Dale York?" Walker asked.

"I knew but I didn't think she'd leave Tim or the girls for him. There had been other men…" She shook her head as Tori realized what that meant. Other men. Not just Ken. Not just Dale. Tori's stomach turned. Oh, God. "Val was never serious about any of them," Celeste told Tori quickly as if reassuring her. "But she said Dale had figured out a way for them to be together, for them to escape Mystic Point. She said they came into some money but I hadn't realized they'd blackmailed Ken for it."

Celeste swallowed. "She was so happy, so excited and all I could think was, how can she be this happy knowing she's leaving her husband? Her children? I asked her about the girls and she just…shrugged. Said they'd be fine with

Tim…that she loved them but she wasn't cut out to be a mother. She needed to be free." Celeste frowned, looked at Walker. "That's what she said to me. *I need to be free. I can't be tied down, not to one man, not to one place. I'm bigger than that. I'm more.*"

Walker nodded slowly. "What happened next?"

Celeste pressed her fingertips against her temples. "I begged her not to go. Told her she was making a huge mistake in picking Dale over Tim and their children but she smiled and said Tim would get over it, her girls, too, because they'd have me, wouldn't they? She said with her gone, the coast would be clear for me and Tim."

Tori gasped. "You and Dad were having an affair?"

"No. God, no. But…I loved him. Valerie knew, of course. She could see it. She'd often tease me about the crush I had on her husband. That night she told me that with her out of the way, I could step into the role of Tim's wife, as a mother to you girls. I was so angry that she'd treat us all that way, I knew how devastated you all would be if she left so when she turned toward the door I…God, I don't know what happened. I don't even remember anything except this utter rage filling me. The next thing I knew, I was standing over her body, holding a lamp in my hand." Tears flowed again. "I'd hit her. Hard. I'd killed her."

"You hit her at your apartment?" Walker asked. "How did she wind up at the quarry?"

"I took her there," Celeste admitted in a hoarse whisper. "I panicked. She wasn't breathing, she was just so… so still and then she got so cold…" She shook her head and when she spoke again it was as if she was far away, her voice monotone, her eyes glazed. "She'd told me she was meeting Dale at the quarry. I dragged her to her car and drove it out there, and put her behind the wheel of the car and then hid in the woods."

"You thought Dale would be blamed for her death," Walker said.

Celeste nodded. "He had a history of violence. I thought she'd be discovered and he'd be arrested once word of the affair came out. I waited for an hour and he finally showed up but when he saw Val, he dragged her body into the woods and just…left her there. Then he took her car. I walked home and waited for my secret to come out, waited for someone to figure out what I'd done."

"Except no one did," Walker said. "Everyone thought Valerie was with Dale."

"I realized I'd been given a second chance," Celeste said. "Everyone already thought Val had just walked away and she would have, she would've left you all," Celeste told Tori as if that made what she'd done all right. "So I kept my secret, my guilt. I buried it and I did my best to be there for you and your sisters, to be the kind of woman Tim needed…the kind he deserved. But it wasn't enough, it was never enough for him," she said hoarsely. "He still loved her. After all this time, I'm still second best to him."

Tori was shaking, her head spinning. "You killed her. You killed her and you left her out there in the woods. My God, how could you?"

"I thought she'd be found. I thought for sure she'd be found."

Tori didn't even realize she was crying until a tear dripped off her chin and landed on the back of her hand. She lifted her fingers to her cheeks, surprised to feel the wetness there, to realize she could cry when inside she was so cold, so numb. "You were her friend. Her best friend."

"I loved her," Celeste said. "I loved her like a sister. I didn't mean to hurt her."

Walker touched Tori's shoulder gently then stepped forward. "Celeste Vitello, you're under arrest for the murder of Valerie Sullivan. You have the right to remain silent—"

"I'm sorry," Celeste said, her eyes locked on Tori's. "I'm so, so sorry."

Tori felt as if she was out of her body, somehow looking down on the scene. The sound of Walker's voice as he told Celeste of her rights faded, time slowed. Walker reached for a pair of handcuffs on his hip even as Celeste moved, bent to get something from the bottom drawer. Some memory tugged at Tori's brain, told her to stop Celeste. Realization had her leaping to her feet.

"No!" she screamed.

Celeste straightened, the gun she kept locked in her desk drawer in her hand. Walker pushed Tori aside as Celeste raised the gun, pressed the barrel against her own temple.

"Forgive me," she said, somehow too calm, too composed, her eyes beseeching. "Please, forgive me."

And she pulled the trigger.

CHAPTER SIXTEEN

WALKER GAVE TORI a day, twenty-four hours, and then he went to her. He couldn't stay away, not any longer than that, not after she'd been so crushed, so traumatized yesterday.

Hell, he'd been traumatized, too. When Celeste raised that gun, his first instinct, his only thought, had been to protect Tori. Which he'd done, he assured himself as he walked up to her house. But he hadn't been able to protect her from Celeste's death.

Or from the truth of what Celeste had done.

He exhaled heavily and then knocked on the door. Cars lined the driveway. He wasn't the only one who'd stopped by to check on her.

The door opened and Brandon stood in the foyer. "Hi," the kid said solemnly. "You here to see Mom?"

"I'm here to see both of you. How are you holding up?"

Brandon lifted a shoulder, looking so much like his mother, Walker's stomach clenched. "I'm okay."

Walker stepped inside, shut the door behind him. "And your mom?"

"She keeps saying she's all right but she's not," Brandon said, sounding older than twelve. "She didn't sleep at all last night and I heard her crying," he added in a low voice. "But no one else knows that," he rushed on.

"They won't hear it from me," Walker promised. He followed Brandon into the living room to find Chief Taylor talking to Tim Sullivan. Tori's dad was tall with graying blond hair and blue eyes. He looked distraught, his face weathered, his eyes weary. Astor Sullivan joined them, said something to Tim and laid her hand on his arm. He patted her hand, nodded then walked away with her.

His brother kept his distance, sat in a chair next to a pretty blonde who was probably his daughter, Erin. Griffin York stood by the window, listening to Brandon's dad and Colleen.

"Bertrand," Taylor said, coming up to him. "Everything in order?"

Walker knew he was asking about the report. "All filed. I recommended that no recourse be taken against either you or Captain Sullivan."

He'd found no reason for charges of misconduct to be filed against either of them. They'd played it by the book during a difficult time. Walker wasn't sure he would've been able to have done the same.

"I appreciate that," Taylor said, as if he meant it. Then he held out a hand. "Thank you."

Walker shook the chief's hand, knew he was being thanked for more than just his findings in the case against him and Layne. He nodded.

Taylor sipped his beer. "Tori's in the kitchen with her sisters."

And how the chief knew she was the real reason he was there, Walker had no idea. Wasn't sure he wanted to know.

He went into the kitchen as Tori slammed down a can of coffee and said, "I'm perfectly capable of making a pot of coffee in my own damn house."

"Of course you are," Nora said in a soothing tone. "Layne was just trying to help."

"I don't need her help," Tori said as if through gritted teeth. She peeled the top off the coffee, waved the scoop at her sisters. "And I don't need you two hovering over me. I'm fine."

"Yeah," Layne said, leaning back against the counter, her ankles crossed. "That's clear." She noticed him, raised an eyebrow. "Detective Bertrand," she said. "What can we do for you?"

All three Sullivan sisters looked at him. He felt edgy and restless, didn't know what to do with his hands, wasn't sure why he was there. He was out of place. Tori didn't need him there, didn't need him at all. She had her family, her sisters. It was them she'd turned to yesterday.

When Celeste fired that gun, the room had filled with the scent of gunpowder and blood and he'd rushed to her, had called in the situation to get an ambulance as soon as possible. He'd checked her pulse but it was too late.

He'd turned in time to see Tori—her face and chest splattered with blood—sway, her eyes wide, her pupils dilated.

Then all hell had broken loose. People had come running, a waitress had burst into the office and he'd barked at them all to get the hell out as he'd gone to Tori, had led her out into the hall where she'd crumpled against him. He'd kept the gawkers at bay. Joe, the cook, had helped calm the waitresses and the customers and, fifteen minutes later, the ambulance had come and Celeste's body had been taken away.

Layne and Nora had arrived within minutes of each other. He'd filled Layne in on what had happened and while she'd seemed as shocked as her sisters, she'd taken control. Had helped Tori to the ambulance where she could be treated for her shock. Nora stood by silently crying.

Walker had left Tori with her sisters, had done his job to make sure Taylor knew exactly what had happened. He'd given his statement, filled out the reports and hadn't made it back to his room until late. Though he'd been exhausted, he hadn't slept. Couldn't stop thinking about Tori.

She'd gotten under his skin. If he wasn't careful, she'd worm her way into his heart.

"I came for Tori," he said, then his neck heated as he realized how that sounded. He cleared his throat. "I came to see you," he told Tori.

"I swear to God," she told him, "if you ask me if I'm fine or if you can do anything for me, I'll shove this scoop so far up your—"

"Hey, now," Layne said, taking the coffee measuring spoon away from her sister. "I'll take over. Why don't you take the detective out back? Get some fresh air?"

Tori stomped out the back door and Walker followed. Found her sitting at the end of a picnic table in a small backyard, her head on her bent arms. He sat next to her. Lightly touched her wrist.

She raised her head. "I'm being a bitch."

He scratched his cheek. "I'm not sure what the proper response is to that."

Her lips twitched. "The proper response is for you to assure me that I'm being no such thing. The honest response is to agree."

"You've been through a lot," he said.

She snorted and leaned back, crossed her arms. "I think my pissy mood has more to do with the fact that they won't leave me alone," she said with a nod toward the house. "The only time I have any privacy is in the bathroom. I took a forty-five-minute shower just to escape them for a little while and Layne broke the lock. Said she was worried I'd drowned. In the freaking shower."

"They care about you," he said, wishing he'd been there for her. Wishing she wanted him there. "They just want to make sure you're okay. Plus, they need you just as much. I imagine this isn't easy for any of you."

Tori tucked her hair behind her ear. "You're right. I just…" She exhaled heavily. "I can't stop thinking about it. I'll forget for a few minutes and then suddenly I'm back in that room watching Celeste pull the trigger. Every time I close my eyes I see her lying there…"

"I'm sorry," he said gruffly, fisting his hands on his thighs. "I shouldn't have let her lead us to the office. I suspected she was guilty. I never should have let her get a hold of that gun."

"It wasn't your fault," Tori said gently, touching him for the first time since they'd made love. "I knew she kept a gun there. It had been her father's and she kept it there for security. We'd all told her it was dangerous to have one in the restaurant but she'd said it made her feel more secure."

"I'm still sorry I didn't stop her."

"Maybe it's for the best. Maybe this way we can finally put the past to rest." As if realizing she was still holding his hand, she slowly pulled away. "So, I guess this means your work here is done?"

"It is," he said, watching her carefully. "I'm leaving today."

She blinked. "Oh." She smiled, one of her practiced smiles that didn't reach her eyes. "Well, I'm glad you stopped to say goodbye before you left."

"I could come back," he heard himself say. Nerves tightened his stomach, had sweat forming at the base of his back. But he held her eyes, saw the question in the brown depths, the unease. "I'd come back for you, Tori."

TORI'S HEART stopped, her mouth went dry. Walker watched her, his gaze intense, the sun catching the gold in his hair.

He was strong and honorable and honest. He was a good man. Dependable and capable.

But the only person she could truly depend on was herself.

She smiled and shook her hair back. "Now, Walker, our night together was lovely and it meant so much to me, but let's not get greedy."

Hurt flashed in his eyes, pain she'd caused but better for him to hurt a little now, she assured herself, than to think there could be something between them.

"So that's all it was to you?" he asked. "Just a one-night thing?"

"It's what it was to both of us," she said firmly, hoping that it was true. "We both knew going into this—"

"This?"

She waved her hand uselessly while searching for the right words. "This…friendship…that it had an expiration date. You have your life, your career back in Boston, and I have my life here."

"And you don't want to see if there's a way for us to combine the two."

It wasn't a question, but she treated it like one. "What good would it do? Look, you're a good guy but—"

"Don't," he said, whipping his hand out and grabbing her wrist. "I'm the guy you slept with two nights ago. The only guy you've been with other than your ex-husband so don't you try to tell me it was because I'm a good guy."

"I choose who touches me and when," she said stiffly, "and I chose you the other night. And now, I'd like you to unhand me."

He stared at her, then slowly opened his fingers, releasing her. Her hands shook and she tucked them into her lap. "As I said, the other night was great, but don't make more of it than there was. I had to get back into the pool at some time."

"So I was, what, your inaugural single-woman screw?"

She flinched, ducked her head so he couldn't see that he'd hurt her. But that's what happened when you loved someone, when you let someone get close to you. They hurt you. You hurt them back. She wouldn't put herself in that position. Look what love had done to her family. Her father had loved her mother to distraction, to the detriment of himself and his pride. Celeste had loved Tim only to always be his second choice.

Tori got to her feet. "This conversation is over. Have a nice life."

She made it to the door before his voice stopped her, the words whipping over her like a brutal wind.

"I'm in love with you."

She froze. Grew dizzy. Locking her knees, she steadied herself and faced him. "Then you're a fool. I'm not interested in love. I don't want to love anyone other than my son." And how dare Walker put her in this position? Love? God, it was the last thing she wanted, to be tied to another man, one who claimed he loved her. No. No, she repeated to herself firmly. Never again.

"Go back to Boston, Walker," she told him. "And don't bother ever coming back. There's nothing for you here."

ANTHONY TOOK A deep breath and then knocked on the door. His hands were sweating and he felt sick to his stomach. But he had to do this, had to make things right. A moment later, Jess opened the door. She frowned. "Layne's not here."

"I know," he said quickly, sticking his foot in between the door and the jamb when she tried to shut it in his face. "I came to see you."

She pushed harder against the door. "Too bad."

"Please," he said, knowing he sounded desperate but not able to care. "Please, Jess. Just give me a few minutes, then I'll go and you'll never have to see me again."

He heard her sigh and then the pressure eased on his foot as she opened the door. "Fine."

He looked behind her into his cousin's house. Bobby O, Layne's dog, barked, stood behind Jess, his tail wagging. "Can I come in?"

She crossed her arms. "No."

"Okay, fair enough." But that meant he had to grovel on the doorstep. He guessed he deserved that and worse. "I'm sorry," he said slowly, trying to remember the words he'd chosen, the apology he'd practiced on his way over here. "I'm really sorry about the other night. I… God…I can't believe I treated you that way, with such disrespect. That I said those things to you."

Just remembering what had happened made him feel sick inside. He'd never, not once treated a girl so badly and while he had been drinking, he wasn't about to blame his bad behavior on alcohol. He was a man. An adult. It was time to act like one.

"I have no excuse," he continued when she remained silent, giving him one of her sneering looks. "And I'm truly sorry. A few months ago, you asked me if I could forgive you. Well, I'm asking the same thing. Can you forgive me?"

She twisted the bracelet on her wrist. "I don't know. Besides, what does it matter? I mean, just because Uncle Ross is with Layne doesn't mean you and me ever have to see each other."

"It matters to me."

"Why?"

"Because I can't stop thinking about you," he said quietly. "Because I miss talking to you. Because I still care about you."

She stepped back. "It doesn't matter. I'm with Tanner now."

"I know, and I respect that. It's just…I'm leaving and I really want to know that you don't hate me before I go."

"Leaving? You mean you're going back to school?"

"No, I…I joined the Marines."

She blinked, her mouth dropping. "What? Anthony… God. Why?"

"You were right. I need to grow up and I can't go back to school and follow in my father's footsteps. Not now. I never wanted to be a lawyer anyway."

"I know that, it's just…the Marines? Are you sure about this?"

No, he was terrified. But despite that terror, he was also determined for the first time in his life to make something of himself on his own. In his own way. "I'm sure." His heart raced and he tried to smile. "If I write to you, will you write back?"

"You're really leaving?" she asked as if she couldn't believe it. Maybe she'd miss him.

A guy could hope.

"Not for a few weeks but then…yeah. I'll be heading to boot camp."

Jess studied him then slowly nodded. "Yeah, I guess I could write you back. We can be friends," she added.

"Friends. Sure." It was a start, maybe more than he deserved after he'd been such an ass to her. "But I think, since we're being honest here, I should tell you that I plan on coming back here in a few years. And when I do," he added, leaning close, so close her eyes widened and she gasped softly, "I'm going to come after you." He flicked his gaze to her mouth then met her eyes again. "I hope you're ready for me."

Before she could tell him to go to hell or that she changed her mind about them being friends, he went down the sidewalk, feeling lighter than he had since he'd discovered what his father had done. He reached his Jeep, unlocked the door.

"Anthony," she called. He turned back; she stood in the doorway, her hand on Bobby's head, her feet bare. "Be careful."

He nodded. Waved and climbed into his Jeep. Before he shut the door he heard her say, "I don't hate you."

Smiling, he drove away, ready to take on his new life.

THE BREEZE PICKED up Tori's hair, blew it into her face. She didn't move, just stared down at the fresh grave. Shivered.

"I still can't believe it," Nora said as she came up beside Tori. "You know, I used to think that nothing was more important than the truth, that no matter what else happened, you could at least count on it. Now I wish the truth had stayed buried."

They stared down at Celeste's grave. They'd held a private service. Tim hadn't attended, he'd felt too betrayed, was too torn up over everything that had happened. It'd just been Tori, her sisters and Ross and Griffin. But Tori hadn't cried. She couldn't. She was all cried out, all she felt was numb.

"I don't know," Layne said from Tori's other side. "When we discovered Mom had been killed, I wanted to deny it. I didn't want to admit that all these years I'd hated her so much, resented her so much and she'd been taken from us. I felt so damn guilty, as if I hadn't had any right to those feelings but they were the truth," she pointed out.

"They were real and honest. She wasn't the best mother. But she was ours."

"She was ours," Tori repeated. "She was selfish and so beautiful and fun and irresponsible."

"She was ours," Nora said softly. "For all her faults, she helped shape who we are, who we turned out to be. For good or bad."

Layne nudged Tori's hip. "Speaking of good, what happened between you and Walker?"

Tori slid her sister a sidelong look. "Now, you know I don't kiss and tell."

Layne rolled her eyes. "Drop the act. We saw your face the day he came to see you after Celeste died."

"What about my face?"

"You were devastated," Nora said gently.

Tori fidgeted, her heels sinking into the soft ground. "Of course I was. We all were. We'd just discovered the woman we'd taken in as part of our family had killed our mother."

"No, that wasn't it," Layne said. "Or at least, not all of it. You were hurt Walker left."

She tucked her hair behind her ear. "Shows how much you know," she said, sounding like a teenager. "I told him to leave."

"Why on earth would you do that when it's obvious you're in love with him?" Nora asked.

Panic slid into Tori's chest, made it difficult to breathe. "Don't be ridiculous."

"What's so ridiculous about it?" Layne asked.

"Because I can't love him," she blurted. "I'll just mess it up."

"Probably," Layne agreed. "But since when has that stopped you from going after what you want?"

Tori laughed harshly. "Are you kidding me? I never go

after what I want. I've stayed in this town, afraid to move forward, my whole life. I got pregnant and married Greg even though I knew it was a mistake, stayed with him for Brandon's sake, though that was wrong, too. For all of us."

"What do you want to do?" Nora asked as if she was really interested.

"I want to run the café," Tori heard herself admit. Then she blushed madly. Forced a smirk. "Crazy, right?"

Nora shook her head. "I don't think that's crazy. I think it's a great idea."

"Me, too," Layne said.

Tori's jaw dropped and she faced her older sister. "You do?"

"Of course."

To her horror, Tori burst into tears.

"Hey, hey," Nora said as she wrapped her arm around Tori's shoulder. "It's okay. Everything will be all right."

She shook her head. "It won't. I sent him away. I was so scared. He told me he loved me and I sent him away." She looked at Nora then Layne. "What do I do?"

Layne wrapped her arm around Tori's waist and squeezed. "That's easy. You get him back."

THE FIRST CLUE Walker had that something was up was when half the department rose as one and stared out the window. Walker continued filling out his report, kept his face turned toward his computer screen. Ever since he got back two weeks ago, he'd kept to himself, had downplayed his trip to Mystic Point.

The second clue came a few minutes later when someone opened the door and the entire room went silent.

The back of his neck prickled with apprehension. With awareness. He stilled.

"Good morning," a husky, familiar voice said, one that

had filled his dreams for the past two weeks. "I hope one of you can help me. I'm looking for Detective Bertrand?"

Walker hunched over his desk, realized he was trying to hide in a room full of people, some of whom had a clear view of him, and straightened to see several of his male coworkers point his way.

Tori. In the middle of his workplace looking like a goddess in her tight, dark jeans and a clinging red top. Their eyes met across the room and it was all he could do not to get up and walk away like she'd done to him after he'd declared his feelings for her like some love-besotted idiot.

"Here," one of his coworkers said, surging to his feet, "I'll walk you over."

She broke eye contact with Walker long enough to smile at the poor fool at her elbow. "Thanks, but I think I can take it from here."

Walker didn't move, couldn't, as she came toward him in that hip-swaying, drool-inducing walk of hers. He managed to tear his gaze from her long enough to note that all the men in the room were checking out her ass—an ass he had firsthand experience to know was top-notch—as she crossed the room.

"Hello, Detective," she said in that purr of hers as she stopped beside his desk.

"Mrs. Mott," he said curtly. He wouldn't ask her why she was there, wouldn't lower himself to admitting how much he'd missed her, how he'd thought of her every freaking day.

"Is there somewhere private we can talk?" she asked.

He flicked his gaze up to her then went back to his work. "I'm busy."

From the corner of his eye he saw her fidget, play with the strap of her purse. She was nervous. Good. She should be nervous.

"Okay, if that's how you want to play this," she murmured, "that's how we'll play it." She inhaled deeply. "I love you."

And once again, the room went silent. Walker's neck heated with embarrassment and he leaped to his feet, wrapped his hand around her wrist and all but dragged her out of the room, down the hall and into the break room. He shut the door and leaned back against it, though he imagined more than one curious soul would be making their way down the hall in the hopes of overhearing his and Tori's conversation.

"What the hell are you doing?" he asked.

"What does it look like?" she asked, sounding slightly put out, as if he was trying to make her life uncomfortable when she'd done nothing but make his life a living hell since he'd met her. Christ, but he'd missed her. "I'm here to win you back," she continued. "Or did you miss the part where I said I loved you?"

"No," he managed to reply through gritted teeth, "I didn't miss it. No one missed it including my coworkers and my boss."

But she didn't seem to care about any of that. "Well?"

"Well what?" he growled.

"Well, don't you have anything you want to say to me?"

"Oh, believe me, I have plenty I want to say, but my mother taught me not to use certain language in front of women." He shoved away from the door. "You hurt me," he said, the words bursting out of him despite his best effort to keep them inside. "I told you I loved you and you threw it back in my face."

"I know. I'm sorry. Walker, please," she said, holding out a hand. "I'm so sorry."

But he didn't want her touching him, didn't want her here, not when he'd been trying so hard to forget her, to pretend his feelings for her never existed, that they weren't real. "It doesn't matter. What the hell was I thinking, anyway? How can I possibly love you? I've only know you a few weeks."

"Don't say that. We may have only known each other a short time but I know you and you know me. Maybe better than anyone ever has. You see me, no matter how hard I try to hide, you see me. I want you to. I want to share myself with you, my thoughts and dreams, my hopes and fears. Everything. Only with you, Walker. Please say you want that, too."

He did. So much it hurt. But it was a risk, being with her. Trusting her.

He wanted to turn her away, wanted to go back to his nice, normal, safe existence but he looked into her eyes. Saw hope there. Saw love there.

And he knew he was a goner. That this woman, this complicated, stubborn, beautiful woman, was going to make his life interesting in the best possible ways.

"Yeah," he sighed, knowing when he was beat. "I want that, too. I want you, Tori."

She smiled; a real smile that lit her eyes and her entire face. Then she launched herself at him, buried her face against the side of his neck and held on as if she'd never let go.

He'd never let her go.

EPILOGUE

Eighteen months later

TORI'S FIRST WEDDING had taken place at the county court-house, the only witnesses her future in-laws, her father and the judge's secretary. She'd been all of eighteen, eight months pregnant and desperate to be loved.

Today she'd stood before a priest at the front of St. Bernard's church, her son and her sisters at her side, and had promised to love Walker Bertrand for the rest of her life.

A promise she knew she'd have no problem keeping.

"You're smiling," Walker murmured into her ear as they enjoyed their first dance as Mr. and Mrs. Bertrand to the sound of Nat King Cole's "Unforgettable." The warmth of Walker's fingers seeped through the silk of her dress at her hips. "You know that makes me nervous."

Tori pressed against him, touched the soft hair at the nape of his neck. "Now why on earth would that make you nervous?"

His grip tightened but he kept their movement slow and easy. "Because it usually means you're up to something. And want to drag me into your plans."

"I don't remember you complaining the other night when my plans included a can of whipped cream and that ugly purple tie you refuse to throw away."

"My mom gave me that tie."

"So I shouldn't mention that it makes an excellent blindfold?"

He blushed and glanced over to where his parents sat with Tori's father. "Shh. Do you want me to be struck dead by lightning?"

She laughed and he grinned. Kissed her warmly. God, how she loved him, this stubborn, gruff man. Her man. She held her left hand out, admired the silver band on her ring finger. Her husband.

Walker settled his hands onto her lower back, his touch now familiar but no less exciting than it had been all those months ago at the Tidal Pool motel. Tori laid her head on his shoulder.

For the past year and a half, her family had been dealing with the consequences of the truth about Valerie's disappearance and death. Tori knew they would always be affected by it in some way. They were scarred and forever changed, but ultimately, they had survived.

She liked to think they were stronger for having gone through it.

Raising her head, she searched out her family. Nora sat across from Erin and Collin, having what appeared to be quite the lively conversation while Griffin held his sleeping eight-month-old daughter. Tori still wasn't sure how much she trusted Griffin, but even she could see he was crazy about his wife and daughter and would do anything for them.

Tori's father, looking handsome in his dark suit, was speaking with Walker's parents while Ken and Astor sat at the table behind them. Unfortunately, not all of her family's wounds had fully healed. Thanks to counseling, Ken and Astor had weathered the storm of his infidelity, but the rift between Ken and Tim remained. And Anthony had yet to forgive his father, but did his best to remain in contact with his mother, sister and cousins—and most especially, Jessica—while stationed overseas.

Tori nodded toward Jess as the teen led Tanner out of the reception hall. "I guess that tells us all we need to know about how that *just friends* thing is working out for them," Tori said.

When Tanner left Mystic Point last fall to attend Belmont University, a small school in Nashville, he and Jess had decided they should be free to see other people. But every time he came home, they were inseparable.

"You have got to be kidding me."

The sound of Layne's loud, flat tone had Tori and Walker stilling. They looked toward the buffet line where Layne stood, a glass in one hand, a plate filled with food in the other.

And a puddle of water between her feet.

"Is that what I think it is?" Walker murmured as Ross rushed to his very irritated, very pregnant wife.

Tori nodded. Her sister's water had broken. "I told her she was going to have that baby today."

"Heading to the hospital," Ross said as he steered Layne past them.

She rolled her eyes. "Ross, I'm not even having strong contractions yet."

"Better safe than sorry," the chief said, looking more nervous and flustered than Tori had ever seen him.

Ross had maintained his position at the police department, but Layne had decided it would be better for both their careers and their personal life for her to accept a position with the county sheriff's department.

"This one's for the newest member of the Sullivan family," the D.J. said into the microphone as Justin Bieber's "Baby" began to play.

"What's going on?" Brandon asked, meeting Walker and Tori as they left the dance floor hand-in-hand.

"Your aunt is having her baby," Walker said.

"Yeah? Cool." Brandon flipped his hair from his eyes. Looked down at his mom, thanks to his latest growth spurt. "You two going to have one?" he blurted. "I mean... it's okay, you know, with me, if you do."

Walker kept his eyes on Tori as he slung an arm around her son's shoulder. "Glad to hear it."

"Me, too," Tori said, kissing Brandon's cheek.

They still had their differences—what parent and teenager didn't? But things were much better between them now. She and Greg had agreed to share custody of Brandon until he was sixteen, at which time they would let him choose where he wanted to live. For now, he spent Wednesdays and weekends at his dad's and the rest of the time with Tori.

"I want another one," Tori said softly as Brandon headed toward his grandfather. Clearing her throat, she faced Walker. "I want a baby."

"What about the café?"

They had talked about kids, of course, but they had planned on waiting. They had only recently moved into their new home, a renovated house close to the beach. Walker still worked out of Boston but was considering moving to a station closer to Mystic Point. Tori had taken over the café, but she hadn't done it alone. Her father had gone into business with her and, while they made their fair share of mistakes, they were muddling through just fine.

"It'll all work out," she said, knowing it was true. "Between Dad and Patty, the café will survive my maternity leave. I don't want to wait. I want it all."

For the first time she believed she could have it all. That she deserved it.

He cupped her face in his hands. "No more waiting." He kissed her. "I love you, Tori."

She held on to his wrists, happier, more content than she'd ever imagined. "I love you, too."

Oh, she still didn't believe in fairy tales—life was too imperfect for that. But looking into Walker's eyes, surrounded by their families and friends, the future a bright promise, she did believe in something else.

A happy ending.

* * * * *

COMING NEXT MONTH
from Harlequin® SuperRomance®
AVAILABLE OCTOBER 30, 2012

#1812 SUDDENLY YOU
Sarah Mayberry

Harry Porter is happy to be one of the guys. No long-term commitments for him. But a chance encounter with single mother Pippa White leaves him reeling. Before he can explain it, he's inventing excuses to run into her, to stop by her place, to help her...anything to see her one more time!

#1813 AFTER THE STORM
The Texas Firefighters
Amy Knupp

Firefighting is dangerous—Penn Griffin knows that. But when he's injured rescuing Nadia Hamlin from a hurricane, he's stunned to find that his career is over. And even more stunned to realize the intensity of his attraction to the woman he holds responsible....

#1814 THE WEDDING PLAN
Abby Gaines

All Merry Wyatt wants is a temporary marriage to Lucas Calder to make her dying father happy. Her need to put down roots isn't a good match for Lucas's military career, but at least it's not forever. Or is it? Because her father seems to be recovering!

#1815 THE LIFE OF RILEY
Lenora Worth

Socialite Riley Sinclair is pregnant. Even more shocking, her long-absent ex-husband is the father of her child. When he suddenly returns, wanting to restake his claim, Riley realizes she has some explaining to do. Now if only she could resist this man she never stopped loving....

#1816 ABOUT THE BABY
Tracy Wolff

Dr. Kara Steward definitely wants her unborn child. But the baby's father, Dr. Lucas Montgomery? Not so much. It's not that she doesn't care for him. It's more that their lives are incompatible. Or so she thought before he began his campaign to convince her otherwise!

#1817 THE CHRISTMAS INN
Stella MacLean

Being a mystery guest at a country inn is Marnie McLaughlan's favor to her brother. Then she falls for the manager, Luke Harrison. Falling for Luke complicates everything because Marnie knows her very presence could compromise his job. But at Christmas, things have a way of working out....

You can find more information on upcoming Harlequin®
titles, free excerpts and more at www.Harlequin.com.

REQUEST YOUR FREE BOOKS!
2 FREE NOVELS PLUS 2 FREE GIFTS!

Harlequin®

Super Romance®

Exciting, emotional, unexpected!

YES! Please send me 2 FREE Harlequin® Superromance® novels and my 2 FREE gifts (gifts are worth about $10). After receiving them, if I don't wish to receive any more books, I can return the shipping statement marked "cancel." If I don't cancel, I will receive 6 brand-new novels every month and be billed just $4.69 per book in the U.S. or $5.24 per book in Canada. That's a saving of at least 15% off the cover price! It's quite a bargain! Shipping and handling is just 50¢ per book in the U.S. and 75¢ per book in Canada.* I understand that accepting the 2 free books and gifts places me under no obligation to buy anything. I can always return a shipment and cancel at any time. Even if I never buy another book, the two free books and gifts are mine to keep forever.

135/336 HDN FC6T

Name	(PLEASE PRINT)	

Address		Apt. #

City	State/Prov.	Zip/Postal Code

Signature (if under 18, a parent or guardian must sign)

Mail to the Reader Service:
IN U.S.A.: P.O. Box 1867, Buffalo, NY 14240-1867
IN CANADA: P.O. Box 609, Fort Erie, Ontario L2A 5X3

Not valid for current subscribers to Harlequin Superromance books.
**Are you a current subscriber to Harlequin Superromance books
and want to receive the larger-print edition?
Call 1-800-873-8635 or visit www.ReaderService.com.**

* Terms and prices subject to change without notice. Prices do not include applicable taxes. Sales tax applicable in N.Y. Canadian residents will be charged applicable taxes. Offer not valid in Quebec. This offer is limited to one order per household. All orders subject to credit approval. Credit or debit balances in a customer's account(s) may be offset by any other outstanding balance owed by or to the customer. Please allow 4 to 6 weeks for delivery. Offer available while quantities last.

Your Privacy—The Reader Service is committed to protecting your privacy. Our Privacy Policy is available online at www.ReaderService.com or upon request from the Reader Service.

We make a portion of our mailing list available to reputable third parties that offer products we believe may interest you. If you prefer that we not exchange your name with third parties, or if you wish to clarify or modify your communication preferences, please visit us at www.ReaderService.com/consumerschoice or write to us at Reader Service Preference Service, P.O. Box 9062, Buffalo, NY 14269. Include your complete name and address.

HSR11

Turn the page for a preview of

THE OTHER SIDE OF US

by

Sarah Mayberry,

coming January 2013
from Harlequin® Superromance®.

PLUS, exciting changes are in the works!
Enjoy the same great stories in a longer format
and new look—beginning January 2013!

THE OTHER SIDE OF US
A brand-new novel
from Harlequin® Superromance® author
Sarah Mayberry

*In recovery from a serious accident, Mackenzie Williams
is beating all the doctors' predictions. But she needs
single-minded focus. She doesn't need the distraction
of neighbors—especially good-looking ones
like Oliver Garrett!*

MACKENZIE BREATHED DEEPLY to recover from the workout. She'd pushed herself too far but she wanted to accelerate her rehabilitation. Still, she needed to lie down to combat the nausea and shaking muscles.

A knock came from the front door. Who on earth would be visiting her on a Thursday morning? Probably a cold-calling salesperson.

She answered, but her pithy rejection died before she'd formed the first words.

The man on her doorstep was definitely not a cold caller. Nothing about this man was cold, from the auburn of his wavy hair to his brown eyes to his sensual mouth. Nothing cold about those broad shoulders, flat belly and lean hips, either.

"Hey," he said in a shiver-inducing baritone. "I'm Oliver Garrett. I moved in next door." His smile was so warm and vibrant it was almost offensive.

"Mackenzie Williams." Oh, no. Her legs were starting to

tremble, indicating they wouldn't hold up long. Any second now, she would embarrass herself in front of this complete and very good-looking stranger.

"It's been years since I was down here." He seemed to settle in for a chat. "It doesn't look as though—"

"I have to go." Her stomach rolled as she shut the door. The last thing she registered was the look of shock on Oliver's face at her abrupt dismissal.

And somehow she knew their neighborly relations would be a lot cooler now!

Will Mackenzie be able to make it up to Oliver for her rude introduction? Stay tuned next month for a continuing excerpt of THE OTHER SIDE OF US by Sarah Mayberry, available January 2013 from Harlequin® Superromance®.

Discover the magic of Christmas with two
holiday stories of love and forgiveness in

CHRISTMAS IN TEXAS

Christmas Baby Blessings

by TINA LEONARD

Capri Snow isn't happy when she discovers
that the Bridesmaids Creek Christmastown Santa is her
almost-ex-husband and cop, Seagal West. But when danger
strikes, Seagal steps in to protect his wife, no matter the cost.

&

The Christmas Rescue

by REBECCA WINTERS

When Texas Ranger Flynn Patterson saves Andrea Sinclair
and her infant child from her stalker ex-husband, he finds
himself in more danger than just losing his heart.

Bring the magic of Christmas home
this November 2012.

Available wherever books are sold.

celebrating 15 YEARS

Kathryn Springer

**inspires with her tale of a soldier's promise
and his chance for love in**

The Soldier's Newfound Family

When he returns to Texas from overseas, U.S. Marine
Carter Wallace makes good on a promise: to tell a fallen
soldier's wife that her husband loved her. But widowed
Savannah Blackmore, pregnant and alone, shares a different
story with Carter—one that tests everything he believes.
Now the marine who never needed anyone suddenly
needs Savannah. Will opening his heart be the
bravest thing he'll ever do?

— TEXAS TWINS —

Available November 2012

www.LoveInspiredBooks.com

LI87776